The Gang That Couldn't Shoot Straight

The Book Trader
1313 Redfield St
La Crosse, WI
1-608-782-9

G·K
Hall
&Co.

Also by Jimmy Breslin
in Large Print:

I Want to Thank My Brain
for Remembering Me

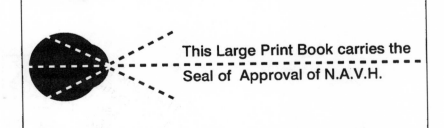

This Large Print Book carries the
Seal of Approval of N.A.V.H.

The Gang That Couldn't Shoot Straight

Jimmy Breslin

G.K. Hall & Co. • Thorndike, Maine

Published in 2001 by arrangement with Little Brown and Company, Inc.

G.K. Hall Large Print Paperback Series.

The text of this Large Print edition is unabridged.
Other aspects of the book may vary from the original edition.

Set in 16 pt. Plantin.

Printed in the United States on permanent paper.

Library of Congress Cataloging-in-Publication Data

Breslin, Jimmy.
   The gang that couldn't shoot straight / Jimmy Breslin.
     p. cm.
   ISBN 0-7838-9391-4 (lg. print : sc : alk. paper)
   1. Organized crime — Fiction. 2. New York (N.Y.) — Fiction.
  3. Criminals — Fiction. 4. Mafia — Fiction. 5. Large type books.
  I. Title.
PS3552.R39 G36 2001
  813'.54—dc21
                                             00-067295

The Gang That Couldn't Shoot Straight

Chapter 1

The idea for the six-day bike race came out of a meeting held in November, in Brooklyn, in the offices of Anthony Pastrumo, Sr. He is a sixty-eight-year-old man who is called "Papa" when he is at home and "Baccala" by his friends and business associates, all of whom share a common feeling toward Baccala. They are scared to death of him.

Baccala is one of the five big bosses of the Mafia gangsters in New York. He is also a very great dog-lover. Last year he bought a Russian wolfhound for his four-year-old niece so she could grow up in an atmosphere of teeth. The dog was stolen. Baccala had somebody write a form letter that was mimeographed and sent to every veterinarian and animal hospital in the New York area. It offered a reward of $250 to anybody who reported if a Russian wolfhound with specific markings was brought around for shots.

"I look to make a stool pigeon out of a dog doctor," Baccala explained. "All he tells me is who the guy is with-a my dog. I pay the $250. I go to the guy who stole my-a dog. I speak to him nice. Then I cut out his heart and feed it to the dog."

The bike race was Baccala's idea. He nominated a chubby real-estate man named Joseph DeLauria to be the actual promoter of the race. DeLauria has made large sums of money fronting for Baccala in business deals. DeLauria also has received many slaps in the face when he has irritated Baccala during these deals.

Baccala's office in Brooklyn is in a building which is listed as the home of the Lancer Trucking Company. There is no trucking company. If Baccala wants a trucking company, he will steal one from a Jew. Baccala held the meeting to deal with a dissident group in his gang: Reform Italians. The gang was headed by Salvatore Palumbo. He is known, among all illegitimate people and cops in Brooklyn, as Kid Sally Palumbo. In Brooklyn waterfront dialect, this often comes out as "Sally Kid." He is twenty-nine and he has a power base of five cousins and sixty others who live on the South Brooklyn waterfront and work, under Kid Sally's direction, at mayhem for the Baccala gang. For some time Kid Sally Palumbo and his group have wanted to get their hands on a major revenue-producing enterprise. Violence still pays less than any other job in crime. Baccala was of the opinion that Kid Sally Palumbo couldn't run a gas station at a profit even if he stole the customers cars. But the level of annoyance from Kid Sally Palumbo and his people was becoming inordinately high. You could see that at a big meeting held to discuss the rift.

"You sit-a here, okay? you sit-a here, okay? you sit-a here, okay?" Baccala was saying, assuming his role of *don cheeche*. One of the major rewards for being a big shot in the Mafia is that you are in charge of seating arrangements at all restaurants or meetings. You tell everybody where to sit and keep the best seat for yourself.

Everybody in the meeting sat down except Kid Sally Palumbo.

"You sit-a," Baccala said, pointing at a chair in the corner.

"I don't feel like sittin'."

"You sit-a."

"I think I'm going to stand."

The two glared at each other. Baccala shrugged and sat down. He is known as the Sicilian Dean Rusk. Be a little smooth and give a little on the surface now. After the conference ends amicably, send in the B-52s.

"So what you want?" Baccala said.

"Do the right thing," Kid Sally said.

"What's?" Baccala said.

"We got to go around with a gun with loaded bullets. What do we get for it? You get everything, we get ungotz."

"You shut up you face," Baccala said.

"You old guys, we got to do deuces and treys

9

in the can and you leave the money for your kids. What's this? You send your kids to West Point. We go to West Point, all right. Sing Sing West Point."

"You show no respect," Baccala said.

"I'm good people," Kid Sally said.

"You no act like good people."

"I'm good people!"

Kid Sally's grandmother, Mrs. Big Mama Ferrara, had rehearsed him carefully. "You just say you good people and you take-a no bulla-sheet," she told him.

The meeting broke up on that note. Baccala, watching Kid Sally and his cousins leave the office, realized they constituted political pressure. As Baccala is sensitive to this sort of thing, he decided to do something about it.

What Baccala wanted to do at first was not good. *"Ciciri,"* he muttered one night. The three people with him at dinner became nervous. The word *ciciri* means bean, but to Baccala the meaning is much deeper. The only history he knows of is the rebellion of Sicilians in Palermo in 1282 against the French. A French soldier tried to rape a housewife in front of her husband in Palermo. The husband killed the soldier and all Palermo took to the streets. They surrounded French soldiers and told them to say the word *ciciri*. It is supposed to be an impossible set of syllables for the French tongue to handle. So the people of Palermo, with a great shout, slit the throats of the soldiers. Baccala, who knows the story by heart, loves to talk about the part where the hero of the uprising, Nicola Pancia, boarded a French ship in the harbor and had seventy French sergeants and their wives and children thrown overboard. Nicola Pancia and his men hung over the side and cheered each time a baby drowned.

"The baby makes-a bubbles in the water," Baccala always says, crying from laughter.

In more recent history, each time Baccala mutters this particular word, somebody in Brooklyn gets invited on a deep-sea fishing trip from Sheepshead Bay. Out in the ocean, a rope is put around the man's neck. The other end of the rope is attached to an old jukebox. The jukebox is thrown overboard. The man invariably follows.

On this particular occasion, however, Baccala spent a week glaring and muttering and then he called in Kid Sally Palumbo again and told him he was getting a chance to make money. A bike race.

Bike-racing is a thing out of the 1930s. It used to be called "the Ride to Nowhere." The only thing Baccala really knows about bike-racing is that Italians ride bikes. But it was indicative of Baccala's age that, when pressed, he went for an idea out of the 1930s instead of something modern, such as selling cocaine to grammar-school kids. During the Depression, when even fine gangsters were broke, Baccala went to a bike race at Madison Square Garden and quickly noticed that when everybody stood up to cheer they left their coats draped over the seats. On the second sprint of the night Baccala grabbed a great camel-hair from Row B, Section 205. A while later he took a black Chesterfield out of the last row of the end arena. He got into the side arena and came off with a terrific storm coat. He happened to look around, and he saw so many guys running around the arena and stealing coats that he thought he was having a vision of heaven.

Over the loudspeaker, later on that night, the announcer for the bike race said, "The score at this point . . ."

"Forty-nine coats!" somebody screamed from the mezzanine.

Despite the different era, Baccala was certain his new bike race would make immense amounts of money. He intended to have open gambling on it. The event would be held in a field-artillery armory in the 91st Precinct in Brooklyn. The only thing not for sale in the 91st Precinct is the captain's bowling trophy. As Baccala saw it, the bike race would be a roulette wheel for six days and nights. He would let Kid Sally Palumbo handle the whole thing and keep nearly all the money. This would keep the fresh bum quiet.

This bike race is another example of how Mafia bosses weave their way into the fabric of society. The Mafia of New York is split into five groups known as "families." The Baccala Family runs all organized crime in Brooklyn. The gang has been in Brooklyn longer than the Ferris wheel at Coney Island. It was formed in 1890 under the leadership of Raymond the Wolf. He ate babies. Raymond the Wolf passed away in his sleep one night from natural causes; his heart stopped beating when the three men who slipped into his bedroom stuck knives in it. Joe the Wop, who had sent the three men, took over the mob. Joe the Wop shot nuns. A year later he dropped dead while being strangled. At this point Baccala heard that three people he had known and loved for twenty years were discussing ways to take over the gang. So was Baccala. This, of course, made his three great friends become treacherous enemies. One night Baccala stepped into the Roma Gardens Lounge to visit the three people. Baccala also brought a machine gun with him. The three old friends were eating dinner. Baccala caught them with the machine gun between the veal. A waiter was so close to Baccala's gun that he got powder burns all over the front of his waiter's jacket.

When the police arrived, they found the waiter nervously twisting a napkin between his hands. An inspector looked at the powder burns on the waiter's jacket.

"What shooting?" Louis the Waiter said.

For several months thereafter, whenever some hero would come into the Roma Gardens Lounge and order a meal, a hand would come up from under the table and set down a dish of veal Parmigiana.

After the machine-gunning was out of the

headlines, Baccala took command of the gang. He has lasted as head of the family since 1944, which is a new record for gangsters, Brooklyn, single individual.

Kid Sally Palumbo came toward the top of the Baccala Family through personal service, great greed, and also great luck. His objectives were the power to say, "You sit here," and money. They go together. The financial structure of the Mafia is the same as in the film industry. Ten stars walk around earning millions, and thousands of unknowns get little pieces of work here and there and mainly earn nothing. They wait for the key role to pop up.

One day, in Kid Sally Palumbo's presence, Baccala announced he was very mad at one Georgie Paradise.

"Georgie Paradise, he's-a no do the right thing," Baccala said. "Georgie Paradise, he's a rat *basset*."

Kid Sally immediately got very mad at Georgie Paradise too.

"That dirty rat bastard Georgie Paradise," Kid Sally Palumbo said. He had never met Georgie Paradise.

Kid Sally called a saloon where he was told Georgie Paradise hung out.

"Hey! Is Georgie Paradise there?" Kid Sally said.

The phone on the other end dropped and then it was picked up again. "Hey! This is Georgie Paradise."

"You be on the corner in ten minutes. We got a important message from Baccala that you got to handle," Kid Sally said.

Georgie Paradise was on the corner in front of the saloon in ten minutes. Kid Sally and three of his people, Big Lollipop and his cousin Little Lollipop and Mike the Driver, who was driving, came to pick up Georgie Paradise.

"Hey!" Kid Sally Palumbo called out from the car.

"Hey!" Georgie Paradise said. He walked up to the car.

Big Lollipop jumped on Georgie Paradise's head as Georgie Paradise came into the car. Little Lollipop put both hands on Georgie Paradise's throat. Sensing something unusual, Georgie Paradise began twisting. Kid Sally Palumbo took a gun out. He tried to hold the gun against Georgie Paradise's head. Georgie moved his head around. Kid Sally's gun slipped off Georgie Paradise's head. Kid Sally fired three shots which went out the window. Georgie Paradise got a hand on the door and opened it and threw himself out onto the street. He began to run. Mike the Driver, who was driving, was afraid Georgie Paradise would start screaming and bring the cops. Mike the Driver put his foot to the floor so he could drive the car away. The car shot forward just as Georgie Paradise was trying to run around it. The car did some job of squashing Georgie Paradise.

The newspapers the next day wrote that

Georgie Paradise had been the victim of a hit-run driver.

Baccala was elated. "You know that Kid Sally, he's a nice-a boy," he told everybody. "He does-a things with style. They no even investigate Georgie Paradise."

This great doing away with Georgie Paradise made Kid Sally a comer in the Baccala Family.

This Mafia of Baccala and Kid Sally Palumbo got into American life the same way the Greeks got into Buckingham Palace. They came by boat and worked their way up. The Mafia is known as the "Cosa Nostra" in publications and on witness stands. In America today it is a federation of gangsters, ninety-seven per cent of whom are Italian or of Italian origin. The other three per cent is comprised of Irish, who run the docks; Jews, who handle the money; and Greeks, who are the most underrated thieves in the world. The members of the federation work together as well, and have the same trust in each other, as members of Congress. At a wake of a Mafia leader who has been shot six times in the head, one huge floral piece always arrives with the ribbon saying, "I'm Sorry It Had to Come to This."

The foundation of the Mafia is its Sicilian blood. Calabrese and Napolitano bloodlines mean very much. But Sicilian stands over all. The older founders of the American Mafia refer to their group as the *onorata società,* or honored

16

society. It was formed centuries ago in Sicily to protect the people from being robbed and tortured by foreigners who constantly invaded and controlled the island. Like any such organization, including the police in America, it was most responsive to the needs of the rich Sicilian landowners. Their property was most protected. The poor were robbed. Soon the rich were robbed too.

The basis of the Mafia was that it ignored all local laws, as they were laws set down by foreigners. The Mafia ruled by its own code. The Mafia liked this way of life so much that it has not given it up through the centuries. A true Sicilian in America today must smoke in the subway. Baccala himself goes three blocks out of his way for the privilege of going the wrong way on a one-way street. At the same time, the Mafia is very strict in upholding its own laws. Once a member of Baccala's gang cheated Baccala just a little bit on profits from a bookmaking operation. Baccala took the man to a dentist's office that night and put the drill just a little bit through the man's tongue.

In Sicily, in one thousand years of existence, the Mafia has never been able to spread from Palermo and Agrigento on the southwestern side of the island. There is no Mafia in Siracusa or any other place on the island's eastern coast. And today, when a Mafia member is arrested in Italy, he is treated with extraordinary disdain by authorities. In Palermo the shifting of the wholesale fruit market to a new location produced a wave of murders. Authorities indicted 118 hoodlums. A high-school gymnasium was used for the mass trial. Bleachers for the defendants were set up along one wall, and plumbers constructed a cage of thick steam pipes around the bleachers. Whenever one of the defendants would jump up from the bleachers and grip the steam pipes and shout out his innocence, policemen would reach up and smash his fingers with clubs. Late one afternoon one of the defendants, charged with cutting off a man's head among the tomato stalls, had to attend the men's room. Guards manacled his hands and ankles, looped a chain around his middle, and walked him like a dog. One of the magistrates, a magnificent gray-haired woman from Verona, watched the Mafioso shuffle helplessly at the end of his chain. In precise, cultured tones, the woman magistrate inquired from the bench as to why the police did not have another chain wrapped around the prisoner's neck so he could be yanked around more easily.

But in America, where violence is loved and respected in all sectors, the Mafia leaped and spread to every major city and its suburbs as the nation grew. When the protection-minded Mafia people came to America, they found the landowners had so many guards it was ludicrous. The National Guard shot down women and children during a strike against a Rockefeller mine in Ludlow, Colorado. The fiercest dons of them all threw up their hands in defeat and admiration. "No can match," Giuseppe (Extreme Unction) Magaddino of the Kansas City outfit said. The Mafia was left with only the poor to protect. As only so much can be taken from the poor by terror, subtler methods must be used. Sell women or narcotics or the chance to gamble or whisky to the poor. So the Mafia originally became a national success during Prohibition, as evil everywhere flourishes under repression. Then there is the matter of Americans relying on a dedicated lawman and lifetime bachelor named J. Edgar Hoover. He is the head of the FBI. The original job of the FBI was to prevent interstate crime, the foremost practitioners of which are the Mafia. But in the years of Hoover the Mafia grew into a crime cartel and an FBI arrest of a Mafia member was rare except on the FBI radio programs and, later, television shows. Hoover himself kept announcing that he did not believe there was any such thing as the Mafia. The answer can only be either that Hoover was a member of the Mafia or that he regarded Communist literature on 14th Street in New York as far more dangerous than narcotics on 108th Street. So many FBI agents penetrated the Communist Party that meeting halls became referred to as "the squad room." The agents, graduates of Catholic colleges in the North or dedicated Southerners, both varieties of which can be counted upon to hate Communism and suspect its presence everywhere, always have been help-less around the Mafia.

"Don't we have anybody who infiltrated this organization these people have?" the new United States Attorney General asked at his first FBI crime briefing.

"We've tried, but we've had no success," the assistant director handling the briefing said.

"Why is that?" the Attorney General said.

"Well, we do have several agents who could *pass* for Italian, but each time one of them gets close he is asked for the names of all his cousins," the assistant director said.

Hoover knows better than anybody that stool pigeons, not electronic eavesdropping, are the backbone of law-enforcement. Hoover himself would be merely another retired cop at the race-track if a girl hadn't once called him up and told him what movie John Dillinger was at. Yet for decades Hoover had no contacts around or within the Mafia, and the Mafia grew into a part of American life. Of course, even with a clear field, the Italians in the Mafia never have come close to the magnitude of larceny committed here by English Protestants, but they have been formidable, given the limits of education and intelligence.

And now, here, in Brooklyn, the Mafia was starting to stretch out and wrap its tentacles, as the newspapers write it, around another part of American life. The Six-Day Bike Race. And Joseph DeLauria was presenting himself around town as a bike-race promoter. He rented an armory, put his name on letterheads, contacted a booking agent in Rome, and awaited other ceremonial duties. The real job of putting on the show, getting the track built, and organizing the gambling was left to Kid Sally Palumbo and his people.

Chapter 2

The cold wind from the mountains ran through the stone streets that have no trees. When Mario Trantino came out of the house into the early-morning emptiness, the air forced his eyes to widen. The street was an alley built on a sharp hill, which started in the center of town and ended in the rocks and mud where the hill became the start of a mountain. The alley ran between attached two-story stone houses which were pastel-colored but tiny and dirty inside and with running water only in the daylight hours. The narrow sidewalks were lined with cars parked half on the sidewalk. A new gray Fiat was in front of Mario's door. The auto-rental agency where he worked had given him its best car, at an employee's rate, for his trip. It was a fine car, but all Mario cared was that the machine knew enough to move. He despised cars. His job was apprentice mechanic and handyman at the auto-rental agency, but he really considered himself a young artist.

Mario always went around town with his shoelaces untied. He did not care for this, because he always tripped on the laces. And then his arches ached constantly because he had to walk in a way that would both get him where he was going and keep the loose shoes from falling off his feet. Mario told everybody that he did not like shoe-laces because this is the first way that society ties up the human personality. When people in town said he was crazy, Mario beamed. He did not need glasses, but he would take his uncle's, thick, silver-rimmed things, and walk with the glasses perched on the bridge of his nose. When Mario had to see, at a streetcorner, he looked over the tops of the glasses. Otherwise, he kept his eyes looking down. The thick glasses hurt his eyes, so he would close them and pretend he was a blind man and concentrate on visualizing things. Mario said this kept the world from dis-tracting him. It also kept the people in town shaking their heads and clucking. This made Mario feel it was the only way he could make people regard him as artistic.

In his town, the town of Catanzia, in Calabria, in southern Italy, there was no way for an artist to subsist or to be recognized, and his chances of developing his talent were limited. So Mario Trantino had to walk around town with his arches aching and his shoes flopping and his eyes closed, tripping over his shoelaces quite often, but his real suffering began when he had to go to work on his job. Every wipe of a cloth and every turn of a wrench at the auto-rental garage went against Mario. Near the end of a day a pain would shoot through the palm of Mario's right hand. The pain was caused by the nail being driven through his hand and into the cross.

A woman came through the doorway curtain of the next house and smiled good morning to Mario in the cold morning air. A nannygoat with straggly hair, black-tipped with dirt, followed her. The woman put a brazier, black from fire, on the sidewalk. The brazier was filled with tree branches broken into small sticks. She stuffed a fistful of balled-up paper into the sticks and put a match to the paper. The nannygoat sniffed at the brazier and then backed up from the flames and went through the curtain and into the house. The woman was starting the morning fire to warm the house. When the paper burns and the sticks first catch, the flames are too high and wavery to bring into the house. The woman stepped away from the brazier to wait for the flames to become low. Using her skirt as a pot-holder, she brought the brazier upstairs in the house and put a little pocket of warmth into the morning dampness. The goats and chickens lived downstairs in the house. Mario's house had a striped curtain, more like a bath-towel, on the door. Behind the curtain a cow stood in straw that was wet with urine. The woman stood and watched the flames. She smiled at Mario again and walked over to the gray Fiat and began polishing the fender with her wool skirt. Southern Italy is the same as the rest of the world. People stroke and polish machines while goats urinate in their houses.

In a few minutes Mario would be using this car to leave Catanzia forever. He was driving to Reggio Calabria and the 9:35 a.m. plane to Rome. At Rome he would transfer to the International Terminal and get on the 1:45 p.m. Alitalia flight to America; to Kennedy Airport in New York, to Manhattan, and to Brooklyn, and to all the great things that everybody said that he, Mario Trantino, surprise third-place finisher in the Milan-San Remo amateur bike race, was sure to receive for placing very high in, or winning, the World Championship Six-Day Bike Race in New York. If Mario failed and had to come home, he would sit down backward on the railroad tracks at Reggio Calabria and eat his sandwich and let the Naples express come from behind and do the rest.

When the letter inviting Mario to the bike race had come six weeks ago, it put a flash of brightness in his chest. The letter was from a booking agent in Rome named Rinaldi, who said he was representing an organization of American-Italian men who were anxious to bring back bike-racing to its rightful place in American sports.

In Europe only a few athletes make more than a champion bike-racer. With bike-racing in America unknown in the last twenty-five years, Rinaldi had to produce contestants at a price American promoters could afford. Rather than contact professionals chasing big fees and endorsements on the European circuit, Rinaldi went for reasonably good amateurs and pointed out to them that nobody would notice they were being paid in America. Besides, there was the free trip to America. Any dreams Mario had of becoming a great rich bike-rider were minute compared to his desire to get to America. Rinaldi wanted Mario to team with another fairly good Italian amateur, Carlo Rafetto of Milano. In his letter he said Mario had a fine chance to win. As the sponsors in America had made it plain that they were not about to turn over much money to some oily Turk, Rinaldi was booking only people learning how to ride a two-wheeler, or advanced tuberculars, from countries other than Italy. He was an expert at doing this. Once, for Rossi, the popular but slightly weak Italian lightweight, Rinaldi brought in a German with a broken hand. Rinaldi told the German that if he punched very fast with the broken hand, he would not notice the pain.

For his trip, Mario was guaranteed all expenses plus $1000 American. If his team won the race, the letter said, prizes could run to as much as $2500. There was even a chance the bike race would go on tour throughout America. When Mario took the letter to the bank to look up the money-exchange tables, the teller hung over his shoulder. The teller began shaking when he saw the amounts Mario was inspecting. The teller blessed himself and kissed his fingers. He leaned over the top of the counter and kissed Mario.

Mario took a deep breath of the cold morning air and started walking down the hill. He took long strides. At twenty-three, Mario Trantino was probably the most striking male in Catanzia. If he had grown up in a freer atmosphere than the vacantness of Catanzia, he would have been on the preferred invitation list of every party that had the chance of becoming an orgy. Mario had a proud body that was a little bit over six feet and was contained in 165 pounds. Black hair clung to his head in waves. Sideburns dropped to a point that was a full inch lower than they were on the picture of Garibaldi in Mario's house. His face was clear and had a tone and life to it that comes from the constant breaking of sweat during some form of athletics. His dark brown eyes gleamed with excitement. His nose, just prominent enough to get into trouble with a fast-closing door, put a measure of Roman history onto his face. He wore his only suit, a tight-fitting pepper-and-salt with double vents.

On his job at the auto-rental agency, Mario took interest only at lunchtime when Savona, the fat manager, would sit at his desk and sip *chocolata* and play cards with Mario. Savona wore eyeglasses that were as thick as wind-shields. The eyeglasses would steam up in the noon heat; Catanzia was very cold at night and on both edges of night and very hot at midday, and at noon Savona would take the glasses off and wipe them. With his glasses off, Savona was technically blind. It is extremely helpful to play cards for money with somebody who is not too good at seeing.

Mario's other small pleasure on the job was to stretch out underneath a car he was working on and pretend he was a gynecologist tinkering with Sophia Loren. When he would get tuckered out from this, he would fall asleep. His head would be on the cement that was covered with oil and grease, but this wouldn't matter to him.

Mario had been putting things on paper since he was eight. Each morning that summer he had bicycled two miles down a twisting road to the small resort hotel on the cliff over the sea. The hotel allowed kids to put out deck chairs and run other small errands for tips. The hotel was out of the way, and the only foreign tourists ever to stay there were a childless couple from Manchester, England. The man was a schoolteacher who liked to paint. He liked vacationing on the Calabrian coast because nobody came up to him and insisted he needed a drink when all he really wanted to do was paint. At first, the kids from Catanzia formed a circle behind the man and watched him paint. They would lose interest and leave. All except Mario. When the schoolteacher came for the second summer, he had a paintbox for Mario. The little boy spent some of his afternoons sitting on the cliffs and putting colors on paper while the man painted. Once in a while he looked at what Mario was doing and made suggestions. The schoolteacher spoke fair Italian and was able to make himself understood. And by the middle of the third summer Mario was starting to pick up enough English for the beginnings of conversation. In the summer of Mario's twelfth year the schoolteacher and his wife did not come, and the hotel never heard from them again. But the man had left his impression on Mario. The boy loved to draw and paint. In school, Mario leaped ahead of the class in English and because it was so easy he worked even harder on the subject. When somebody's relatives from America came to Catanzia for a visit, Mario would show off and talk to them in English that was a couple of shades better than that used by the relatives.

Mario also showed off his art work. He brought a pencil sketch of Christ on the cross to the rectory, and it still hangs in the front room of the rectory. Another of Mario's sketches was far more famous in Catanzia. Mario made the sketch when he was sixteen, and he did it carefully and slowly over several weeks of peeking at his uncle and aunt on Sunday afternoons in order to obtain an immensely detailed sketch of the two of them steaming through knockout sex. When Mario showed it around the street for the first time, so many kids collected around him and made so much noise that a fight started. A stumpy old man named Doto got up from a cane chair in front of his house and waved a stick at the boys and chased them. When Doto saw Mario's sketch, he pretended to go into a rage. He grabbed it from Mario and told him to go to confession. Doto took the sketch and tottered down to the *pasticceria* and passed it around to the old men having coffee, and the old men choked and doubled up and coffee ran down their chins. Doto brought the sketch home, and he keeps it in the top drawer of his bureau. He looks at it every Sunday afternoon in hopes of being stimulated.

There was no impetus at home for Mario to do anything but work at a job. His mother had died when he was six. His father was a name on a birth certificate, put there for form. He was raised, with four cousins, by his uncle and aunt. The seven people lived on one large bed, and on three cots, in three rooms in the tiny house. Whenever Mario drew anything around the house and showed them his work, the uncle would say, "That's nice, but come with me today and do something good. Pick up almonds with me today." Then Mario had to go out with a burlap sack and long sweepers made of sticks and scratch almonds from the ground and into the burlap, while his uncle walked around hunting chipmunks with a .22 rifle. The family ate the animals and sold the almonds.

There was a girl in town named Carmela and she worked at the dry-goods store, and Mario asked her to go to the movies one night and Carmela's aunt, who was called Zia Nicolina, showed up as chaperon. Zia Nicolina did not look like a chaperon. She looked, from neck to midsection, like a cow. Her stomach looked like a steam boiler wrapped in black cloth. Zia Nicolina was unmarried. During the war, when there had been Italian and then German and then American troops in the town, Zia Nicolina had been able to take care of entire regiments. The Germans used to send a command car to pick her up. As a chaperon, Zia Nicolina was a large bulldog. At the movies she sat directly behind Carmela, with her fat hands draped over the seats between Carmela and Mario. Every time Mario shifted his weight, Zia Nicolina's hands dug into his shoulder. "Stay on your side," Zia Nicolina rasped. The walk home was excruciating because Zia Nicolina got between them, one hand tightly gripping Mario's arm, and she complained of arthritis until they reached the door; then she shooed Carmela inside and told Mario to go away.

Mario endured it because Carmela was the only girl in town who seemed to find any amusement in his untied shoelaces and his eyeglass habits. One night, when he had a date to take Carmela to see a picture billed as *Gangster Story*, Mario arrived to find Zia Nicolina standing outside the house.

"Carmela's sick," Zia Nicolina said.

"Oh," Mario said.

"You can't see her, she sleeps," Zia Nicolina said.

"Well, tell her I was here and that I hope she is better," he said.

He turned to go.

"Hey!" Zia Nicolina said.

"Yes?"

"You take Zia Nicolina to the movie instead?"

A vise closed around Mario's throat and he nodded yes, and Zia Nicolina grabbed his arm and he walked her down to the movie house. She sat next to him all night, her fat legs brushing up against his, her hand grabbing his arm when anything happened. Her face, which needed a shave, was shiny with sweat. Carmela and her family lived in a house at the top of the hill, on the edge of town. On the way home Zia Nicolina made Mario go a block out of the way because she wanted to find a hoe she said she had left in the field her family tilled. Zia Nicolina stepped into the field, and Mario, one hand on her elbow, followed her. Zia Nicolina went a couple of steps and then backed into Mario like a truck. Mario was off balance when Zia Nicolina twisted around and put her hands on the back of his neck. She fell backward, and Mario came down on top of her.

Mario despised the night with Zia Nicolina. He had a great love for the earth and the colors and shadings of ground in the sunlight, and he loved the symmetry of a girl, not just her body, but her hair and her eyes and her mouth and the depth that her face could show, and he loved his mornings up on the hills, with the sounds of his work, the tinkling of water running through the brushes when he rinsed them, the tiny sound of a pencil biting into good paper. Every morning he rode up the road winding along the mountain, pushing his legs until they were on fire and then became numb. When he could go up no more, he stopped and drew. When it was time to leave, he turned and came flying down the mountain and onto the hill at the foot of the mountain and down through the town, and he always headed for the start of the road which led out of town and while he was racing on his bike through the town he imagined he was leaving it forever. At the last corner he would turn and slow down and pedal sullenly to his job at the auto-rental agency.

Riding through the hills made him the best bike-rider in Catanzia by the time he was sixteen, and he entered and won several small races sponsored by the church societies. He entered a townwide race and won that too. Savona, from the auto-rental agency, was a bike-racing fan. The day before Mario stumbled out of high school, Savona offered him a job. Mario took the job and continued bike-racing on weekends. He began entering amateur races all over Italy. He received expenses and also placed in the first twenty finishers often enough to earn silent bonuses. He earned $200 for his first major victory, the 25-kilometer race.

He spent most of this money on expensive art paper. Mario's drawing was put to uses of sorts around Catanzia. At a charity carnival for one of the churches he sketched faces and took in more money for the church than the weight-guesser did. Once Mario did a poster for a local bike race and a man from the race committee in Naples liked it so much he gave it to a sporting newspaper in Naples. The sketch ran in the paper, and when Mario got the clipping in the mail he walked around looking at it so much that the newsprint began to disintegrate.

For one big championship race Mario went to Rome, and he took a guided tour of the Cinecittà film studios. In one building dozens of people were sitting in an air-conditioned room and working at drawing boards. They were animating comic strips that ran on television. One of the artists, about twenty-five, had long straggly hair and wore a flowered shirt, tight chino pants, and cowboy boots. He was whistling while he cut out little strips of gray-speckled cellophane and carefully glued them over parts of the comic strip. The tour conductor was talking about the hard, precise work going on in the room. Mario jumped when he heard the word "work." When he got back to Catanzia and was polishing his cars, he kept hearing the tour conductor say the artists were working.

When he was in Rome, Mario took a walk on the Via Veneto and dawdled in the light from the kiosks on a big corner newsstand across the street from the Hotel Excelsior. Mario's eyes jumped when he saw an entire rack of magazines with titles: *Il Giornale di Artista*, *The Artist*, and

Studio International of Modern Art. Mario liked the American magazines best. In one of them the first article was titled, "A Basic Approach to Composition." It was written by Grant Monroe. A picture of Grant Monroe, with great bushy hair and in a T-shirt, ran with the article. The caption read: "Grant Monroe at his studio on 10th Street in New York's East Village." Mario read the article, which was difficult because it referred to a thing called the "Golden Section," which is a triangular way of arranging scenes so that people look into them, rather than see a flat, straight-up-and-down arrangement. He read the magazines for months, always returning to the picture of Grant Monroe and his bushy hair, and he dreamed of meeting him one day. Then the letter from Rinaldi came, and Mario walked around with the magazine under his arm. He would go to America and see Grant Monroe and become an artist and never leave America and never see Catanzia again.

Now, in the cold air of his last morning in Catanzia, Mario walked down the hill from his house as quickly as he could and he came around a corner and went down the block toward the church, which stood facing a square.

Father Marsalano was pacing up and down with the chickens in the cobblestone piazza in front of the church. He carried a prayer book and a Polaroid camera. When Father Marsalano saw Mario turn the corner and come into the square, he brought his hand to his mouth and let out a yell. The chickens flapped up and hung around Father Marsalano's ankles. If he could ever get them to go higher and begin flying in circles around him, he would claim he was Saint Francis of Assisi.

Eleven heads poked from doorways. Father Marsalano pointed to a boy of about seven, who was standing in his bare feet. The boy had short pants and a thin white shirt ripped at the elbows. Black uncombed hair fell onto his face. The boy came running across the square and followed the priest and Mario to the back of the church. A muddy lot covered with rocks and tin cans ran up the hill behind the church.

Father Marsalano held the camera out to Mario. The priest stepped into the lot, and the boy came through the cold mud after him. Father Marsalano grabbed Giovanni's thin shirt and ripped the front of it. Giovanni made a face. Father Marsalano ran a hand through the mud. He wiped his hand on the front of Giovanni's shirt and smeared the mud across Giovanni's face. The kid's mouth almost formed a word.

"All right," Father Marsalano said to Mario, "take the picture."

Father Marsalano stood with the prayer book in his left hand and his right hand on top of Giovanni's head. Father Marsalano's face became somber. Giovanni stuck his tongue out at the camera. Father Marsalano's hand lifted from the top of Giovanni's head. Then it came down hard enough to cause a concussion. Giovanni winced. Mario took the picture.

While Mario was flipping and pulling and peeling to get at the picture, Father Marsalano was on him like a blanket. The priest started saying, "Good! Good!" when he saw the picture. It was nearly as good as a Dr. Tom Dooley poster. Father Marsalano's face was pleading. Giovanni looked only like early death.

Father Marsalano took Mario by the arm and started walking him to the back door of the church. Giovanni stood in the cold mud and made a fist with his right hand and brought his arm up and bent it at the elbow. Giovanni's left hand slapped the inside of his right elbow. This is the classic expression of true Italian regard for the clergy, which first began to appear when Innocent IV was Pope.

Inside, Father Marsalano began writing in pen on the back of the picture:

Dear Friends Who Left Catanzia to Go to America and Become Rich, the Mother of God is watching always. So is Saint Angelo, who is the patron of Catanzia and everybody who ever lived in our town. This picture on the opposite side shows the place where your beloved church is going to erect a new orphanage. This poor little boy standing with me has no place to sleep or eat. He is very hungry now. Also very cold. Someday when we have the new orphanage which we will build this little boy will be warm and fed.

It is good to hear from you. Send me some good news in the mail. Then I will have good news for the homeless little children of Catanzia.

Yours in the Lord,
Father Giuseppe Marsalano

The priest put the picture into a manila envelope. The envelope was already stuffed with addresses of people who had gone to America directly from Catanzia, or who were members of families started by people who had gone to America from Catanzia and were now dead.

"All right, you go now?" the priest asked Mario.

"Yes, Father."

"You know what to do in New York?"

"Go to the mailbox with them to make sure they send the money."

"Good." The priest cleared his throat. "Now, I tell you something. You be a good boy."

"Yes, Father."

"Don't steal."

"No, Father."

"Respect womanhood. Remember. Every woman you meet will be the mother of somebody some day. You respect that. Just remember, the Virgin Mary watches when you're near a woman who will become a mother."

At the airport Mario checked his baggage through to New York. He sat in the little waiting room with his ticket in his hand and looked out the window. The whitecapped, very blue waters of the Strait of Messina ran against the edge of the airport. Across the water the dark mountains of Sicily climbed straight up. Mount Etna, dark at the bottom, misty and snow-covered at the top, had gray smoke billowing from its crater.

Mario looked at Sicily. He had been there once, for a bike race at Palermo. The night before the race he had gone into a *pasticceria* on a little street near the hotel and he stood at a table and played brischola with a priest. The priest was cheating, but when Mario complained a man said he would cut off Mario's ears if he complained again. Mario turned white, but he stayed and kept playing with the priest until there was a power failure. Palermo has three or four of them a night. While the owner was getting out his hurricane lamps, Mario's hands swept the table. He scooped up all the money and ran out of the place. The next day, when the bike race started through the streets of Palermo, Mario put his head down in case the man who had threatened him was in the crowd. He did not lift it up until he was out in the hills of the countryside. Sicilians were strange people.

As Mario looked at the water he heard the noise of the plane. A twin-engined Convair was coming out of the sky. It was the plane which goes from Messina to Reggio Calabria to Rome. The date was January 23. In airports all over Europe, in Belgrade and Turin and Warsaw and Copenhagen, there were bike-riders waiting for planes to America and the many thousands of dollars which the six-day bike race would bring.

Chapter 3

Baccala, the executive producer of the six-day bike race, was at home asleep in his $175,000 brick house in Beachhaven, Long Island. Baccala is 5-foot-5. He was in bed on his back with his arms flung out and his mouth open. He looked like a rolled stuffed pork. His wife, Mrs. Baccala, was asleep on her side next to him. Baccala had his toes stuck between the calves of Mrs. Baccala's legs so he would be warm all night. Mr. and Mrs. Baccala were the only people in the nineteen-room house. They had raised three children: Anthony Jr., who attended Georgetown and became a lawyer in Maryland; Vera, who attended Mt. Carmel College in New Hampshire, and now teaches in San Leandro, California; and Joseph, also known as Zu Zu, who dropped out of high school at the behest of a judge who sentenced him to six months in the reformatory. Zu Zu, twenty-six, is a very promising young shylock in Miami.

Of his three children, Baccala is proudest of Zu Zu. "He's a good nice boy," Baccala always says. All Mafia people succumb to an insidious urge to make their children respectable. But they are never comfortable with it. When the dons sit down for coffee and discuss their children, there are many baffled gestures made with the palms up.

"What do I know what he do?" Baccala said to Louis the Chink one day when asked about his decent son. "All the time he read a book. What do I know? He goes to the school."

But when Zu Zu was fifteen and he had just stood his first pinch, felonious assault with a tire iron on his continuation-school teacher, Baccala came bounding into a restaurant and ordered everybody to drink up.

"What do you think-a my kid does today?" he said. "That little rat-a basset. What do you think-a he does? He breaks his teacher's head!"

"A salut!" somebody called out.

"Aha!" Baccala said. He threw down a straight scotch.

With the children gone, Baccala's house, with its bowling alleys in the basement, stereophonic-fitted bar and study, and square foot after square foot of Italian marble floors, was silent and empty. Outside, floodlights glared on the fenced-in grounds. Two tawny German shepherds loped around the grounds, ready to chew on anybody coming over the fence. Baccala does not rely on the dogs to wake him up if trespassers arrive. He has every inch of his windows and doors wired. The central alarm system is on the floor under Baccala's bed. Its major component is an air-raid alarm. Next to it are two loaded shotguns.

At eight a.m. Baccala was out of bed and ready to leave for the day. He was standing just inside the kitchen door while his wife, Mrs. Baccala, went out into the driveway in her housecoat. Mrs. Baccala slid behind the wheel of a black Cadillac. Baccala sat down on the kitchen floor and closed his eyes and folded his arms over his face. Mrs. Baccala started the car. When the car did not blow up from a bomb, Baccala got up from the kitchen floor and walked out into the driveway, patted Mrs. Baccala on the head as she came out of the car, got in, and backed down the driveway and went off to start another day.

Baccala was beautiful in his big black car. Covered with pressed black Italian silk, he looked stumpy, rather than dumpy. His head was stuck inside a tiny black fedora. The next size after Baccala's hat is a college beanie. He sat on two overstuffed pillows. Without the pillows, Baccala would be so low in the seat that he would have to peer through the steering wheel. Even with the pillows, Baccala has a big wooden block strapped to the gas pedal.

Baccala pressed a $125 black alligator tasseled loafer onto the gas pedal. The shoes were, after Baccala's heart, the most important part of his make-up. New shoes are the badge of the Mafia. Gangsters come from families who went barefoot in southern Italy and Sicily. The children were raised in America in worn sneakers, summer and winter. The first dollar they steal, on growing up, goes to a shoe store. Even old Mafiosos, the ones who have lived to pile up fortunes from narcotics and shylocking, cannot pass a shoe store without going in and buying a new pair. The danger in this is considerable, and many good law-enforcement people feel the way to break up the Mafia is to hit them in the shoes. This was borne out when a joint venture of Baccala's and the Philadelphia mob's turned into real trouble. Representatives from the two mobs shot four major welshers. Three men from each mob were assigned to a burial detail. The graveyard was a field in Rockland County. The six gravediggers who showed up with the bodies all wore $110 pebble-grained Bronzini customs. They walked on their toes through the mud. When they began digging, they tried to push the shovels down only with their toes. They kept stopping to rub their shoes on the backs of their trousers.

"Dig deep down," one of them said.

"I got a fresh shoeshine," somebody muttered.

"Mud gets in the lines around the dots," one of them said, referring to the pebble grain.

The body never did get down very far. A good rainstorm a week later uncovered the bodies, and the FBI moved two mobile laboratories into the field.

As Baccala drove to work, the hopes of three personal families and of his whole Mafia family rested on him. He has the three personal families because he has two other wives, aside from Mrs. Baccala. One of the other wives is a twenty-nine-year-old cocktail waitress who is in a split-level house which Baccala bought for her in Teaneck, New Jersey. The other is twenty-four and redheaded and she wears fur coats and lives in an apartment on East 56th Street. He also has a sixteen-year-old high-school senior as a friend. The wives are absolutely legal wives as far as the government is concerned. Baccala files joint income-tax returns for all three families. Local authorities might require a divorce in here some place, but nobody has ever complained.

Baccala got married three times to solve a great problem which came to a head one night in 1955. The cocktail waitress he was to marry was sixteen. Baccala had her at the bar of a Chinese restaurant. They were sitting on stools and facing each other. The girl rubbed her young knees against Baccala's. His body started to glow. He swallowed his vodka. It created a stirring in his loins. He waited until the Chinaman behind the bar was busy, and he slipped out of the place with the girl. Baccala would stiff a bishop. They walked up to Seventh Avenue, to the Park West Hotel. Baccala went into the cigar store on the corner. He stuffed a handful of twenty-five-cent cigars in his pocket. He took one from the fifteen-cent box and held it out to the clerk. He gave the clerk a dollar for the cigar. While the clerk made change, Baccala hit the candy stand

45

nd came off with six rolls of butterscotch Life Savers. He got the change and grabbed a *Daily News* on the way out.

He took the girl into the hotel lobby. The clerk pushed the registry pad at him. Baccala picked up the pen. He shot his cuffs and held the pen way out. He arranged his feet so his weight would be evenly distributed. Then he bent over the registry pad and brought the pen to it.

Make-a two sticks and put a little v between them, and that's a big M.

He began drawing a capital M, the first letter of "Mr. and Mrs. John Smith."

Baccala's knuckles whitened as he pushed the pen. After he had the capital S in Smith he broke into freehand.

Make a couple of mountains.

He made two mountains for the small m in Smith. It didn't seem right. He went back to make another mountain, and his hand was tired and it slipped and made a mess of the card. Baccala could feel the reservation clerk's eyes boring into him. Baccala dropped the pen and shook his hand. He was angry and too embarrassed to look at the clerk. He put his hand into his pocket and pulled out a roll three inches thick, with hundreds on the top, and snapped a five dollar bill off the roll.

"I got arthrite. You write in for me."

The clerk looked at him haughtily. Baccala was crushed. For his pride, he wanted to bite the clerk on the nose. When he got upstairs with the girl he didn't want to take his clothes off.

After that, Baccala wanted permanent lodgings for his romancing. So he married his two girl friends. Baccala stays home with Mrs. Baccala three nights. The other four are divided among his two other wives and the sixteen-year-old coed.

Baccala is in complete command of his business life. He never touches anything that is illegal. Every year, on Christmas Day, his chief shylock, Moe Fein, arrives with an envelope containing $50,000 in cash. The $50,000 is Baccala's interest for the year on the $250,000 he gave the shylocks a year ago to put on the street for him. The shylocks loan it out for whatever interest they can get. But the first $50,000 must go to Baccala. And the $250,000 can be recalled at any time. Baccala passes on narcotics importing, but is never in the same room with narcotics. It takes large amounts of cash in small bills to pay for a shipment of heroin or cocaine which could earn hundreds of thousands of dollars. If Baccala feels a shipment is worth it, he sends Moe Fein on a plane to Lucerne, Switzerland, to withdraw the money from Baccala's numbered accounts. The accounts total over eleven million dollars. In Switzerland, Fein meets somebody from the Corsican drug-factory organization. Fein and the Corsican are bonded with their lives. Fein flies home, the Corsican disappears, and the narcotics shipment comes into New York from Montreal by car. The narttics seep down to the street, where Negroes do the selling and much of the using. "We don't hurt-a nobody, we only sell to-a niggers," Baccala reasons. The money rises to Baccala. He is silent about it. But as nobody sees anything wrong with gambling, Baccala openly admits he runs all bookmaking and policy numbers in Brooklyn.

Baccala is one of the many Mafia bosses who generally are depicted as controlling sprawling businesses. He has been involved in a number of legitimate enterprises. At one time he was one of the city's largest dress-manufacturers. He used threats, acid, and non-union help. People in the garment industry referred to a Baccala dress as "the buy or die line." The chief assistant in the dress factory, Seymour Lipman, had a brother-in-law named Dave, who also was in the garment business. Dave sold Seymour material. It took four sets of books to do it, but Seymour Lipman and his brother-in-law Dave wound up with houses in Miami. Baccala was losing eighty cents each time he sold a dress. At the first-anniversary party for his dress business, Baccala arrived at the factory with a can of gasoline in each hand.

In another business venture, Baccala and the chief of the East Harlem mob, Gigi off of 116th Street, entered into what they felt would be a gigantic stock-swindling operation. They were doing business with, they were assured, complete suckers. "High-class Protestant people, what could they know?" Gigi off of 116th Street said. Then the high-class Protestants went to Nassau for a week. Baccala and Gigi suddenly lost $140,000 each in the market and were indicted for illegal trading in potato futures.

After being arraigned, Baccala growled, "I shoot-a somebody, but first I gotta find out-a who I shoot-a and what for I shoot-a him."

It cost him another $35,000 in legal fees before the indictment was dismissed.

But as money makes geniuses of all men, Baccala is known as an immensely successful real-estate holder in Brooklyn. The first thing a Sicilian in America seeks is property. This is a reaction to centuries of peasantry. Baccala's first money went for a small house with a back yard in Canarsie. He planted fig trees in the back yard and when it got cold he covered them with tar paper and put paint cans on the tops of the trees. This, along with religious statues and flamingos on the front lawns, is the most familiar sight in an Italian neighborhood. Baccala bought all his property through Joseph DeLauria. In New York State it costs $100 to form a corporation. Shareholders in the corporation do not have to reveal themselves. They can nominate a person to represent them in a realty corporation. In buying realty, DeLauria forms a new corporation specifically to purchase one parcel. He then nominates his secretary to be the name of record for the new corporation. Anybody attempting to check a realty deal runs into a secretary. She

49

traces back to another corporation. Baccala's name is nowhere, and he owns land worth millions. Many business people understand the connection but don't mind doing business. Money is money.

In the course of the years, many lawyers handling real estate in these deals went on into politics. Joseph DeLauria always came around with good campaign contributions. They usually were accepted with deep thanks. Gullible Italians regarded the Mafia as a Knights of Columbus that got mad. They believed that if there were no Mafia, the closest many Italians would come to holding office in this country would be supervisory jobs in the Department of Sanitation. Of course the Mafia gave Italians a bad name. Their money, which was supposed to go to Italians to fight the prejudice the Mafia fed, was being grabbed by Irish and Jewish politicians who didn't like Italians. Frank Costello, the Italian mobster who did the most in politics, did his political fixing through Jewish bagmen and Irish judges. His pushing of Italians for judges was mainly done out of pride for his people. If one of his Italian judges could handle a contract, that was fine. But it was more important that they were Italians and they were judges and that their children would be the children of Italian judges.

But his love for his own dissolved when he and Baccala, if presented with a choice between a fine, highly promising Italian candidate and a dislikable, shifty Irish thief, would at all times go for the Irishman. Baccala's political theories were simple. He had Joseph DeLauria try to bribe every public official in Brooklyn, but he did not expect an inordinate number of breaks to come his way as a result of the bribery. He learned over the years that when it is important, a politician performs for the Mafia about as well as he performs for the public. The popular story is that every big Mafia boss owns one or two appeals-court judges, a few Congressmen, a raft of prosecutors, and, for important contracts, one Supreme Court justice. Now maneuvers with quite a bit of sophistication always do occur. An assistant United States attorney in New York deliberately made reversible errors during a trial so that the Mafia defendant would be certain to win an appeal on a case which was hopeless to win with a jury trial. But endless tales of the Mafia reaching everybody in the world are the result of rumors and fantasies and false promises as much as anything else. Baccala was a political realist. Sure, he'd love to get to a judge. Even higher than that, if possible. But he settled for full ownership of one freshman New York State Assemblyman. The moment the Assemblyman took office, he introduced a private bill which would allow Joseph DeLauria to purchase most of the land under the Hudson River.

In personally vetoing the bill, the Governor remarked to people in his office, "The last person who tried a thing like this was my grand-father."

The drive to the office on this morning took Baccala forty-five minutes. He used the parkway to get to Brooklyn. He came off it onto narrow, puddle-filled streets of warehouses. On one dull street he pulled the car into the empty loading space in front of the dingy two-story Lancer Trucking Company building.

When Baccala came into the building, chairs scraped on the floor of the first-floor office. Four guys jumped to their feet.

"Hey!" Baccala said to them.

The faces of the four screwed into deep thought. Finally one of them said something.

"Hey!" he said to Baccala.

"Hey!" Baccala answered.

"Hey!" another one said.

"Hey!"

"Hey!"

"Hey!"

"Hey!"

The four black suits stood at attention while Baccala started up a flight of narrow wooden stairs. Baccala stamped his Cuban heels on each step as he came up. The noise sounded through the stairwell. A water buffalo in a light blue suit with silver threads appeared at the top of the stairs.

"Hey!" Baccala called out.

"Hey!" the Water Buffalo said.

Baccala walked into the morning silence of his

office, which is a sea of snake plants, lamps with ancient frilled shades, and a large wooden desk. Religious statues were everywhere. When Baccala flicked on the light, the room was alive with multicolored lights arranged around the statues. A bank of red imitation candles glowed in front of Saint Anthony. In cream face, brown robes, yellowing Easter palm tied around the waist in big loop knots, Saint Anthony stood directly behind Baccala's desk.

Baccala whipped his hat off for Saint Anthony. *"Buon' giorno,"* he said.

He held his hat against his chest. He bowed his head and started praying out loud.

"Saint Anthony, let me make the good-a living today. And Saint Anthony, let me tell-a you something. I know they a lot of people, they tell you that Baccala is no good. Tell you that I'm bad. Well, you listen to me, please? You remember one thing. Baccala he's on your side. You need, Baccala he goes out and gets it for you. Don't worry about Baccala. He's with Saint Anthony. So Saint Anthony, you be sure you on Baccala's side. Don't listen to these-a creeps. You understand? All right. Amen."

Chapter 4

At midnight that night, twenty miles away from Baccala's big house, on Marshall Street in Brooklyn, smoke from the first cigarette of the day came against the film of toothpaste on Kid Sally Palumbo's capped teeth. He had just gotten up. Kid Sally straightened his collar. His shirt collar came hallway up the back of his neck. It grazed his ears and came around to a powerful silver tie. He smoothed his hair back. His hair was black and gleamed with brilliantine. It was cut in Madison Avenue buttondown. The day Kid Sally saw Artie the Chink, one of the big guys in the East Harlem outfit, walking around with a button-down, he went into Manhattan and got his hair cut at the same barbershop Frank Sinatra uses. The buttondown seemed a bit off-center for Kid Sally's face. He has a scar running through his right cheekbone. High cheekbones give his deep brown eyes a hard look. His square chin toughens the look of his mouth. He took another drag on the cigarette. It was an English Oval. Frank -

Costello smokes English Ovals.

He blew the cigarette smoke at his face in the mirror. His top lip came up in a careful sneer. He giggled. It was a terrific interpretation of Tommy Udo. Tommy Udo is a gangster in an old movie called *Kiss of Death*. Richard Widmark played the part. The big scene in the movie is when Tommy Udo, sneering and giggling, pushes an old lady in a wheelchair to her death down a tenement staircase. Kid Sally Palumbo loved the movie the first time he saw it. He loved it so much that he came back to the movie house that night and saw it again. The next day he was first in line when the movie opened. Kid Sally was fifteen at the time. For the next fourteen years, less twenty-two months in various prisons, Kid Sally Palumbo saw reruns of the movie wherever it played, so he could learn to imitate Tommy Udo. It was not a waste. As Kid Sally looked at himself in the mirror now, he thought he was seeing Tommy Udo, he was giving such a terrific imitation.

One of Kid Sally Palumbo's main men, Tony the Indian, was standing in the bedroom doorway. Tony the Indian is called the Indian because he looks like an Indian. He has olive skin and black hair that combs straight back on either side of his part. Tony the Indian also acts like an Indian. When he is out collecting gambling debts, he comes into a place with a knife between his teeth.

"So what's doin'?" he said to Kid Sally.

55

"What's doin', I'm gettin' dressed," Kid Sally said. He fingered the tie. He craned his neck to make sure the tie knot and shirt collar sat just right.

"You got a real good *eagle*," Tony the Indian said.

"What should I do, go around thinkin' like I'm a ragpicker?" Kid Sally said.

"That's what I mean," Tony the Indian said. "You got a real terrific *eagle*. You let yourself know you're somethin'."

"You got to get respect off of people. You can't get no respect if you come around actin' like you're just a guy in off of the street. You got to have some class."

"Well, you could *axt* anybody, Sally Kid, they all tell you, that Sally, he got a real *eagle*."

Kid Sally tilted his head to look at himself from another angle.

He and Tony the Indian are always talking to each other. They have stirring conversations, particularly on any telephone they suspect is tapped. Three weeks ago the two spoke over Kid Sally Palumbo's line, which is jointly tapped by the New York City police, the Treasury Department, the FBI, and the Immigration and Naturalization Service.

The phone rang, and a voice the lawmen could identify as Kid Sally Palumbo's answered.

"Yeah," Kid Sally said.

"Hey! What's doin'?" the other voice said. The wiretappers did not know who it was. Kid

56

Sally knew it was Tony the Indian.

"I know you," Kid Sally Palumbo said.

"You do?"

"Yeah, I know you," Kid Sally said.

"All right," the other voice said.

"How we doin'?" Kid Sally said.

"What's goin' on?" the other voice said.

"Did you see that other fella?" Kid Sally said.

"Yeah, I seen him."

"Do you want to see me for somethin'?" Kid Sally said.

"Yeah."

"Meet you right where we was the last time," Kid Sally said.

"You mean the place where that guy —"

"No, not that place. The other place," Kid Sally said.

"What place?"

"The place where we went after the place you're talkin' about."

"Oh, I know that place. Yeah, I was in that place with you."

"What time you be there?" Kid Sally said.

"The same time we was in it last time," the other voice said.

"All right, that's a meet," Kid Sally said.

"We got a meet," the other voice said.

"Take care," Kid Sally said.

"Take care," the other voice said.

When Kid Sally hung up, he stuck his chin out proudly. "Now let them rat mothers, they think they all so smart, let them figger out what that was about."

"Who was it?" one of his men, a dwarf named Beppo who is called Beppo the Dwarf, said.

"Tony the Indian. He seen the guy Levy from Thirty-eighth Street what owed the twenty-five hundred. I got to meet Tony at Ciro's at ten-thirty tonight."

The bug the New York police had put into Kid Sally's desk picked this up. That night two detectives were at the bar when Kid Sally and Tony the Indian came in. The next day a marginal dress manufacturer, David Levy, was brought in for questioning by the District Attorney. Levy said just enough to provoke a new investigation into shylocking.

Kid Sally always seemed to have troubles of this sort. Baccala gave him a clear field in the jukebox business in a few busy sections. Kid Sally established the Ace Vending Machine Company. One of his main men, Joe the Sheik, was in charge of supplying records. Joe the Sheik detested any loud, fast music that reminded him of niggers. "There ain't enough of niggers in the world, people havin' to go around soundin' like them," Joe the Sheik said. Ace Vending juke-boxes carried only Italian numbers. Many people say this is what led to the resurgence of weekend piano-players in Irish bars. Ace Vending went broke, and Baccala laughed openly about it.

Baccala did not laugh so much when Kid Sally

Palumbo, without official sanction, tried to take over businesses by using only muscle. This style went out with Al Capone. The Mafia today tries to emulate Protestant bankers. First, loan money. Then collect souls as interest. Kid Sally Palumbo tried to do it with beatings and acid and terror.

He became particularly attracted to Weight Watchers clubs, which were springing up throughout Brooklyn. The clubs were run at great profit by reedy Jewish women who warned clients, mainly fat Italian women, that "your husband is going to get himself a little girl friend so he can feel her ribs." Weight Watchers profits soared and pasta sales slumped. Soon Kid Sally Palumbo began making visits to the Jewish women running the clubs. He dropped veiled hints: "You could be dead in a bomb accident."

The most faithful member of the Weight Watchers club on Saypole Street was Carmela Russo. At thirty-five, she was 5-foot-2 and weighed 217 pounds. When Carmela Russo bent over to touch her toes, her breasts hit the floor before her fingertips. She regarded Weight Watchers as the last chance for her marriage; two months ago her husband, Tony, had started buying dirty books. One afternoon Carmela Russo was in the Weight Watchers club, exercising very hard. She glanced up and saw Kid Sally Palumbo and two of his group swagger in and begin shouting at Mrs. Millie Lewin, who ran the club. Carmela Russo picked her chest off the floor and let out the first of many loud hollers, the last several of which were heard by the District Attorney's office.

However, as a gangster, Kid Sally is very good at some of the basics. The big thing was his knowledge of Good People. In his circles, you say, "He's good people" when you speak of anybody who has at least one legitimate extortion murder under his belt. Kid Sally is the Walter Winchell of the Good People. When he goes to the jukebox he always plays a record by Phyllis McCarthy because she goes out with Sam Giardine, who is the big guy in *Chick*-ago. He knows that Gigi from the Bronx takes out a barmaid from the Silhouette Lounge. If Kid Sally is in the area he stops in at the Silhouette and leaves the barmaid a $10 tip and says, "My regards to your friend." He knows the barmaid will describe him to Gigi and Gigi will say, "That's-a that nice-a kid, Sally. He's a real nice-a boy." And Kid Sally knows other important things, such as that Georgie Brown from Mott Street lives in Seaview, Long Island; Johnny Brown from Bath Beach lives in Greendale, Long Island; Jackie Brown from East Harlem lives in Pelham Park, Westchester; and Tommy Brown, Eddie Brown, Tony Brown, and Jimmy Brown all go to New Jersey to play golf. Kid Sally never met, but knows all about, Rocky from Detroit, Rocky from Buffalo, Rocky from Cleveland, and Rocky from Topeka.

While Kid Sally stood and looked at himself in

the mirror, he began his crap-game singsong. Until he handled the Georgie Paradise contract, he was best known in Brooklyn for the way he could remember all the sayings and keep saying them, over and over, at the crap games he worked at for Baccala. Kid Sally's job was to stand and watch and keep his right hand ready. At the first squawk from a player, Kid Sally would make a V for victory with the two fingers of his right hand and then jab them into the player's eyes. And while he stood and waited to poke eyes, Kid Sally would singsong to the players. When Kid Sally began doing it here in the bedroom, Tony the Indian smiled. He liked Kid Sally to do this.

"Hey! The game's not hard and nobody's barred. . . . Pick a hunch and grab a bunch. . . . Hey! The more you bet, the more you get. . . . Let it go and watch it grow. . . . Hey! Slow it down. Bet fast and you can't last, bet slow and you got to go. . . . We go every night at ten, come along and bring a fren. . . . Hey! The game's not hard and nobody's barred. . . ."

"Who's got the moneys?" Tony the Indian said.

"Yeah, who got the moneys?" Kid Sally said. "I know it ain't us."

Kid Sally took the English Oval and put it in his mouth. He clenched the cigarette between his teeth. He wanted to see how he looked with the cigarette like this. It was all right, but the cigarette was too short. You can put your teeth on a filter cigarette. But who can smoke filters? You got to smoke English Ovals. Frank Costello smokes English Ovals. Kid Sally let the cigarette hang from his lower lip. He looked through the smoke. That's pretty good. Kid Sally thought he looked pretty good. He felt real good.

Then, as it always happens to him, he became uneasy. Somewhere in his mind, just beneath where he is thinking of all these big things and how he looks, there is this jumbled scene that always lies there waiting for him to come on it, and he always seems to come on it and it makes him feel uneasy.

It is a rainy day in Samuel J. Morse High School. The grade adviser for the first-term boy students has gone over the charts, trying to find a class in which Salvatore Palumbo can sit for the 1:45 to 2:40 period. Salvatore Palumbo has already been placed in all the shop courses and gym periods available. The grammar-school record and Youth Court probation notice attached make it plain that Salvatore Palumbo belongs in chains, not classrooms. The grade adviser notes that Salvatore is only two months away from being sixteen, when he can be ejected from school. "You like Spanish?" the grade adviser says finally. Kid Sally shrugs. "He says he likes Spanish," the grade adviser says.

Kid Sally comes into the Spanish class in his sneakers and brown corduroy pants and blue windbreaker with RED WINGS S.C. printed across the back. The S.C. stands for Screwing

Club. The class is made up of Jewish girls in neat blouses and plaid skirts and they peer through Chinese-slanted eyeglasses when Kid Sally comes into the room. The boys are thin Jewish kids who sit erect and with their eyes riveted on the teacher, a tall, balding man named Goldstein. Goldstein grimaces when he sees Kid Sally. Then Goldstein walks slowly back and forth in front of the classroom and starts the lesson. Kid Sally Palumbo sits down and hunches his neck inside the top of his windbreaker and goes into a trance.

"Wouldn't you say so, Mr. Palumbo?"

There is a roar from the class. Kid Sally Palumbo looks up, and all these black-haired girls are looking at him through their Chinese-slanted eyeglasses and the boys with the bumpy noses are looking at him and everybody is laughing at him. Laughing loudly, and laughing down their noses at him. In the front of the room, Goldstein is smiling.

"Well, give us your answer to the question, Mr. Palumbo," Goldstein says.

Kid Sally Palumbo, flustered, his face red while everybody laughs at him, pulls himself together and does the only thing he knows how to do.

"You could go and fuck yourself!" he shouts at Goldstein.

Every time Kid Sally comes onto this scene in his mind, his stomach begins turning over and he has trouble thinking, and he snarls at Goldstein and the snarl comes up out of Kid Sally's insides and right into the present. And Kid Sally, standing in front of his mirror, moves his mouth around the cigarette. He snarls.

"You could go and fuck yourself!"

"Hey! What you say this for?"

Big Mama had come into the bedroom with her hands on her hips.

"Nothin'," Kid Sally said.

"You watch-a you mouth in the house," Big Mama said.

Big Mama is a short, wrinkled woman with a parrot's bill for a nose. Her gray hair is pulled back in a bun. Her dark brown eyes move quickly. She was dressed in traditional Italian mourning black: black dress, black stockings, black tie-lace shoes. Big Mama's husband, a game but inept extortionist, died twenty-three years ago.

Kid Sally calls her Big Mama because he grew up in an apartment with both his mother, whom he called Little Mama, and his grandmother, who became Big Mama. His mother died of pneumonia when he was nine. The father, Papa Albert Palumbo, did nine years in jail for being an accessory after the fact of a murder. Albert got to the scene too late to do the thing himself, as contracted, but he did arrive just in time to be seen stuffing the body into a cement-mixer. He died a year after he got out of prison. Big Mama raised Kid Sally Palumbo and watched with pride while he headed for stardom, with her urging him on.

"Now you know what to do?" she said to Kid Sally.

"Yeah."

"Make sure you know what to do."

"Yop."

She whispered, "Just remember, all these others, they *bassets*. Rat *bassets*."

Kid Sally's face brightened. Big Mama always made him feel strong. Like the day he was sitting in the back of the courtroom with Big Mama while they waited for an assault case to be called. It was one of Kid Sally's first contracts for Baccala, and he had beaten up the wrong guy. The victim let out a sucker's holler. Kid Sally and Big Mama sat in the brown-paneled court- room and there was a case on before Kid Sally's and the lawyer in the front of the courtroom was questioning a Negro kid who was on the stand.

"Now the racial tensions in your neighbor- hood are the result of it being a Negro neighbor- hood, isn't that correct?" the lawyer said.

"*Ahont* know," the black kid said.

"Well, are there many Negro families living in your neighborhood?"

"Guess so."

"Tell me about the block you live on. What kind of people live on your block?"

"Le's see. There's eight houses that got all Negro people livin' in them, then there's one white family, and then we got one eyetalian family."

"Mulagnon!" EGGPLANT Big Mama screamed from the back of the courtroom.

"Rat *mulagnon basset!*" Big Mama was on her feet now, shaking a finger at the black kid on the witness stand.

"You, you, you — you get you ass whipped."

The judge was directing a court attendant to grab her, and the lawyer, a little man with a mustache, whirled around and shouted, "Please!"

"Jew mocky lawyer!" Big Mama yelled.

The judge, Irish, took no real offense at this. He only had Big Mama and Kid Sally thrown out of the room.

Out in the hallway, Big Mama got up on her tiptoes and looked through the small pane in the door and put the Evil Eye on everybody inside. Kid Sally stood next to her and felt great.

Kid Sally ran manicured fingernails, the polish glistening in the light, over the scar on his right cheek. The scar was one of the prices he has paid for this uncertainty that runs through him sometimes. Once, very early in his career, he was assigned to a good arson job by the Baccala family. His job was to do whatever the arsonist, Benny the Bug, wanted. A row of five attached shops, all losing business in a changing neighborhood, had formed a sort of association and paid Benny to turn their businesses into a large empty lot. Benny spent hours splashing gasoline in the cellars of the stores. He had Kid Sally flatten out the empty gas cans and take them to Erie Basin and throw them in the water. If a fire marshal finds an old gas can in the ruins, he will report this to the police, which is very bad, and to the insurance company, which is far worse. After careful checking, Benny the Bug left the scene and repaired to an el station overlooking the stores. One of the merchants, who had the dry-goods store on the end of the row, was with him. The merchant was worried about a good fire wall in his store.

"You're dealing with professionals," Benny told the merchant.

Presently flames began showing in the windows of the first four stores. Nothing showed from the dry-goods store. "I tol' you," the dry-goods-store man wailed. Benny took out a dollar cigar, licked it with his tongue, then put it in his mouth. All the stores erupted in smoke. The dry-goods shop remained solid. "Ohhhhh!" the shopkeeper moaned. The front of the dry-goods store then blew out into the middle of the street. The roof turned into a geyser of timbers, bricks, and tar paper. A side wall exploded and disintegrated. The flames licked at the fire wall like it was candy.

Benny the Bug took the cigar out of his mouth and sneered at the merchant next to him.

"Nuclear," Benny the Bug said.

Kid Sally Palumbo thought he knew the whole game after that day. He pestered Baccala for arson jobs he could handle himself. Baccala gave him a special, a nightclub in Greenwood Lake which was owned by a cousin of Baccala's and which was losing money. This made the night-club a candidate for the usual restaurant fire, a grease fire in the kitchen, helped along by fifteen gallons of gasoline. Kid Sally sloshed gasoline all over the place late one night. He kept remembering all the things Benny the Bug had done. He was satisfied that he had done everything. He started a small fire in a corner and stepped outside. He strode out like Mussolini. "Beautiful," he said to Tony the Indian, who was waiting in the car. Kid Sally's foot hit something. He looked down to see a gas can. He had forgotten to pick up the gas cans. Kid Sally ran back to the nightclub just as the place exploded. Flying glass cut Kid Sally's face. The next day fire marshals found four gas cans in the embers.

"If Eisenhower owned the place we wouldn't pay," an insurance adjuster said.

Kid Sally looked carefully at the scar on his cheek, then stepped back and put the English Ovals in his inside jacket pocket. Sinatra keeps his cigarettes there.

"Take care," Kid Sally said to Big Mama.

He walked out of his bedroom and into a hallway. The staircase going down to the street is in the middle of a dark hallway. Tony the Indian went down the stairs first. As Kid Sally started down, a door at the far end of the hallway opened and a girl with a pink quilted robe pulled around her stood with the light from her room flooding around her. She had long black hair and off-olive skin. Oriental eyebrows slashed away at

68

an angle from long narrow eyes.

"You going out this late?" she said.

"He got business," Big Mama called out. "You in college. You keep studying. That's-a you business. He got-a his business."

"Take care," Kid Sally said.

"You take care," the girl said.

She shut the door. Kid Sally started down the stairs. Big Mama leaned over the banisters. "You forget," she whispered. She was holding out a black pistol.

"I don't need it," Kid Sally said.

"All right. But you watch you ass."

Chapter 5

Kid Sally bounced down the stairs and through the scarred vestibule and came out onto the street. The building Kid Sally lives in is two stories of old brick with a storefront office taking up the first floor. Gold lettering on the streaked window says ACE VENDING MACHINE. This is a business he ran. His people stole pistachio nuts from the big Washington Market and filled machines with them and put the machines into bars. It was a fair business, but then the Washington Market moved up to the Bronx and security was tighter at the new place and nobody could steal pistachio nuts, so Ace Vending went out of business.

Beppo the Dwarf, with hair hanging in his face, sat in the office. The office was a good place to sit because it wasn't cold like the street. The dwarf had on a plaid short-sleeved sportshirt. He sat at a scarred desk. The wall behind the dwarf was covered with a poster of the front of a nude girl lying on a fat right hip. When the dwarf saw Kid Sally standing outside the office, he twisted around in the straight-backed chair. He got onto his knees, stood up straight, and then got way up on his toes and leaned out and kissed the girl on the poster somewhere around the top of the legs.

"That Beppo, he's crazy," Kid Sally said.

"You bet he's crazy," Tony the Indian said.

In the office, Beppo the Dwarf stood clapping his hands. He had just touched on one of the major sore points of all gangsters, and he knew he was small enough to get away with it. From the day a man is inducted into the Mafia he feels he is God or, at the very least, Saint Michael the Archangel. This ego, coupled with the normal lack of imagination and caring which goes with his IQ, makes the average hoodlum the worst sex partner imaginable. "I'd rather have a cold German than a hot wise guy," Sandra the Hooker announced one night. To overcome this, the wise guys will do anything to leave a girl feeling thrilled, up to, including, and mainly the little scene Beppo had just acted out with the poster. If there is one thing a Mafia guy fears, outside of a narcotics conviction, it is having the girl tell anybody what he does to her.

"If you ever tell," Tony the Indian warned his girl friend one night, "I'll choke you on the throat and make your eyes fall out."

The building Kid Sally lives in is in the middle of the block. The block is made up of single-story tan stucco laundry-truck garages set

71

between four- and five-story tenements that have fire escapes creeping down their fronts. The block seeps to an end against dreary wharves which are part of the South Brooklyn waterfront. A lone tanker, with only a couple of small lights showing on the bridge, sat in the oil-covered water.

On Marshall Street, men could get up in the morning to work with baling hooks as longshoremen. Or they could go out at dusk with a gun. "We got to steal because they don't let us in, we're Italian," Kid Sally said. Of course, Italians were spreading rapidly through politics, medicine, and law. Any bad name was coming from the two thousand mobsters who sullied millions. Upon arrest, Mafia hoods screamed discrimination.

This situation once led Nathan Glaser, director of the Brooklyn Regional Social Security Office, to observe, "These people don't take out Social Security cards even once in their lives. If we had a few more places like Marshall Street we'd be mailing tambourines to retired people."

Kid Sally Palumbo and Tony the Indian started up the cracked sidewalk toward the corner. Kid Sally's shoulders swung, and his legs were close together. His steps began with the toes and the balls of his feet pushing against his big black thick new shoes. Kid Sally had spent a long time learning how to walk this way. An alert, quick walk is rare in a poor neighborhood.

People usually react to environment right down to their feet. In crumbling surroundings people walk with a wide, aimless gait. On Marshall Street a woman going to buy tripe for dinner slumps into three or four people each way. On Madison Avenue, women coming for fittings swing their legs out of taxicabs and flick across the sidewalk through a wall of businessmen without bumping. On Marshall Street, only Kid Sally Palumbo, who is trying to be a general in the Mafia, has direction to his stride.

Tony the Indian went to one of a row of brown-doored garages near the corner. He opened the doors and went in and backed out a black Cadillac. Kid Sally shut the doors and got into the car. Ten minutes later Tony the Indian slowed the car as it came to the corner of a dark street. He inched the car past the building line of a red brick supermarket. Kid Sally looked down the neon-lit sidewalk of Flatbush Avenue. It was empty. Tony the Indian hit the gas and the car swerved around the corner and came to a stop, tires squealing, in a flood of neon formed by a long sign:

THE ENCHANTED HOUR

A poster in one window said:

INDOOR CLAM BAKE, SUNDAY AFTERNOONS.
CHICKEN CACCIATORE, LINGUINE
AND GO GO GIRLS!

73

The noise of the tires squealing made the people near the windows in the Enchanted Hour look out. They saw Kid Sally Palumbo step out onto the sidewalk and march like Mussolini to the door. Tony the Indian swung around the car after him. Kid Sally waited at the door for Tony to open it. Kid Sally arranged his lips in a Tommy Udo sneer. Then he walked into the Enchanted Hour and he could feel everybody in the place looking at him.

"Hey!" somebody said to Kid Sally. He nodded and kept walking.

"Hey!" somebody else said. Kid Sally nodded again.

Kid Sally went down the bar to an empty black leather stool. He stood alongside the stool. Never sit. You sit and you look all bent over. Kid Sally stood at the bar with the English Oval hanging from his bottom lip and his chin out and his chest out and his shirt cuffs showing nice, feeling real soft and good on his wrists. The mirror behind the bar made everything look blue because the place was so dark. Kid Sally tilted his chin higher, and the smoke came out of his nose and mouth at the same time. One stream of blue smoke running up and one stream of blue smoke coming down. In the mirror, Kid Sally saw a guy who really knows what he's doing. *Good People,* Kid Sally said to himself.

He put a hundred-dollar bill on the bar. His index finger waved. "Take care of us, here," he said.

The bartender flung himself in front of Kid Sally. "Scotch?"

"For me and my friend." The finger waved. "And buy the bar a drink."

The bartender nodded. He threw straight scotches and water in front of Kid Sally and Tony the Indian. Then he ran up and down the rest of the bar, filling the order. Kid Sally would borrow at shylock interest rates before he would put anything less than a hundred-dollar bill on the bar at the Enchanted Hour.

A short guy in a black suit came down the bar and stood with him.

"You got somethin' for me, pal?" Kid Sally said.

"The guy give me long stories," the little guy said.

"What stories?" Kid Sally said.

"I think he's a broken-down suitcase," the little guy said. "I don't know if he got."

Kid Sally was leaning against the bar. He pushed away from it and stood up straight, his shoulders squaring.

"Who does this guy think he is? I'm going to break both his legs and throw in a arm for good measure," Kid Sally said. "Who is this guy, not payin'? Does he know who he's doin' business with?"

"I told him it was good people," the little guy said.

"I'm gonna do what I have to do," Kid Sally said.

"I tol' him," the little guy said.

Kid Sally looked at the little guy. "All right," he said. The little guy left. Kid Sally turned back and looked at himself in the mirror. Huh. The whole place was looking at him. They all got respect for Kid Sally Palumbo, he told himself. He began to think of the day when he could walk into the big places in Manhattan, the Copa and Jilly's, and get the respect the big guys over there get.

At his left elbow was a small railing that separates the regular bar from the service bar. The service bar has an aluminum top for draining. The red and blue neon from the jukebox was reflected in watery light on the aluminum. The waitress, her long black hair swinging across her shoulderblades, brushed behind Kid Sally and came up to the service bar, just on the other side of the little railing. She put a tray down on the aluminum.

"One C.C. and water, a vodka gimlet, and two Dewar's on the rocks," she said.

Kid Sally took his shot glass of scotch and flicked it down in a gulp.

The waitress stood at the aluminum with her lips pursed. She clucked in rhythm to the music from the jukebox.

The bartender was reaching for a bottle on the back bar to start filling her order. Kid Sally put his shot glass down. He waited until the bartender was right in the middle of reaching for the bottle.

"Take care of me and my friend," Kid Sally

said. His finger waved.

The bartender stopped in the middle of his motion. He grimaced. Then he turned around with a big smile. "Sure, Sally Kid," he said.

The waitress looked at Kid Sally. "Really!"

Kid Sally made his Tommy Udo sneer.

"You!" the waitress said.

Kid Sally felt great. He loved being a big shot like this.

Tony the Indian tapped him on the arm. "That guy is in the booth waitin' for you."

Kid Sally threw down his drink and lit a fresh cigarette. He squared his shoulders. This was a very important match for him. He walked to a booth in the back of the place. He slid in on the empty side. The man sitting opposite him grinned. The man was wearing a hand-stitched light brown glen-plaid suit. His reddish hair was closely cut. He wore hornrimmed glasses. His name was Izzy Cohen and he was Baccala's chief Jew. The Mafia relies heavily on Jews. Boss gangsters are usually able to count only when they take off their shoes and use their toes. Every big outfit has a Jew who can count money and mastermind gambling and swindling operations. As the hoodlums do not understand exactly what the Jew is doing, but suspect the worst, they threaten the Jew periodically. Baccala always tells Izzy Cohen, "You steal and I make you put you tongue on the third rail." Izzy Cohen throws up his arms in horror. The next morning he takes out his Jewish revolver, a ballpoint pen, and goes to work and steals some more. Izzy comes out of a family of pushcart peddlers on the East Side of Manhattan. The north end of his brain has clear, almost impressive university tendencies. The south end is cluttered with worms which become active only when the word larceny is programed into them. This situation makes Izzy Cohen a literate thief. As the master figure man for the Brooklyn mob, he is thought to be as brilliant as the late Abba Dabba Bernstein. Abba Dabba worked for Dutch Schultz and became famous for his ability to fix the Cincinnati Clearing House total, used for policy numbers payoffs.

"Where do we stand?" Kid Sally Palumbo said. He wanted to let Izzy know who was in charge. Kid Sally was. Kid Sally had a button in the Mafia. Izzy was only a Jew. They can't join.

"My work was finished before it started," Izzy said.

"What do you mean?" Kid Sally said.

"I know my business. Let me ask you something. Where do you stand?"

"Stand where?"

"Stand with everything."

Kid Sally reached inside his jacket for his cigarettes. He carefully took one from the pack. He picked up his lighter and flicked it open. He wanted to show this Jew who he was.

"You want a Monte Carlo made up around a bike race, right?" Izzy Cohen said.

"Right," Kid Sally said.

"I got that already," Izzy said. "Now let me ask you one thing. Suppose a chain breaks? What do you do then?"

"A chain? What chain?"

"The chain on the bike breaks. What do you do then? You can't have a price on a bike-rider if his chain breaks. What do you have for that?"

Kid Sally felt all this uncertainty running through him.. He put the cigarette in his mouth and gave Izzy the Tommy Udo sneer.

"I got the fat man takin' care of all the details. What do you think, I'm some little kid runnin' around fixing bikes?"

"What do you mean by everything?" Izzy Cohen said.

"Just what I said. The fat man does all my work for me. He's terrific at takin' care of things like this."

The fat man was Big Jelly Catalano, and he is 425 pounds slabbed onto a 6-foot-3 frame and topped by a huge owl's face with a mane of black hair. He looks at the world through milk-bottle eyeglasses. What he thinks the world should be has made him, at thirty-two, a legend in South Brooklyn. In grammar school, with 280 pounds of him lopping over both sides of his seat and blocking the aisles, he spent his years with his hands covering his mouth while he whispered to the girls:

"Sodomy!"

"Period!"

"Come!"

Since that time he has done so many bad things that Judge Bernard Dubin, Part 2B, Brooklyn Criminal Court, one day was moved to observe, "If this man ever could have fit on a horse, he would have been a tremendous help to Jesse James."

While Kid Sally guaranteed on this night that all things were being handled by Big Jelly, while the bike-riders were due in the country in a matter of hours and the race was only a week off, Big Jelly was doing what he always does at night.

"I'm telling you it's all right," Big Jelly was saying to the maitre d'. The maitre d' was nervously fingering three menus while he stood in the foyer and tried to block Big Jelly's entrance into the Messina, a restaurant on East 55th Street in Manhattan.

"Meester Jelly, please, we got a nice-a place here. You a circus."

"Carlo, will you stop it," Big Jelly said. "This is my wife. Say hello to Carlo, honey."

A thin ebony-wood carving with a tremendous chest bursting against a white blouse held out her hand to Carlo.

"*Howyou,* my good man," she said.

"And this here is my mother-in-law," Big Jelly said.

A cocoa-colored girl built like a middleweight and dressed in a blond wig and yellow miniskirt began to giggle. "If Jelly my son-in-law, then that make him a mother-in-law fucker!"

Carlo turned his head to see if anybody inside had heard her, and the two girls began to shriek and Big Jelly reached out and mussed Carlo's patent-leather hair, and he pushed past Carlo and the two girls came with him and Carlo had to trot to get ahead of them and he was scowling while he led Big Jelly and his two girls to a table in a corner in the back of the room.

Big Jelly sat down and untied his pearl-gray tie. He took off the jacket of his size-64 black mohair suit. He unbuttoned his white shirt and took it off and arranged it over the back of the chair. Big Jelly now sat in a T-shirt that had broad pink stains on it from some previous powerhouse linguine sauce which would not come out in the wash. Big Jelly always takes his clothes off when he eats because his stomach and chest stick out so far that the fork always brushes against them and food drops down his front. So Big Jelly strips down and lets the linguine sauce fall where it may.

All around the carpeted dining room people were looking at Big Jelly in shock, then smirks and a chuckle or two. Big Jelly's mother-in-law leaned across the table and began rubbing the two cow udders that Big Jelly has for a chest.

"You make a girl for somebody," the mother-in-law said.

Big Jelly laughed loudly. He cupped his hands under his cow udders and he swung back and forth in his seat.

"That's it, that's it," the mother-in-law said.

81

The wife began to clap her hands and sing a smoker song.

Carlo came plunging between tables, running his hands over his hair and then waving them.

"Please, please."

"Please what?" Big Jelly said.

"This is no pigsty," Carlo said.

"A pig!" Big Jelly shouted. "You call me a pig? Who's a pig!"

He picked up a butter plate and bounced it off Carlo's head. Carlo grabbed a glass of water and threw it in Big Jelly's face. Big Jelly got his size-13 shoe out from under the table and he kicked Carlo in the ankle. Carlo let out a scream and clutched his ankle. Big Jelly bounced another plate off Carlo's head. A waiter in a red jacket came over and grabbed Big Jelly. The girl with the big breasts got her nails into the waiter's face. He screamed. Another waiter grabbed the girl. Big Jelly missed a right-hand punch but he got a fork in his hand and brought it down hard into the waiter's hand. The two girls got up from the table. Big Jelly grabbed his shirt, tie, and jacket and fought with one hand while he and the girls made their way to the door. Big Jelly came out into the cold air in his T-shirt, and his hair was all over his face.

"I'll burn that joint down," he screamed.

The two girls waved a cab. The three of them got in, and Big Jelly said he wanted a drink. They went to Clarke's on Third Avenue for straight vodka. The cab waited outside. Then Big Jelly took his girl friends to a place on Madison Avenue, where he drank scotch with a wine chaser. They told the cab-driver to take them to Jilly's on 52nd, but they made a stop at the Wagon Wheel on the way, and now Big Jelly was clapping his hands and rolling his eyes and saying, "Sodomy!" and the two girls slapped their thighs and the wife fished into her purse and Big Jelly yelled, "Find it for paper." When the cab-driver saw the girl come out with three marijuana cigarettes and pass them around, he stopped the cab and got out and leaned against the hood.

"If I'm goin' to take a pinch, it's goin' to be for my own habit, not yours," he announced.

"It's all right, I'm with my mother and she lets me," Big Jelly said.

At 6:30 a.m. the two girls were standing naked in Room 625 of the Hotel West Virginia. The bathroom door opened and Big Jelly came out naked with a black beret tilted over his right eye.

"Ooooooo la la," he said.

Chapter 6

At 7:05 p.m. Alitalia flight 101 came in on its approach to Kennedy Airport. The plane whined across the last of the Atlantic with its landing floodlights striking the black water and then running onto the gray sand of Rockaway Beach. In the tourist section of the plane Mario Trantino and seven other bike-riders tumbled around the windows like monkeys, trying to see America for the first time. The plane came down on the winter-wet runways and Mario Trantino came down the steps with his eyebrows up, mouth open, eyes afire.

Joseph DeLauria was waiting in the lobby in his function as president of the bike-race association. A crowd of men stood with him. When the passenger agent brought Mario and the other riders out, DeLauria pushed through people and hugged Mario. He stepped aside, and a thin old man wearing the red, green, and white sash of the Society of San Gennaro kissed Mario on both cheeks. Two fat doctors wearing reception-committee rosettes waited in line. Another man in a sash stood behind them.

Joseph DeLauria was next to Mario, rattling off names, "Mr. Riccobona . . . Mr. Scola . . . Mr. Cirillo . . . Dr. Palermo . . . Mr. DiLorenzo . . ."

Mario jumped. "Mr. DiLorenzo!"

The fat man hugging Mario nodded eagerly. Mario reached into his jacket pocket for the list from the priest. "DiLorenzo, DiLorenzo," he said. His finger shook while it went over the list and stopped at the name.

"Are your people from Catanzia?"

The fat man nodded yes. His eyes became filled. He hugged Mario tightly. Mario put the list back in his pocket and wrapped his arms around the doctor.

"You know Father Marsalano? He put your name down on the list here."

The fat man pushed backward against Mario's arms.

"He said you'd help," Mario said.

The man broke out of his arms and went backward through the crowd.

"Hey!" Mario called out to him.

"Bafongool," the fat man said. He fled into a crowd.

Mario tried to follow him in the crowd, but his eyes fell on two Air France stewardesses. The committee led Mario out of the airport while he kept twisting to see the stewardesses, and when Mario got into Manhattan the lights in the theater district, and the crowds walking in them, made him dizzy.

Mario passed out when he got to the room. He woke up in the morning with his head under a pillow. He rolled over on his back and began to run his legs back and forth against the white sheets. His body tingled with its first brush of luxury. He swung out of bed and went over to the window. Manhattan in the morning in the silence drifts across the eyes, and the buildings seem to be moving into each other. Beyond the buildings was the river. The river water was winter-gray and the January wind blew onto the water from an angle and made a windowscreen pattern on the surface. Mario went into the bathroom and unwrapped the soap. It was the biggest bar of soap he had ever seen. He held the soap to his nose. There was a clean smell with an undertone of cologne. It did not have the cleaning-fluid smell of Italian soap. He twisted the shined silver handle in the stall shower. Warm water, becoming hot, came down on him. He turned and let the water fall on his neck. He stood there with the hot water hitting his neck, and he was using more water with this one shower than entire families use during a day in Catanzia. Mario began thinking while the hot water fell on his neck. He began thinking of the same things anybody who lands in America thinks of. Mario was thinking about staying in America forever.

He came out of the shower and sat on the edge of the bed and flipped through the telephone directory. He was surprised to find Grant Monroe listed. He dialed the hotel operator and gave her the number.

"You can dial that yourself," she said.

"I'm blind," Mario said.

"Oh, I'm sorry, I'll get it for you," she said.

Mario spoke away from the phone. "Do your own work, I don't do it for you."

Grant Monroe's number rang several times. Finally a foggy voice answered. Mario stood up in excitement.

"Mr. Grant Monroe?" Mario said.

"Of course, he's always up answering phones this time of day."

"Oh, good," Mario said. "Could I please to speak to him?"

"Oh, I see. You're not putting me on. You *are* sick."

The phone clicked.

Mario got dressed and went downstairs, where he waited for Joseph DeLauria. Since Mario could speak English, DeLauria was taking him around town for publicity interviews. When DeLauria arrived he was grumpy because he didn't like being an errand boy, and he was also afraid the bike race would be a flop and he would be blamed for it. "My guys don't even know what a bike race is," Bobby Scola of Hodcarriers Local 43 told DeLauria. DeLauria gave the desk clerk envelopes addressed to the bike-riders. He handed Mario one. It contained a hundred-dollar bill for expenses. Mario put the bill in the watch pocket of his suit. He went to the news-stand and took two Hershey bars for breakfast. He stepped aside so DeLauria could pay. DeLauria remained immobile. Mario made a face like a beggar in pain. DeLauria muttered and fished in his pocket for change.

DeLauria took Mario to the offices of a scratch sheet which ran little sports-news items, to two small radio stations, and then to the big chain afternoon newspaper. By custom, it was the easiest to crack for publicity. The custom called for DeLauria to step into a small office with the sports editor and pay money. The sports editor then called out to a young guy who was sitting at a desk and writing a headline for a basketball story. The headline said, "St. John's Splinters Holy Cross." The young guy put down his work and interviewed Mario.

Back at the hotel, Mario called Grant Monroe again. There was no answer. He watched television all afternoon. At night three fat men on the race committee took the riders to dinner at a restaurant across the street from the hotel. The riders, mixed up by the time changes, began to fall asleep at the table.

In the morning Mario called Grant Monroe again. After many rings, the foggy voice answered.

"The wake is tomorrow," the voice said. "He died yesterday. He cut his throat." The voice trailed off. "Hey, it's seven-thirty in the freaking morning. Are you crazy? What do you do, sleep in the streets?" The phone clicked.

The bikes had arrived by air freight. They were being kept in a park building at Central Park. Mario and the other riders went for a workout at ten. Many of them were asking when the indoor track would be ready for practice. Joseph DeLauria laughed and clapped a few of them on the back. After the workout DeLauria walked out of the park to hail a cab. Mario, who was wearing a black sweatsuit and had sweat dripping from his chin, ran after DeLauria. He got in the cab with him. Mario showed DeLauria Grant Monroe's address on 10th Street.

DeLauria shook his head. "Puerto Rican neighborhood."

Mario did not answer.

DeLauria held his hands out. "So go get killed." DeLauria told the cabbie to go down the East Side to 10th Street.

Tenth Street was narrow, and tin cans and spilled garbage bags were on the curb and in the gutter. The blacktop was covered with swatches of broken glass, which glistened in the pale winter-morning sunlight. The sidewalks were empty in the cold. The houses were five- and six-story adjoining walkups, some dirty red, some dirty brown, some dirty tan, with chalk-marked stoops and high, bare soot-covered windows. Number 288 was dirty red. The brass mailboxes in the vestibule were scarred and bent from being pried open by junkies. The names on some of them were printed by hand on cardboard and were so smudged Mario had to look closely to see Ruiz and Torres and Maldonado. The other slots had no names on them. Mario couldn't find Monroe. He tried the vestibule door. It was unlocked and he came into a lightless hallway with a staircase in front of him and an apartment, the door half open, on his left.

Mario knocked on the half-open door. There was no answer. He stepped inside. He was in a bare-floored front room. The walls were covered with floor-to-ceiling posters of pop art. One showed a caveman chiseling "Nobel Peace Prize" onto a stone tablet. An old bathtub was against one wall. It had a curved lip at the top and it stood on ornate legs. The bathtub was painted in psychedelic swirls. In the middle of the room were easels and tables with brushes and paints and palettes. A high stool was placed in front of the three windows looking onto the street.

"Hello," Mario called out.

There was a muffled sound from the back of the apartment. A door opened and a little man pushed himself into the room in a wheelchair. He was bald and wore glasses and he had a brown bottle of whisky in his lap and a cup in his left hand. He pushed the chair with his free hand. He brought the chair to a stop at a long table.

"In that case," he said. He put the cup and the whisky bottle on the table. He opened the whisky bottle and poured into a glass. He swallowed the whisky in a gulp. He picked up the cup and spilled something on a large sheet of art paper on the table. He began rubbing his fingers on the wet paper.

"He knows I only want tea and the son-of-a-bitch doesn't buy me any and he tells me use coffee. Use coffee, and he'll see what he gets."

"What's that?" Mario said.

The little man kept rubbing the paper. "Tea, I said tea, can't you even hear? He wants something to look ten years old. I use tea on the new paper to make it look old. Tea does it good. This son-of-a-bitch, what does he care? He says use coffee if I don't have tea. Oh, he's a lazy bastard."

"Who?" Mario said.

"Who? Who do you think? What's the difference anyway? I'm so freaking stewed now I don't care."

He poured himself another drink. After he swallowed it, he ran his hands over his face.

"All night I work, and twice in a row now some dirty bastard calls here early in the morning and wakes me up. Two days in a row. So this morning I said to hell with it. I just took myself into the kitchen and had a pick-me-up. And I'm still picking myself up. Freaking telephones."

The little man's head was flopping toward his left shoulder, and he had to raise his eyebrows to focus on Mario.

"Where are you from, dressed like that?"

"I'm Mario Trantino. I am from Catanzia in Italy."

"How's the Pope?"

"His Holiness?"

"Yeah. I think he wants to make sex a contest. See whose wife gets caught tonight."

He spun around in the wheelchair and whirred over to the bathtub. He fumbled with his fly and went in the bathtub. He ran the water, shut it off, and whirred back to the table.

He held the bottle out to Mario. "Treat it like it's your own."

Mario looked at him. "Come on," the man said. Mario walked over to him, took the bottle, and put it inside his mouth as if it were a tongue-depressor. He was not going to do anything to have this man in the wheelchair get mad and make him go away. With his lips outside the bottle, there was no way for Mario's mouth to close by reflex and block the flow of whisky. When he tilted the bottle, the whisky poured free and a string of small bubbles beaded through the bottle, and then more of them came, and finally an air pocket gurgled through the whisky.

"Hey," the man said. "When I was young I was taught that whisky is better for you than jerking off, but you're ridiculous." Mario's stomach was turning. He breathed out of his mouth so he wouldn't gag.

"Now what do you want?" the guy said. He took a drink for himself. "You want Grant?" Mario said yes. "Then what the hell are you doing here? Don't you know him?"

"Oh, yes, I know him very well," Mario said.

"Well, then, you know that he's never here. What the hell would he do here? There's work here. He can't do any of this. He doesn't even know to pour tea. Use coffee if you don't have tea, he says." The little man looked up. "Say, what the hell is that outfit you got on?"

"It's a — well, the clothes I wear, in the — ah — they are my clothes — ah —"

"It's your game, not mine," the little man said. "Jeez, I'm stewed. And I got to have this work done by tomorrow morning. An early work. Huh. Where is the thing now?" He leaned over and went through a pile of paper on a small table and pulled out a street scene that was obviously New York. "Here we are," he said.

"It's very nice work," Mario said.

"Nice work? It's great work. The guy broke his back doing things like this. But people are pigs. You know he never sold this? He never knew how to push himself, so he never sold this? That's one thing you can say about Grant. For somebody who never drew a stroke in his life, he has taste. He knows where to get some obscure thing and sell it around. Hell, we'll push ten of these things out. I can do one of these in a day. Just as long as we don't get jammed. Jeez, I *am* stewed." He picked up the bottle.

"He leaves me here with nobody. Christ, he wants nobody around to see. All right. But get me somebody to bring me tea. He forgets about me being in the chair here. You know what he said to me once? He said, 'Meet me uptown right away.' Me. How'm I going to get down the stairs here? I told him, if I could just leave here like that, I would be playing football and screwing young cheerleaders. When do I get out of here? He's supposed to come around and he never does. He sends a cabbie to take me out. I go up to Harlem. The Glamour Inn. You get stewed and they let a broad wheel me into the back room. Beautiful. So what does the cabbie do? He takes a fare and he leaves me there. I'm trying to get a cab from the curb and all these bastards are pullin' the money out of my pockets and I can't stop them. Son-of-a-bitch. Then I ask him for an answering service and he won't even get me that. So freak him. I got woken up two mornings in a row, freak him. I'm drunk."

He stopped talking and looked at Mario. "If you go to the Plaza and see him, don't start telling him Sidney is sitting here drunk. Sidney is good and drunk. Only don't tell him."

He frowned for a moment and looked cock-eyed at Mario. "Say, how did you get in here? Did Grant give you a key?"

Mario smiled and decided not to tell him the door was just open. He said good-by and walked backward out of the room. He waved good-by at the door. "Don't say I'm drinking," Sidney called after him. Mario shut the door.

Mario went outside and walked the streets in his black sweatsuit, asking directions for his hotel every few blocks. In the lobby he asked where the Plaza was and what it was and the bellhop told him it was a very good hotel. Mario went upstairs, showered, and changed into his suit. At two, he went to the Plaza, with its horse-carriages and Rolls-Royces and hot-dog venders parked around a fountain, and the scrubbed steps, under an ornate heated marquee, leading to the lobby. Mario asked at the desk for Grant Monroe. He was not registered. Mario began to walk around the lobby.

Grant Monroe was sitting at a small table in the corner of the Palm Court. His long fingers, which had a couple of dusty orange paint streaks on them, were wrapped around a small china coffee cup. Grant Monroe was dressed in a shapeless tweed topcoat that was splattered with red and blue and gray paint. His hair was uncombed and it came down the back of his neck and stood out where the coat collar brushed up into the back of his neck. Underneath the coat he had on a gray turtleneck and an array of multicolored love beads. He sipped the coffee, put it down, and peered through his glasses. His left hand went into his topcoat pocket. It twisted around inside. It came out slowly, while Grant looked around to see who was watching him. The hand came up holding a tugged-off piece of salami sandwich on rye bread. He pushed the whole piece into his mouth, and his jaws worked violently to compress the salami and rye bread before they choked him.

The minute Mario saw Grant, he brushed

through a row of potted palms and came up to the table. Mario was starting to introduce himself when the violins struck up and his words were lost.

Grant was up on his feet, pushing Mario away with one hand and waving with the other. "Oh, Mrs. Tyler! Here, Mrs. Tyler. Essie, right here!"

A tall slim woman in a white wool coat with black leather trim waved a gloved hand at Grant and walked toward his table. Grant began pushing Mario hard. "I'm quite busy at the moment; oh, you look stunning, Essie. Come sit." Grant Monroe put his hand onto Mario's chest and gave a shove.

The woman slipped into a seat at the table and opened her coat, and Grant helped her put it on the back of her chair. Grant then reached under the table and brought up a huge black leather folder and pulled a chair up next to the woman, and he sat down and held open the folder and spoke excitedly to her while he showed her the painting. It was the same street scene Sidney had just shown Mario. He could hear snatches of Grant talking.

". . . You see, I am accepting a Guggenheim to work abroad and I just felt I could not simply leave and have this hanging nowhere. It was always my favorite and now that I have my Guggenheim I feel I must dispose of it . . ."

Mario stepped through the potted palms and onto the carpeted walkway which goes around the Palm Court. The walkway was empty. Mario bent over and snatched at his shoelaces. He pulled them open and out of the holes so they flopped loose. He reached into the breast pocket of the suit and took out his uncle's eyeglasses. He pulled his tie half open and out of his jacket. Feet flopping, his eyes shut, Mario pushed back into the Palm Court.

He opened his eyes and looked over the top of the glasses once so he could aim himself at Grant Monroe's table.

"Grant Monroe?" he said.

"Yes, I'm quite busy now if you'll excuse me," Monroe said. "Now, Essie, this is the perfect thing for your sitting room."

"It *is* charming."

"I saw Sidney and he told me where you were," Mario said. Grant Monroe's eyes became large behind his glasses. His mouth became set.

"Grant," the woman said, "now you must talk to me sensibly about price. I can see that it's . . ."

Mario stumbled away from the table and went out into the lobby.

"Say there!" Grant Monroe rushed into the lobby behind him. Grant was breathing quickly. He took Mario by the arm and walked him to a row of telephone booths.

"Now where did you see Sidney?" he said.

"This morning."

"This morning where?"

"At your place where he works. On Tenth Street."

Grant Monroe's lip was trembling. His eyes

flashed. He ran a hand through his hair. He plunged into a phone booth. His paint-streaked, bony fingers fumbled a dime into the phone and stuttered through the dialing process.

"Come on, answer the phone, come on, come on, oh, hello, Sidney? . . .

"Sidney? Who do you think it is? Of course. Sidney? What's the matter with you? Sidney, are you drinking?" Grant put a hand over the phone and looked at Mario. "Was he drinking?" Mario nodded yes. Grant went back to the phone. "Sidney, listen to me. Did a person come in this morning, a person from Italy? He did? Well, Sidney, how many times have you been told . . . Hey! Don't you say that to me. Sidney! Sidney, don't you ever talk like that to me. WHAT! What did you just say? Sidney, that goes for your mother too. Sidney?" He looked at the phone and hung it up.

Grant Monroe slumped in the phone booth. His legs stuck out. He was wearing chino pants and white socks and loafers. His hand dug into the coat pocket and came up with the torn salami on rye. He took a bite of it.

"The first thing you do," Monroe said, talking with his mouth full, "is to bring your own lunch. You order a sandwich in there, they charge you two-fifty for a piece of Kraft's cheese on bread. The coffee is bad enough. A dollar."

He looked at Mario. "Now I have to go back in and talk to that woman. What is it you have on your mind?"

"Nothing, I just wanted to meet you," Mario said.

He who catches a thief at work and who wants to take part in the work must show patience or risk disturbing the entire operation. Mario did not have to be taught the basics of larceny. He nodded good-by and left. Back at the hotel, a note in his box said there would be a cocktail party at 5:30 the next night and all riders were asked to attend. Practice as usual in Central Park in the morning. Mario thought for a while. It was just as well. He'd need a couple of days to get an idea together and then he could take it to Grant Monroe for help. He went to a movie and to bed early and he woke up in the morning feeling very happy.

Chapter 7

The police dog had the garbage bucket over-
turned on the sidewalk and he had his head flat-
tened and his nose was rooting at the garbage
when Big Mama came out on the stoop with a
broom to start the morning. Big Mama pulled
the black shawl around her and came clumping
down the steps with the broom held out.
"Shooooo!" she was saying. The dog's head
stopped twisting inside the bucket. He watched
Big Mama out of the sides of his eyes. "Shoooo!"
she said again. The dog's lips parted and long
yellow teeth showed. A growl came through the
teeth. Big Mama stamped her foot on the pave-
ment. "Shooo! The dog's head came up and he
growled loudly and his teeth reached for Big
Mama. Big Mama let out one yelp in outrage.
She swung the broomstick with her right arm.
She swung it so hard the broomstick whirred in
the air, and when it caught the dog in the mouth
the dog's head turned and the growl became a
whine. Big Mama swung the broomstick back-
handed and caught the dog in the face again.

The dog was trying to get away when Big Mama got both hands on the broom and hit the dog across the back with a full-armed shot. The police dog howled and scrambled away. "Shoooo, sonomabeetch!" Big Mama said.

Big Mama, muttering to herself, swept the garbage back into the can. She righted the can, covered it, put the broom up against the building, and began carrying the can out to the curb. She had to arch her back against the heaviness of the can. Other women were out in the street, dressed in the black uniform of old Italian women. They came up cellar stairs or down stoops or out of doorways, and they all carried garbage cans in hands that had deep wrinkles over the knuckles. After this they walked slowly up to the corner and turned onto Columbia Avenue to buy bread for breakfast.

The avenue runs parallel to the river for the entire length of the South Brooklyn waterfront. It is made up of stores set into the bottom floors of five-story brownstone walkup buildings which have flat tar roofs, and jutting out from the roofs are cornices of cement swirled into faces of kings and lions, or scrolls and tablets. The buildings were put up at a time when design was as important to a workingman as wash-up time is today. In the summer Columbia Avenue has pushcarts set up on the curbs and crates set up under the awnings in front of the stores. People walk on the narrow aisle in the sidewalks between the pushcarts and the crates. They walk with bright fruit piled up to form a wall on each side of them, with cheap dresses at their fingertips and cheeses and bright pink pork hanging from the awnings and the merchants talking in Italian into their ears. In the winter the sidewalks are empty and newspapers blow in the wind which always comes off the river. The shop doors are closed and the windows are steamy. When you reach the corner of Marshall Street you turn right and walk halfway down the block to the bakery, Cafiero's bakery. The neighborhood stops at the building line which ends at Cafiero's.

The next store after Cafiero's was empty, and beaverboard covered the broken windows. Once it was Bisceglia's jewelry store. The big clock which had been put into the curb in front of the store, a clock that goes high into the air and can be seen for blocks, was plastered with ripped political campaign posters. The store next to Bisceglia's had a green bread-delivery box on the sidewalk, and a sign in the window read: BODEGA. Across the avenue, directly across from Cafiero's, was Pagano's shoe store. Next to Pagano's was a store with a shabbily painted sign which said, TV REPAIR, and a poster in the window advertised Chu Chu Perez singing on WHOM, a foreign-language radio station.

In the reghettoization of New York, a knife comes down the middle of a block and leaves the last of the old minorities on one side of the blade and the new minorities on the other side of the blade. And both sides live together and apart and they hate each other in a way which only people who are the same and will not admit it always hate each other. On one side of the knife cutting through the building lines, and stretching for blocks, are Italians: Italians in stores and in the linoleum-floored apartments over the stores, Italians in the tenements on the blocks running off the avenue. On the other side of the knife, and running for many blocks, are Puerto Ricans: Puerto Ricans in stores and over the stores in the broken, community-bathroom apartments. Puerto Ricans living in the tenements on the blocks running off the avenue. Puerto Ricans with dented, ripped, used convertibles parked at the curbs, the willowy radio antennas they like so much sticking out of the rear fenders. Puerto Ricans standing in garbage in the doorways and on the sidewalks and in the gutters. Drinking from beer cans in brown paper bags and throwing the cans in the bags out into the middle of the street. In San Juan you get a ticket if you do not throw garbage into the middle of the street, because the trucks pick up garbage by moving down the middle of a street with a cowcatcher and a brush. In Brooklyn you are called a pig if you do this. And the Puerto Ricans do not understand, and the sanitation workers, mainly Italians, do not understand and they will collect garbage on Columbia Avenue past Cafiero's building line only when inspectors come around and force them.

Big Mama bought three loaves of bread and

some rolls in Cafiero's. When she came back to the apartment, Angela had the refrigerator open and she was looking into it. She yawned and clasped her hands and stretched them high over her head. The skirt of her short blue woolen dress came up to her thighs and left a bit of white girdle gartered to white net stockings showing.

"Hiya," Angela said.

"You go to school like that?" Big Mama said.

"Uhuh." She brought her arms down. "It's only when I stretch."

"What do you do, tempt?"

"Mama, nobody even cares any more. The whole world is short skirts."

"I fan you behind."

Angela laughed and sat down to a cup of coffee. "Did brother bring home a paper?"

"No," Big Mama said.

Kid Sally Palumbo always falls asleep with the *Daily News* over his face or on the covers next to him. The paper always carries its share of headlines saying such things as: RAID "KID SALLY" HANGOUT. And particularly now, with Sally doing exactly what Big Mama wanted him to do, pushing to get into the real money, she didn't want Angela seeing any newspapers until she had checked them, and there was no time for checking them this morning. And over the years Angela knew enough never to buy a paper unless it had been read through. It was one of the silent understandings by which she lived.

Angela drank her coffee quickly. She went into

her room and came out in a dark blue coat and with a brown briefcase, thick with books, crooked in her arm.

"I go to the corner with you," Mama said.

Angela came onto the sidewalk waving at two kids looking out the windows from across the street and a fat woman who opened her window and waved a bare arm out into the cold air. A college student on the block is still an adventure on Marshall Street. Toregressa stood guard duty halfway up the block. Toregressa leaned on a cane. He had a cap pulled down over his ears and a plaid scarf covering his chin. It was his third day out of bed after the flu. Yesterday he had spent an hour telling people on the block how he had resisted death. When he saw Angela he let his mouth sag and he began blinking his eyes to show pain. He shuffled his feet and inched the cane along the sidewalk.

"Oh, you look good today," Angela said to him. "By tomorrow you'll be as good as new." She was smiling and walking quickly and she and Big Mama moved past Toregressa while he was trying to make himself cry so Angela would stop and pet him.

Up at the corner, Beppo, eyes roughed up from sleeping on his face on a couch in the back of the office, was standing in his shirtsleeves.

"Learn the lessons," he said.

Big Mama waved a hand. "Shut up-a you, I teach you."

"I'd tell you to be a good boy," Angela said.

105

"Tell me then," Beppo said.

"I don't think you'd know how."

Beppo giggled. Angela laughed. She came onto the avenue laughing and waved a hand at Mama and began walking toward the subway four blocks down. Big Mama stood on the corner and watched her granddaughter and shook her head at the amount of legs a girl shows today.

"Saint Anthony protect," she mumbled.

New York University is in reclaimed office buildings that face the grimy frost-yellowed grass of Washington Square. It is an impersonal place to go to school. Thousands of students come out of the subways, cram the hallways from morning until late at night, and then go back into the subways. The campus hero is the job they get when they graduate. For Angela, the impersonalness was important.

In grammar school, in the fourth grade, when she was ten, there was an afternoon when one of the boys in the class walked around filling the inkwells with a large smeared bottle of ink and the ether smell of ink was all over the room, and the nun looked around when the front door to the classroom opened. Big Mama looked into the room. When Angela saw her, she became afraid, the way all kids do when their world is suddenly disturbed. The nun went over to the door and Big Mama whispered to her and the nun turned around and told Angela to get her coat and go with her grandmother. Big Mama kept Angela home, in the house, until the next Monday, when the stories about Kid Sally Palumbo being sentenced to thirteen months were gone from the newspapers. When Angela got to school at twenty of nine on Monday, the girls clustered around two eighth-graders who were twisting a rope all turned and looked at Angela as if she had polio. The ether smell of ink came into Angela's nose, as it was to come into her nose for years when she was frightened.

Angela always went home from school wordlessly, head down, books held up to her face. When she came across the avenue and turned onto Marshall Street, the books would come down and the chin would go up and life would flood back into her eyes and mouth. At home she was kept away from everything, and she knew everything.

In poor neighborhoods everywhere, there were signs hanging out to welcome kids back from the Korean war. On Marshall Street one night, everybody hung out signs saying, WELCOME HOME SALLY and flags hung from windows and there was a big block party for Kid Sally Palumbo, who was home from the battle of Sing Sing. The kids Angela played with ran around getting sips of red wine from the adults drinking on the stoops. Then they all went up to the corner and told strangers passing by, "Her brother come home today." And the strangers would say, "Oh, isn't that wonderful." And Angela and all the kids would shriek, "He was a prisoner!" Laughing, they'd run down the block again. If Big Mama had heard this, she would have erupted into hand-swinging anger.

As Sally and the five cousins on the block grew older and were involved in continuous trouble, Angela thickened the screen around herself, and her life became the books on the table in her room. In school she became the moody little girl who made the honor roll. In high school, at the Dominican Girls' Academy, she outgrew her head-hanging walk. She began to notice that girls either were overfriendly to her, which she knew was an expression of superiority, or went out of their way to ignore her. Boys, who understand power, always treated her with deference. In her third year of high school her class of thirty-eight girls sat and talked before class started, and it was February 15 and they were talking about Valentine cards they had gotten. A redheaded girl in the front of the room called out, "How come Angela got Valentine Day cards with a picture of a garage?"

Laughter fell around Angela. For a small instant she was nervous and confused. Then the embarrassment ran out of her face and her eyes narrowed. When the laughter stopped, she called out, saying each word by itself, "You . . . rat . . . stool . . . pigeon . . . son . . . of . . . a . . . bitch."

Nobody was overfriendly and nobody made a show of trying to ignore her after that. Everything became correct, and Angela spoke to girls only when she felt like it.

In her neighborhood most of the girls went to vocational or commercial high schools and spent their afternoons smoking cigarettes in Di-Lorenzo's candy store with boys who had dropped out of school and were waiting to get into jobs or trouble. The girls went to filing-clerk jobs in insurance offices in Manhattan, or, mainly, into knitting mills. They rode in cars with boys, and sex and marriage came quickly. Angela found she had nothing in common with the girls. And the boys were overly careful of her because Kid Sally Palumbo had promised to cut the fingers off anybody touching his sister. For a few years Angela was close to Carmine Pollino, who lived at Number 25 Marshall Street and attended Brooklyn Automotive High. Then one afternoon she was coming home from school and she stopped to talk to Carmine, who was sitting on the stoop doing homework.

"A composition, I don't know why I got to do a composition," he said. "You don't have to write no compositions to fix up cars."

She came up and sat next to him on the stoop and looked at his composition.

My friend Jonny Lombardo isn't nervouse of anything. The other day he sent away for a brochure on a fuel injector. Then the mailman came in the morning and what did Jonny receive but the brochure. It was outasight and he come right over to the house to show it to me so I could see what a outasight thing he had received in the mail.

Carmine's budding masculinity crumbled away in Angela's eyes as she read the painful scrawl.

"Is that how you spell Johnny?" she said.

"Yeah, Johnny," he said. "J-o-n-n-y. That's right, isn't it?"

"An H," she said.

"H?"

"Oh, you know that," she said.

Carmine shrugged and crossed out the name the first time and wrote it out correctly and then he skipped over the second misspelling and resumed his scrawling. After this, Angela found she had very little to say to him.

At school she went to basketball games on Friday nights at Bishop McCarthy Boys' High School. After the games she danced with Irish boys who were breathing heavily even before the music started. She did not see the boys at any other time. When one of them asked for her phone number, she told him she had no phone. One of the things Angela knew without being told was never to use a telephone. At home, Angela was always given a running lecture by Big Mama on the evils of Irish boys. Big Mama kept saying that Irishers take the bread out of their children's mouths to buy whisky. Big Mama said this in a high-pitched voice, with her hands waving. Among the most overlooked racial problems in the country is the division between Irish and Italians. "Go with nice Italian boys," Big Mama said.

The trouble was, Big Mama's idea of a nice Italian boy was a strangler's son. For the big event of Angela's four years in high school, Big Mama went to the South Brooklyn version of the *Social Register*. Just as any decent Protestant would enter the hospital if his daughter tried to make her debut on the arm of somebody with an unknown family name, so do the old-breed Mafia try to match their offspring with children of other Mafia families. Royal blood can be preserved only with the strictest of breeding. Big Mama insisted Angela invite to her prom a nice Italian boy named Henry Gallante. He was the nineteen-year-old son of Sammy (the Timber Wolf) Gallante, the Canarsie section of Brooklyn's answer to John Dillinger. On the night of the dance, Henry Gallante arrived with three huge orchids. He gave them to Angela reluctantly because he really wanted to wear the orchids himself. One strangulation too many in the yard behind his house had turned Henry Gallante very far from violence.

Outside of trying to steer her toward Italian boys of shaky antecedents, Big Mama went to great lengths to shield Angela from what was going on around her. Kid Sally Palumbo never spoke of what he did for a living, in front of his sister. And by her own instincts Angela never went into the vending-machine office. She developed the habit of never walking past it, either. She did not want to see or know what was going on in the office. At the same time, she knew everything. There was an organization of Good People and it was an old Italian thing and her brother and his cousins were in it some place, and Big Mama knew all about it, and so did Angela. But the Kid Sally Palumbo in the newspapers was not her brother. Her brother was the person in the house with her who could make her laugh.

One day, in the spring of her last year in high school, she came into the vestibule to go upstairs and the sound of loud voices came through the wall from the vending-machine office.

"Do the right thing," her brother's voice shouted.

"I'm trying to do the right thing," another voice said.

"Then where's the freakin' money?" Big Jelly's voice said.

A chair scraped and there was the sound of flesh being slapped. Then another sound. And then a loud shriek. "You Jew mocky son-of-a-bitch!" her brother shouted. "Oh, you dirty bastard."

"Are you all right, Sally Kid?" Big Jelly's voice yelled.

"My hand, the dirty bastard. Kick his head in."

There was a commotion, and through the door Angela saw a man in a neat gray suit running onto the sidewalk. Big Jelly ran after him and threw a kick at him that missed. The man got into a car at the curb and pulled away.

Angela went up to her room and dropped her schoolbooks on the bed and sat there for an hour. When it was out of her, she left the room as if nothing had happened. Her brother came home that night with his hand in a cast. Kid Sally Palumbo had a willing, but inaccurate right hand. In the afternoon melee he had bounced a punch against the edge of the desk and broken two knuckles.

When she graduated from high school, Angela had the marks and units to enter several colleges. But the Palumbos were not yet in the stratum of gangsters who sent their daughters in fur coats to exclusive schools. Angela entered NYU. She liked the idea of being swallowed in its size. Only people directly familiar with her from months of sitting in the same class knew that she was the sister of New York's reputedly roughest young racketeer. She kept an uninterested attitude about everything but the classwork. One boy, Robert Dineen, who was in her late-afternoon classes, always spoke to her. One day at the end of class he asked her if she felt like a cup of coffee. He took her to a bar that was three steps down from the sidewalk of Sheridan Square. Angela drank Coke. Dineen drank beer with a motion that caused the rim of the glass to strike the bridge of his nose so hard Angela was afraid he would wound himself. After that she met him one time at the Brooklyn Public Library on a Saturday night. They walked to a place on Flatbush Avenue called Flynn's. Dineen drank beer and talked sports with the young guys in the neighborhood who hung out in the place. He had his back turned to Angela much of the time. She noticed the bar was filled with young girls whose companions treated them the same way. But when she walked to the jukebox Angela could feel Dineen watching her very carefully. She went home alone by cab that night. She met Dineen there a couple more times. She liked his openness and the way everybody else in the bar was open and spoke out. Nobody was withdrawn and there was no whispering.

One day after school, when they were going out that night, Angela said she had to go and change and Dineen insisted on coming with her. Angela said yes. She was empty while she rode the subway with Dineen and then walked him down the street to the house.

Big Mama got Dineen in the front room. She sat directly across from him.

"You want a pear?"

"No, thank you," he said.

"Where you go tonight?"

"To a movie, I guess."

"Then you be home by eleven o'clock?"

"Well — uh — I guess around then."

"You name Dineen. What's-a you mother's name?"

"Collins."

"Uh. You go to mass?"

"Yes, ma'am."

"Our family goes to church." Big Mama turned and looked at a picture of the Sacred Heart. "You want a sandwich?"

"No, thank you."

"What's-a you father do?"

"Oh, he's dead."

"Oh, that's-a bad. I'm sorry."

"That's all right."

"What did this-a father do?"

"Policeman."

Big Mama said it very slowly. "You . . . father . . . cop?"

"He was a sergeant. I have two uncles on the job in Long Island."

Big Mama blessed herself and looked up at the ceiling. *"Gesù Cristo,"* she muttered.

When Angela came out, dressed, and started to leave with Dineen, Big Mama snarled at them, "You be home eleven-fifteen the latest."

Angela looked at her, puzzled. "All right," she said.

They were halfway down the stairs when Big Mama leaned over the banisters.

"No fagia mal!"

"Pardon me?" Dineen said.

"Never mind. She know."

Later, when Dineen brought her home, they stood inside the vestibule talking to each other quietly. Through the wall came the well-enunciated words of her cousin, Larry (Kid Blast) Palumbo.

"I still think we should go and shoot his whole freakin' head off. Then set the son-of-a-bitch on fire. That's what I say we should do."

Dineen grabbed the doorknob for support. He stuttered through a good-by. As Angela started up the staircase, a light flicked on and Big Mama looked down the stairs at them.

"You kiss-a her?"

"I'm afraid to close my eyes here," Dineen said.

Dineen kept going to school in the summer so he could finish quickly and go on to law school. Angela stayed in school for the summer too. On Friday nights Dineen drove her to Sheepshead Bay for clams and beer. Afterward they sat in the car, looking at the lights on the dark water which ran up to the fishing-boat piers. On the first night there Dineen leaned over and kissed Angela and she brought up her face to his and he ran a hand over her body for the first time.

On the July Fourth weekend Dineen took her to a beach party at Breezy Point. His cousin had a house three doors from the beach. There was a big crowd of people Angela knew from Flynn's. Dineen started the night off by drinking beer from a keg and talking to the other boys. He came and sat on a blanket with Angela for a while. Then at 11:30 he said he wanted to go up to his cousin's house for cigarettes. He took Angela by the hand and they walked away from the wood fire and across the dark sand to the street. Dineen said nothing. He was breathing too hard to talk. The house was a one-story white wooden bungalow with a screened-in porch. A lamp on the porch was the only light in the house.

"I'll wait outside," Angela said. She said it automatically. Dineen held her hand and took her up the walk and held the screen door for her. On the porch he took her hand again and started into the darkened living room. Inside, he headed for a door. "Where are we going?" Angela said automatically. And he opened the door and led her in by the hand and he was kissing her and she went down onto the bed on her back with him still kissing her, and she wriggled her legs onto the bed. He was surprised when she did not stop him. His hands were at the top of her blouse and he was pulling at it so hard it was lifting her shoulderblades off the bed. The button went in his hands.

"Stop it," she said. He was tugging at the next button. "Stop it!" she said sharply. Her tone brought Kid Blast's voice back into his ears. *She'll have my head cut off.* Dineen tumbled from her and stood next to the bed.

"Don't get mad," he said.

"I'm not mad, I just want to have clothes to wear," she said. She unbuttoned the blouse and reached down and unzipped the side of her Capri pants.

"Don't tell your brother," he said.

The day Angela was supposed to have her

period, the phone rang at eight a.m. Big Mama looked at the phone suspiciously. Kid Sally was inside, asleep. The few people who called never called before noon. Big Mama picked it up. It was Robert Dineen, calling the house for the first time.

"Well, how do you feel?" he asked Angela.

"Fine," she said.

"Everything's all right?"

"Oh, that? Oh, I don't know. No, not yet. Don't worry about it."

"I do worry."

"Oh, stop."

"Stop? I don't want to get strangled."

For three days Robert Dineen called in the morning and saw Angela during the afternoon at school, and each time the answer was no. He began to look like a defendant. On the fourth day Angela told him everything was all right. Dineen went to the bar on Sheridan Square and drank whisky. By seven p.m. he was looking at himself in the mirror behind the bar. "I play with death!" he said.

Chapter 8

A few months after this, a man named Theodore Kaplowitz, who owned four bars in Brooklyn, walked into the office of the District Attorney. He said that Kid Sally Palumbo and three others had come into his best place, the Esquire, and walked behind the bar and opened the cash register and taken half the money. Kid Sally Palumbo announced he was a partner in the place from now on. Kaplowitz began to argue. Kid Sally Palumbo took Kaplowitz's arm and tried to break it over the edge of the bar.

The assistant district attorney handling the complaint had bodyguards placed on Kaplowitz. He also had him wired for recording in case Kid Sally Palumbo returned. Kid Sally had intended to return and get some more money and give Kaplowitz another beating, but he never got around to it. The police thought Kid Sally was smelling the trap. The assistant district attorney, Frank Rogin, twenty-nine, decided to bring in Kid Sally for questioning. Assistant Chief Inspector Cornelius J. Gallagher, fifty-nine, commanding officer, Brooklyn South detectives, had Kid Sally picked up. Kid Sally came into Rogin's office at eight p.m. Gallagher and two detectives stood in the doorway. Kid Sally was chewing gum. The 100-watt bulbs in the cracked plaster ceiling made Kid Sally's black hair glisten.

"What could I tell you, Mr. Rogin?" Kid Sally said. "What could I tell you?" He held his hands out and sat in silence while Rogin kept asking questions.

Gallagher lit a cigarette. His pouchy eyes became slits as the smoke ran over his face.

"You're just a guinea," he said to Kid Sally.

"All right on that stuff," Rogin said.

"Why not?" Gallagher said. "Why be nice to a guinea like this?"

"I said forget it," Rogin said sharply.

Gallagher glared through the slits of his pouchy eyes. Gallagher went into another office and sat with his two detectives. Gallagher leafed through the file on Kid Sally Palumbo. "What's this with his sister?" he said.

"She goes to school," one of the detectives said.

"She must do the bookkeeping for them," Gallagher said. "You know these other guinea bastards can't read or write."

"I just know she goes to school," the detective said.

"Uhuh," Gallagher said. He went back to the doorway of Rogin's office.

"Sally?"

Kid Sally Palumbo didn't turn his head. "Yeah?"

"Does the sister handle the money for you, or does she just keep the records?"

Kid Sally Palumbo swung around in his chair with his eyes flashing wildly. "Your mother!"

Gallagher smiled. "No, your sister, Sally."

Rogin's hand slammed the desk. "I'll do the talking here," he said to Gallagher.

When Kid Sally Palumbo left, Rogin told Gallagher, "I'm very interested in this guy we had here. I'm not interested in anything else. The sister doesn't interest me. Am I understood? Leave the girl alone. I don't do business this way."

Gallagher looked at Rogin the way every man who is fifty-nine looks at a twenty-nine-year-old who is above him in life. Driving back to the precinct, Gallagher said to the two detectives, "Bring the sister in tomorrow."

"Where do we get the warrant?" one of them said.

"You don't need a warrant for a guinea. Pick her up after school and bring her to the Charles Street house. I'll use the office there."

Angela Palumbo was coming out the back door of the English 101 classroom at 3:40 the next afternoon. The ones in front of her were having some kind of trouble getting out the door. Angela stood in line and shuffled forward. When she saw the two faces in the hallway, her

121

breath caught in her throat.

Two Irish faces, tilted back to look past the crowd, and also tilted back with the sense of authority all policemen like to use. Angela stopped just outside the door. The other students were walking past, but going only a few steps and turning to watch. One of the detectives, the one in a black topcoat with the collar turned up, held out his right hand with a gold shield in it. Angela was shaking. She felt a hand on her shoulder. Robert Dineen stood with her.

"Could you come with us, please?" the detective said.

"It'll just be for a little while," the other one said.

The hallway was crowded now. Faces were looking at Angela from everywhere. Her hands began to shake. She couldn't speak.

"Do you have a warrant?" Dineen said.

"It's okay, don't worry," the detective said. He was ignoring Dineen and looking at Angela. The other detective put a hand on Dineen's arm. "You can go," he said.

"Let me see the warrant," Dineen said.

"Why don't you come with her, then?" the detective in the black coat said. "Then you can see that it's nothing."

With the crowded hallway watching her, Angela went with the detectives and Dineen. Outside on the sidewalk, all the heads turned to watch her get into a black unmarked Plymouth.

She sat in the back seat with Dineen. They were driven to the Charles Street precinct house, which covers the NYU area. The precinct house is at the end of a block of warehouses. The flag hanging from the second-floor window whipped in the wind coming from the Hudson River, a half-block away. Angela Palumbo walked into the station with her schoolbooks huddled in her arms and her head down, and the detectives guided her toward the metal staircase in the lobby. One of them turned around and put a hand on Dineen's chest. "You wait here," he said.

Cornelius Gallagher sat in a bare upstairs office. He wore a brown suit, a drinker's stomach pressing against the middle button.

"Sit down," he said. He pointed to a chair next to him. You always sit next to a girl when you question her. It gives that little intimacy women need. If you sit across a desk from her, it puts everything on a cold business basis. Women cannot react to it.

"Here, let me take your books," Gallagher said.

Angela shook her head.

"All right. Would you like a cigarette?" He held out a pack of filter cigarettes. Angela's hand shook and her fingers fumbled with the top of the pack while she took one. Gallagher lit it for her. He put a tin ashtray in front of her. He reached over and put the match into the ashtray. Always use the same ashtray with a girl.

"Angela, I just wanted to ask you a few things," he said. "You can answer if you want, and if you don't want, you don't have to answer. But you don't have to worry about what you say. We're just having a conversation here."

The cigarette shook in her fingers and she had trouble getting it into her mouth.

"You know, Angela, I've been around a long time and seen a lot of things. There's nothing you could tell me that I don't know already. Oh, I tell you, the things I've seen in my life. I couldn't be surprised by anything you tell me. I've heard it all. Why, you could sit there right now and tell me that your brother killed Georgie Paradise and I wouldn't get excited at all. Sally killed Georgie Paradise? What's it mean to me? I've been all through it."

The voice was rasping and unreal, and Angela Palumbo's breath kept falling to the bottom of her stomach.

"What's he waiting for?" the desk sergeant asked a patrolman downstairs. The sergeant nodded at Robert Dineen.

"I don't know," the patrolman said. "Hey, buddy, something you want?"

Dineen had been standing against a rusted radiator. "I'm waiting for somebody," he said.

"Waiting for who?"

"Somebody upstairs."

"Well, you better wait outside, then. This isn't a waiting room."

The patrolman's voice went through Dineen.

It carried the sharpness a cop puts into his voice when he is carrying out an order for somebody he wants to impress.

Dineen waited on the sidewalk. Newspapers blew down the street in swirls of dust. The flat late-afternoon sun came through a garbage-strewn alley between two warehouses. Late-afternoon sun in the winter depresses anybody watching it. After a short while it makes the person feel sick to his stomach. Dineen felt like he had been riding in a closed car filled with exhaust fumes. Fear and disgust mixed with the sickness. The detectives' and desk patrolman's voices kept running through him, and the fear grew stronger. What the hell was he doing in a thing like this? He could get in trouble in law school.

The street was empty and the shadows were becoming longer when Robert Dineen began walking toward the subway five blocks away.

It was 5:30 when Angela Palumbo came down the stairs alone. She had her face buried in the books. She had not spoken a word since she came into the precinct house. She had sat in a trance while this red pouchy face cooed at her and smiled and showed her reports she looked at but did not see. Now she walked through the lobby and stepped outside and she needed Robert Dineen badly, just to hold her arm and talk to her, and she came out into the evening on the sidewalk of the empty street.

Angela Palumbo did not mention the precinct

questioning to anybody when she got home. She went to her room. In the morning she did not go to school. She did not go to school for the rest of the term. When Big Mama and Sally tried to talk to her, she said she didn't feel well. When they told her to see a doctor, she shrugged.

"Girls," Big Mama said to Kid Sally one night. "Girls can be strange sometimes. She get over it."

One day in late December, Angela was coming back from the store and as she came into the vestibule she heard shouts coming through the wall and the sound of somebody being slapped, and one of the voices started pleading. When she heard another slap, she spat a word out of her mouth.

"Good."

In January she went back to school. Robert Dineen was not in any of her classes, and she did not see him in the hallway because she never looked up when she walked from room to room.

On a Thursday night, at the midnight show at the Copacabana, she sat at ringside with Buster Capanegro, a bookmaker and shylock with the East Harlem mob. The comedian told a joke. "Kids from mixed marriages are very confused. I tell you. I know a kid who had an Italian father and a Jewish mother. Every time he passes a department store he doesn't know whether to buy it or rob it."

"Hey! What's so funny about that?" Buster Capanegro snapped.

The comedian looked at him. Buster looked at the comedian. The comedian nearly fainted.

"I didn't like that at all, that fresh punk," Angela said.

When Big Mama told her one night that there would be some nice Italian boys around for a big bike race soon, Angela shrugged. When Big Mama told her it was important for her to go to a cocktail party and be Mama's eyes, Angela was more interested.

"It be good if you go," Big Mama said. "You watch and come back and tell me what everybody does."

Angela nodded. Now she wanted to go to the party.

Chapter 9

The press cocktail party for the six-day bike race was held upstairs at Keefe's Steak House. The crowd featured some newspaper and television reporters, many copy boys from the *Daily News* who passed themselves off as sports reporters and drank whisky with a beer motion, the president of the Queens chapter of a Greek society, and several stumpy members of the Polish Eagles of Greenpoint.

Several young girls were interspersed through the crowd as hostesses. Name cards were pinned to their dresses. When Angela Palumbo came up the stairs to the room, she automatically looked away from the table that had the name cards. She knew there would not be a card for her. If one happened to be there by mistake, she knew enough not to wear it. She was dressed in a short canary-yellow coat. Her black hair fell onto her shoulders. Joseph DeLauria saw her and left the bar and came up to her.

"I'm Joseph DeLauria," he said. "Here, let me take your coat." She turned and began to come out of the coat. She was wearing a matching dress. "God bless, you're pretty," DeLauria said. She saw his eyes go to her shoulder to make sure she wasn't wearing a name card. Then to her hands, to make sure she wasn't holding one of the cards and about to put it on.

She went to the bar and ordered ginger ale. She was not going to start drinking around this DeLauria. He began introducing Angela to people: a gray-haired man who was the New York correspondent for *Il Giornale* of Milan, one of the Polacks from Greenpoint, and a chubby kid with a crewcut whose face was beet-red from the unfamiliar brandy hitting a system used only to tap beer. He said his name was Tommy something and that he worked for the *Daily News*. Angela looked away. Another Irisher drunk.

She stiffened when DeLauria took her arm. "I want you to meet some of the great riders from Italy," he said. He began showing her around the room. "Here, Carlo Rafetto, I'd like you to meet Angela." DeLauria was careful to give only the first name. "And, hey, this is Mario Ciariello. Mario, meet Angela. And now where's the other Mario? Mario Trantino. Oh, there he is in the back. Look at this."

Mario was sitting alone at a table in the back of the room. He was bent over and had the table-cloth pulled up, and he was working with a pencil. Under his left hand there was a small picture, torn from a sightseeing book, of a $35,000 Modigliani which had hung in a Madison

Avenue gallery. With his right hand Mario was just doodling a little, trying to see if he could copy even a bit of the Modigliani. *Who knows, Sidney says they all have the taste of a pig. Maybe you just make a little change here and there and they don't even know.*

When Mario saw DeLauria leading a girl in a yellow dress toward him, he quickly pulled the red-checked tablecloth back into place over his work.

DeLauria made introductions and patted Angela on the back. "Why don't you sit down and visit with Mario? He's all alone here. We can't have that, can we?"

"Am I supposed to make him buy me champagne?" Angela said.

Joseph DeLauria laughed with his mouth and called her a son-of-a-bitch with his eyes. He walked away.

As Angela started to sit down, she looked directly at Mario. The casualness went out of her body and she slipped into the chair with her hands smoothing her skirt and coming up gracefully and her eyes staying on Mario's face. Mario caught an impression of her as she started to sit down, and his eyes ran from her hips to her chest and onto her face. A picture of his hotel room came into his mind.

"Hello," she said.

"Hello."

She thought for a moment. "Uh, *si recreon'?*" She said it stiffly and with the key syllables slurred. Her Italian was terrible.

"Nice," he said.

"Oh, you know English?"

"From the school and this man teaches me home."

"That's good. Do most of the young people speak English where you come from?"

"Young people go away."

"Oh, I'll bet they do. But they have to go to Germany or Australia, don't they? Nobody can get in this country any more."

"You must do a special thing to stay here," Mario said.

"Well, if you win the race that will make you special maybe," she said.

Mario pulled the tablecloth back and looked down at his drawing. He took a pencil from his breast pocket and copied a little curve from the Modigliani. This was the something special that was going to keep him in the country.

"What's that?" she said.

"Nothing, nothing." He pulled the tablecloth back quickly.

He's sitting there probably drawing dirty pictures for the whole time, Angela thought. *I'll bet you he's got me in them.* She picked up the glass to finish it. It's always easier to leave when the glass is empty. *Moron,* she said to herself.

"Well, have fun," she said. She got up.

He looked up, flustered. "No, I just was . . ." his hand made a pinwheel motion.

"What is it?" she said.

"Oh . . ." His hand said it was nothing.

"Oh, what is it?" she said. She decided she'd embarrass him. She came around the table. He put both hands on top of the cloth. Angela grabbed an edge of the tablecloth and pulled the whole thing out from under Mario's hands.

When she saw what he had been doing, she was surprised. "Oh, I couldn't imagine," she said. "You're an artist?"

"I am going to be one," Mario said. "I am going to stay here and work to be an artist. This is — uh — just — uh — trying to — uh —"

"Practice," she said.

"Yes, practice." He stuffed the two sheets of paper in his jacket pocket.

"It's wonderful," she said. "Where did you study? What university did you attend?"

"In Catanzia nobody goes to the university," he said.

"Mario," Joseph DeLauria called. "Mario, come over here for a minute. I want you to meet somebody."

"Don't get up," Angela said.

"He wants me."

"Don't get up."

Mario shrugged. Angela glanced at DeLauria and turned her head from him. She sat and thought about what she could do to upset DeLauria. She had met him today for the first time. He was a bastard, and he also worked for Baccala. She didn't know Baccala, either. But she knew he was the "people" her brother and grandmother were arguing about.

"Why don't you go somewhere where you can do what you want?" she said to Mario.

"I stay?" he said.

"No, let's go some place else," she said.

She got up and began walking through the tables. Mario bent over quickly. He pulled his shoelaces open. He got up and followed Angela. Joseph DeLauria caught a glimpse of them while they were leaving. "Smart," he said to himself. "That's nice and smart."

Out in the street, Mario put on his uncle's glasses. He took a step and tripped on a lace and bumped into Angela.

"Excuse," he said.

They began walking down the street. She glanced down. "Your laces are untied," she said.

"That is the way I have them," he said.

"Oh," she said. She saw he was walking with his eyes closed. "Do you have something the matter?" she said.

"I save my eyes for looking at colors," he said.

"Oh," she said.

He had no coat.

"You'll freeze," she said.

"I think of hot colors and they make me warm," he said. "I sweat."

"Oh," she said.

He felt good. He was impressing her very much that he was an artist.

They rode the subway downtown and came

onto the narrow tenement streets of Little Italy. On Mulberry Street, Italian music came from a record shop. Cheeses hung in the store windows. A meat-delivery truck was parked in front of an Italian butcher's. The white-coated deliveryman was carrying sheep's heads, *capozzelle,* into the store. The red vein lines ran in a spiderweb over the white bone and fat of the sheep's heads. Water was dripping from the back of the truck and turning to ice on the curb. The butcher from the store was shaking a bag of rock salt onto the freezing water. Mario put his hands deeper into his pockets.

"Oh, you'll freeze," she said.

He closed his eyes. "I think of hot colors," he said.

She took him into a place called Raymond's, which is on a corner. Raymond's has a bar on one side and a clam bar on the other. Tables are in the rear. Three men work behind the clam bar, putting breaded shrimp and *calamare* and blowfish tails into wire baskets. They drop the wire baskets into boiling grease and the grease turns to brown foam over the cold breaded fish, and in a minute or so one of the men pulls the wire basket out and dumps the fish on a plate. He covers it with red sauce and slaps it on the counter. The sauce is made of red peppers and cayenne primarily, with a little tomato in passing. The signs behind the counter say: SAUCES: 1. HOT. 2. MEDIUM. 3. LIGHT.

Raymond's is one of the places in New York

tourists and out-of-town businessmen hear about. One of the hobbies of the people in the neighborhood is to sit in Raymond's and watch one of these visitors go against the sauce. Angela slid onto a stool at the clam bar. Mario sat next to her. Angela nudged Mario when a man in a plaid hat called out in a flat Midwestern accent for number-one sauce on his shrimp. They put the plate in front of the man. The plaid hat forked a shrimp dripping with number-one sauce into his mouth. His mouth clamped down on the shrimp. He started his first chew. He then made a face as if he had just been shot. He opened his mouth and made a sound like a trombone. The counterman automatically gave him a glass of Coke. The man swallowed it. The plaid hat now bellowed as the sauce bit into his tongue. The counterman gave him another Coke. The man drank it, paid for the shrimp, and walked out of the door. He stood on the sidewalk. Everybody inside could see the man's shoulders heaving while he gulped in the cold air.

"Another score for the house," the counterman said. Everybody laughed.

Angela and Mario ate *calamare* with number-one sauce and a side order of linguine. The linguine was slick with olive oil, and the bottom of the bowl was covered with clams and parsley. Italians being immune to sauce, they happily swallowed the *calamare*. The counterman wrote out the check and put it on the counter and

Mario reached for the watch pocket. Her hand stopped him.

"Now, don't be silly," she said.

"Oh, no," he said.

"I said."

She picked up the check and went through her purse and paid. They left and she guided him by the elbow around the corner to Ferrara's, which has show windows that take up half the block. The windows are filled with speckled cookies and pastries that have cream coming out of both ends. Inside, brilliant lights glare from the ceiling and come off the mirrored walls and spill onto the white tile floor and polished tabletops. The place smells of whipped cream and coffee. They ordered *cappuccino*, heavily creamed coffee that froths at the top of the glass, and *cannoli*, which are filled with thick rum cream.

"Now tell me," she said.

"With the painting?"

"Yes."

"It must come from here." He held his hands to his stomach. "It must come from me. There is nothing to put down if it does not come from me. There is no way for this to happen at home. We eat chipmunks in Catanzia. You must spend too much time hunting them to be an artist."

"Chipmunks! Still?" she said.

"Oh, and dandelions. Or the good grass," he said.

"Oh, really now," she said.

"No, it is true," he said. When he saw how she

was reacting, he thought of saying he had a brother who died because he had no food.

"When are you going to do any painting here?" she said.

"Tomorrow maybe," he said.

"I'd like to see what you do, but I have school all day. Then I have to go right home."

"You could come another day," he said. The picture of his hotel room came into his mind again. There were, his instinct told him, great resources in anybody who seemed to like him and was this beautiful. But Mario's mind operated one step at a time, and his vision of a future with Angela consisted of her in his hotel room.

"What other day?" she said. "You have the race."

He shrugged.

"I'll see you at the race, and when it's all over I'll come and watch you paint," she said.

"You'll be at the race?" he said.

"Every night," she said.

She paid the check on the way out and walked to the subway with him. She pointed to the entrance for the uptown trains. She started to walk across the street to the Brooklyn train entrance and then she turned around and came back. "Do you have change for the subway?" she said.

Mario said yes.

She said, "Let me see to be sure you've got the right change."

He showed her his silver. She nodded and

went to the subway. When her head disappeared down the stairs, Mario put his hand into the watch pocket and began looking for a taxi. The hundred-dollar bill was still intact. He decided to keep it that way. When the taxi got him to the hotel, the doorman held the door and Mario took out his change. There wasn't enough. He looked at the doorman. "You put it on my room bill?"

"We don't do that here," the doorman said.

"In Italy, yes," Mario said.

Mario showed the doorman his key. The doorman and the cab-driver looked at each other. Mario got out of the cab and walked into the lobby and went to the elevators. When the doorman came in and asked the desk clerk for the cab money and told him what room to charge, the clerk shook his head.

"One of those bike-riders they booked in here. The bastards sure come with nerve."

"They know," the doorman said.

When Angela got home, Big Mama called out from the kitchen. "You have a nice time?"

"It was all right."

"Who you meet there?"

"Some boys."

"Italian boys?"

"I met one. A nice young Italian boy."

"Young?"

"A kid," Angela said.

Chapter 10

When the job of producing a sports event had started, several weeks before, Kid Sally Palumbo and Big Jelly arrived at the 987th Field Artillery Armory with two carpenters named Mulqueen and Keefe. The carpenters had a superior reputation, particularly for their work on the chapel of Attica State Prison, where they each spent thirty months for poor usage of a gun. Big Jelly and the carpenters stood with an armory worker who unrolled the floor plan and went over it with them.

Kid Sally Palumbo walked away. The click of his heels sounded throughout the gloomy armory. Kid Sally lifted his feet up and brought the heels down harder. The sound went high up, to the olive steel beams that crisscross in the pale light coming through the windows. Now Kid Sally started taking big tramping strides and he walked the length of the armory listening to his footsteps making the only sound in the place. Trucks and jeeps, with 105-mm. howitzers coupled to them, were parked along the armory walls. At the far end of the floor a green corrugated-metal sliding door was halfway down from the ceiling. When the green corrugated door came all the way down to the floor it chopped off the armory floor. The area behind the door was the motor pool for the field-artillery outfit housed in the armory. The equipment now happened to be parked out around the floor. But it was always kept in the motor-pool area.

Kid Sally Palumbo didn't bother with any of this. He just kept walking and listening to his footsteps echo around the building. Big Jelly and the carpenters stood and went over the plans. The carpenters were taking notes and Big Jelly was waving his arm around the empty building like a foreman. The armory worker had gone back to his office. He left Big Jelly and the carpenters to work out the floor plan for the track and bleachers. When they told Kid Sally they were through, Kid Sally said he was tired from all this detail work and he needed a nap. The carpenters, holding paper with floor measurements, said they were going to get the lumber and the workers needed to put together a fine track for bike-racing. Big Jelly looked at his watch. It was 2:30. He was just in time to meet his new girl friend. "She gets off in half an hour," Big Jelly said. His new girl friend was in her third year in high school.

With three days to go before the race, a final

140

meeting was held in Baccala's office.

"I don't know where we stand," Joseph DeLauria said. He held his palms up. "I do the right thing every day, that's all I can say."

"I go to a joint yesterday," Big Jelly said, "and I tell the guy, 'Hey, take some tickets,' and he says, 'Who tickets?' I tell him for the bike race, make the waiters go, and he says to me, 'Hey, believe me, they'd rather get shot than have to go to a bike race.' "

"That's what everybody says," Kid Sally Palumbo said. "*Axt* anybody, they tell you, get lost."

"So you get two *tousan*, three *tousan* people," Baccala said. "They all bring money. Be plenty for everybody."

"Who wins the race?" Kid Sally said.

"Whoever wins," Izzy Cohen said.

"Why?" Kid Sally asked.

"Because we have six sprints a night. The riders bunch up so's they're all even and then we announce odds on each rider over the loudspeaker and then you guys make book in the stands and we run the sprint off. What do we care who wins? We got them bettin' into our odds. We take off the top. You got to give a man some kind of a shot for his money. If we try to screw them completely, they walk out on us and then where are we?"

"All right," Kid Sally said.

"One-a thing," Baccala said.

"What?"

Baccala leaned forward with his chubby hands clasped together. "What about the bike-riders looking to rob us?"

"How could they rob us?" Izzy said.

"Never mind, trust in-a only Christ and Saint Anthony." Baccala's eyes narrowed. "We make sure. We lock-a them in the cage."

"What cages?" Kid Sally said.

"We get cages, regular cages with-a bars on them. When the rider is not riding the bike, he goes into the cage. He can no talk to the other riders. When it is time for him to come and ride, boop! Out of the cage. He rides."

"Where do we get a cage from?" Kid Sally said.

"That's your job," Baccala said.

"I got all the jobs," Kid Sally said. "I don't like the jobs and I don't like the whole idea. This race is gonna get us nothin' but grief. A breadline, we could do better on a breadline than with this thing."

"Shut up-a you face," Baccala said.

"I say what I freakin' please," Kid Sally said.

"Shut up-a you face."

"Go screw," Kid Sally said.

Baccala's face did not change expression. The Water Buffalo, standing by the door, took his cue from Baccala. He kept his face straight too. Izzy shrugged and looked at the newspaper. Big Jelly looked through his glasses, unblinking.

Kid Sally took out a cigarette. He opened the lighter with a loud snap. His thumb hit the wheel

142

and the flame shot up. He put the lighter away. He took the cigarette in the thumb and fore-finger of his left hand and held it to his mouth. Smoke hung in front of his face. He stared at Baccala.

He stood up. "Well, the thing better be right, what else could I tell you?" he said. He and Big Jelly left the room, slamming the door after them.

"*Ciciri*," Baccala snarled.

Kid Sally and Big Jelly spent the afternoon in the vending office, looking through the Yellow Pages for cages. Big Jelly finally found two theat-rical renting places. Between them they had eleven circus cages which they could rent for two weeks. They needed them back for the Ed Sullivan show. This left the bike race one cage short. There were twenty-four riders, divided into two-man teams. While one rider was on the track, the teammate would be in the cage, sleeping on the cot. A woman at one of the agen-cies suggested they call Thompson's, a large pet-supply house in Manhattan which services zoos around the country. The man at Thomp-son's said he had one cage he could lease for a week. Sally and Big Jelly drove over to Thomp-son's. It was in a warehouse. A man in the office took Sally and Jelly through a triple-locked steel door and into a hot cement room that was smelly and filled with the squeal of birds. In a tall cage at the front of the warehouse, a zebra shouldered against thick bars. Next to him, in another cage, an antelope stood quietly. Cages filled with multi-colored birds, were stacked on top of each other. Up against the back wall there was a small cage on wooden blocks. Next to it was a big circus cage. A tan form was rolled up in one corner of the cage.

"Here's the cage," the man said, stopping at the small one.

"Not big enough," Big Jelly said.

"We need it big enough for a guy," Kid Sally Palumbo said.

"We're startin' slavery," Big Jelly said.

"Well, that's all I got," the man said. "If I move the lion next week, you could have the cage then."

"Who lion?" Kid Sally said.

The man pointed to the larger cage. "That's a lion in there." The tan form in the corner stirred and came up on four legs. Wisps of mane, darker than the coat, straggled from its head. It stood on four puppy legs that were too long. The lion had feet too big for the body.

"That's a real baby, only five months old," the man said.

Kid Sally slapped his hand on the bars. The lion jumped up and pushed into the corner of the cage.

"What's a matter with him?"

"He's scary. He's only a baby."

"He looks like he could eat my freakin' leg," Big Jelly said.

"You have to put meat in front of him," the man said. "He'll be afraid of people for a few months yet."

Kid Sally yelled at the lion. "Yaaaaaahhhh!" The lion shook. The left side of Kid Sally's mouth came up in a sneer. His eyes squinted. He began to giggle.

"Yaaaaahhhhh!" Tommy Udo snarled.

"You sell him?" Kid Sally said.

"Sure, he's for sale. Two hundred and fifty dollars."

Kid Sally kept giggling and looking at the lion. "Give him the money, Jelly."

At six p.m. there was a roar and then a scream which ran through Marshall Street. People rushed to the windows. They looked out to see Kid Sally Palumbo, giggling, dragging a lion across the sidewalk from a panel truck. Women, screaming, ran away. The lion had a rope attached to a makeshift leather collar around his neck. Kid Sally pulled on the rope. The lion, head down, fear sounding from his throat, tried to dig into the sidewalk. Kid Sally Palumbo began yelling at the lion and pulling hard on the rope. The lion roared in fear. Big Jelly got behind the lion and pushed. They got the lion into the vending-machine office, opened the door to the cellar, and pushed the lion down the stairs. Kid Sally slammed the door and giggled. Big Jelly went out and waddled back with a paper bag, meat in waxed paper showing at the top.

"Eight pounds of chopped meat, that should fill his belly," Big Jelly said. He opened the cellar door and ripped the top of the waxed paper. He threw the bag down the stairs. The meat scent hit the lion while the bag was still in the air. Two floppy paws slapped down on the bag the moment it touched the floor.

"Look at that," Big Jelly said.

"Wait'll we feed him *people*," Kid Sally Palumbo said. He began to giggle.

Kid Sally and Big Jelly locked the office and went out for their night's business. They drove to a lumber mill. The lights were on. Mulqueen and Keefe were hammering bolts into a section of boards planked together to form a curved section of track. All over the lumber mill pieces like this were stacked or sat on sawhorses. A table in the middle of the floor was covered with a layout of the armory.

"We're right up to here," Mulqueen said. He put his finger on a spot in the plans. The spot was even with the doorway for the motor pool. The white lines on the blueprint paper, with long arrows and short arrows and numbers with apostrophes after them, irritated Kid Sally. He didn't know what they meant. He wanted to go back and play with the lion. "We just have to get the turn done, it goes in here," Mulqueen said, tapping his finger on the motor-pool area.

"It looks good," Kid Sally said. "Just don't let us down."

He and Big Jelly went out and sat in the car.

"We got things to do yet," Kid Sally said.

"What?" Big Jelly said.

146

"Well, we got to do things."

"I know what we got to do," Big Jelly said. "We got to go and do things to a couple of girls. Do them certain things to girls, that's what we got to do." He started the car.

Izzy sat in the Enchanted Hour from midnight until 1:30 a.m. He had an important appointment with Kid Sally Palumbo. At 1:30 he told the waiter to give him the check. *This kid is going to make a good memory of himself,* Izzy thought.

At seven p.m. on Friday, January 23, the World Championship Six-Day Bike Race, sponsored by the Americans of Italian Descent Amity Committee of New York, was one hour away from its official start. Only a few people were coming up the brightly lit armory steps. Ticket clerks began to shift uneasily and talk about a small crowd. When Izzy walked into the armory, he asked the head clerk what the advance sale was. The clerk said 1100. Actual attendance usually works out to be double the size of the advance. This would mean a crowd of about 2200 for the night's racing. Opening night. It all goes downhill after that. The ticket clerk laughed at the ridiculous situation. "Don't laugh," Izzy said. "Right now they don't have enough to pay you."

Inside, banners from Italian, Greek, French, and Polish societies hung from the balcony. Smoke from the first few black DeNobili cigars came up from the seats and hung in the flood-lights. The old men smoking the cigars obviously were bike-race veterans. They kept their over-coats on.

In the middle of the floor, directly in front of the center of the grandstands, were twelve red, yellow, and blue circus cages with black bars. Each cage had a cot in it, and a folding tray for eating. The cages were in a General Custer circle. One side of each cage, the side facing the stands, was open. The other side, the side facing the inside of the wagon-train circle, was boarded up. In this way the riders in the cages would be unable to talk to each other through the backs of their cages.

Around the cages ran a beautiful wooden track. Neat, varnished pine wood gleamed in the light. The track had straightaways gently bending into a fine saucer curve. The lip of the saucer was banked high up from the bottom of the track. This was to create thrilling scenes of bike-riders seemingly on their sides, but protected by simple speed while they raced around the curve and came zooming into the straightaway. The straightaway ran the full length of the armory. The other turn of the track was not yet down. The beautiful curved boards that would form the turn were piled atop each other in front of the green corrugated-metal door, which was pulled down to the floor.

Mulqueen and Keefe stood with ten workers. "Get the door up now so we can finish this thing," Mulqueen was telling an armory worker dressed in fatigues.

The armory worker pressed a large button. Black, heavily greased chains began to make a zzzzzzzzzzng sound. The green corrugated-metal shed door grumbled up from the armory floor. It rose steadily to reveal, foot by foot, first, five 105-mm. howitzers, neatly spaced, canvas tied to the muzzles. The howitzers were attached to five half-ton trucks. As the door rose more, the rest of the scene came into view. Packed together in neat rows, shining dully in the dim light, were the jeeps, half-tracks, ambulances, and trucks of the 987th Field Artillery Regiment, New York National Guard.

Mulqueen spat out curses. "Look at this. It'll take a half-hour to move this mess the hell out of there."

"Move them?" the armory worker said. "You don't move anything in there. That's the motor pool. Everything in there stays where it is."

"No, you don't understand," Mulqueen said. "We need that space for the track."

"That's the motor pool," the armory worker said. "It don't move."

It was now 7:15 p.m. Mulqueen walked the length of the armory floor quickly. He went out into the lobby. He saw Joseph DeLauria, dressed in a tuxedo, greeting old men who had sashes draped over their shoulders. Mulqueen tried to talk to DeLauria. DeLauria shook his head and wouldn't listen. Mulqueen saw Izzy leaning against a wall. "I don't do woodwork," Izzy said. Mulqueen finally saw Kid Sally Palumbo standing in the middle of a circle of his people.

"That's nothin', just have them move the trucks," Kid Sally Palumbo said. He turned back to his people.

"They won't move the trucks," Mulqueen said.

"Hey, that's nothin'," Big Jelly said. "Sally Kid, go over to the office there and tell the guy and he'll do it for you."

"It's always me," Kid Sally said. "I got to do everything." He stepped through the people and went into the armory office.

"You got to move the cannons for us," Kid Sally said. A man in civilian clothes sat at the desk.

"Where to?" the man said.

"Out in the street, anywhere, I don't care. Just move them."

"Move our motor pool? That's the property of the United States government. We can't move one jeep."

Kid Sally closed his eyes and ran a hand over them. "Who's in charge of this place?"

"The colonel."

"Where is he?"

"Home."

"Get him on the phone and straighten this thing out."

The man dialed a number. "Hello, is Colonel Rudershan there? Oh, I see. Yes, I forgot all about that. Well, thanks, I'll try him tomorrow then."

He hung up. "The colonel went to a movie with his wife and his brother and sister-in-law. It's the sister-in-law's birthday."

"Move the cannons," Kid Sally said.

"That's government property," the man said.

"MOVE THE CANNONS!" Kid Sally screamed.

"Hey!"

Baccala stood in the doorway, shoes gleaming, black hat tilted on his head, a DeNobili fuming in his mouth.

"How you no measure the track right?"

"This guy won't move the cannons," Kid Sally said.

"So he no move the cannons, then you move the track," Baccala said. "Make the track little."

Mulqueen, the carpenter, closed his eyes. "You can't do it. The thing is measured to fit like it is."

"Fix," Baccala said. His eyes were narrow. He walked out of the office.

A haze formed inside Kid Sally Palumbo's head. The haze solidified and turned into a throbbing knot in the middle of his forehead. He began to punch himself on the forehead. He didn't see Baccala walk away.

Down at the end of the armory floor, Mulqueen and Keefe stood and looked at the track.

"Eight hours," Keefe said. "Eight hours at least."

It was 8:17 p.m. now. Nearly 2500 people sat

151

in the stands. In the age of numbers, 2500 at a sports event is painfully few on paper. But when you have 2500 people sitting and waiting for an event to start that you can't get started and you stand in the middle of the floor and look up at these 2500 people, they look like a million people.

A voice from an empty part of the balcony started it. *"Hey, what you do?"*

A growl ran through the rest of the people. A Polack jumped up in the end balcony. *"Come on."*

The Greeks in the seats behind their society banner began to clap their hands. The clapping spread and now the whole place was clapping, and then the people started stamping their feet and the noise sounded like a building coming down. Kid Sally Palumbo stood in the infield with his eyes shut. His cousin Albert Palumbo said he had an idea. Albert went downstairs to the locker room and called the riders, who were sitting on wooden benches between the green lockers and looking up at the ceiling. The stamping coming through the ceiling had them frightened. Albert led them up the stairs and onto the armory floor. The rhythmic clapping turned to cheers for the riders. Albert led them across the track and into the infield.

"All right, inside," Albert yelled. He began motioning to the riders. The riders looked at the cages and did not move. Big Jelly and Carmine and Albert had to come and start pushing them into their assigned cages. Grumbling in several languages began. The riders got into the cages, and the doors were slammed.

Bike-riders race in T-shirts and black knit swimming trunks. Because they sit on hard bike seats for hours at a time, they stuff things down the front of their trunks to cushion themselves against the steady chafing, biting motion of the bike seat. In a normal six-day bike race, the riders, by the last day, have so much stuffed down their fronts that they appear to have elephantiasis. Towels are used for stuffing. Many old-time bike-riders used to stuff steaks into their trunks. They found the grease was very good for the insides of their thighs. Also the steaks could be eaten after the race was over.

The riders were in the cages and the crowd stirred and again began to clap. At 9:30 p.m., a Greek in a cage started it. Contestant Constantine Caras turned his back on the audience and stuffed three large bathtowels down the front of his trunks. Proudly, Caras turned and faced the crowd with this great bulge between his legs.

"Yip, yip," the Greek yelled. He gripped the bars and began jumping up and down in the cage. He stopped jumping and started scratching behind his neck. He scratched under his arms. He had his hands down and he was scratching his waist when the crowd saw what was coming. A roar went out when the Greek stuck his tongue out of one side of his mouth and

153

his hands began tearing at the bulge between his legs.

Caras' Greek partner had been sitting on the edge of the cot. Now he came off the cot onto all fours. He padded up to the bars and began barking like a dog. He raised one leg into the air.

The crowd was in tears. People were standing, bent over, and slapping their thighs.

Mario Trantino and Carlo Rafetto, who were in the cage next to the Greeks, saw the crowd becoming helpless with laughter. Mario took the folding tray and began banging it against the bars, the way he had seen them do it in American prison movies. The sound of the tin tray carried. One of the Polacks on the other side of the circle of cages picked up his tray and began banging it. Soon the steady rhythm of trays banging against the bars sounded everywhere and the people in the seats clapped along with the banging trays. Up at the end of the armory Mulqueen was ripping out sections of track and scratching his ear while he tried to figure out what to do, and then the clapping from the crowd started to die down and the first people got up and began to file to the exits. More people started to file out. There was a tangle at the exits because people were turning back from the exits, growling, and trying to push their way back into the arena. Everybody was pushing and getting nowhere, and then one old Italian, face shaking with anger, threw his cigar into the air and held out his hands like the Pope and screamed in Italian that the ticket clerk wouldn't give him his money back.

An old woman in a black cloth coat was out of the grandstands first. She came with a stumpy walk. She came with a shopping bag filled with food for the entire night in her right hand. She came across the track with this stumpy walk and with the shopping bag full of food in her right hand and she saw Joseph DeLauria standing in his tuxedo and she went right for the tuxedo and swung the bag of food and the bag broke on Joseph DeLauria's head. Sausage sandwiches with rich red sauce flew all over the place.

A fat man in a truck-driver's cap came running across the track. He began skipping around with his right leg drawn back. He was trying to figure out who to go after when Albert Palumbo came around the side of the cage, and the guy looked at Albert and then let go and kicked Albert in the ankles. A fat, bald Greek came pounding over the track with a folding chair held over his head. He swung the chair at Big Jelly. The Greek missed, but he kept the chair in motion and the chair caught Tony the Indian on the head and he went down like an air-raid victim. Now people were coming from everywhere, throwing punches and chairs, and the bike-riders held their bulges and jumped up and down like monkeys.

An old man in a cap and overcoat grabbed a bike from the front of the Polish riders' cage. The old man walked the bike onto the track and got on it. He started pumping the bike up to the

155

turn. He hit the saucer and pumped wildly around it and then shot down onto the straightaway and flew along it. There was a rumble from the far end of the armory. The big green corrugated door was coming down and the carpenters and workers ducked under it and into the safety of the motor pool. The door came all the way down the floor. The old man riding the bike was in ecstasy while he shot down the straightaway. Three-quarters of the way down he felt the handlebars for brakes. Then he pushed the pedal backward. This made only a zizzzziiiing sound. The bike did not slacken.

The old man got excited and his foot fumbled and pushed the pedal violently forward by mistake. When he and the bike hit the green door, he went halfway up the door like a human fly. He fell like a sack of cement.

The first call was made to the 91st Precinct by the man in the armory office. When the squad car responded, the patrolman took a look at the crowd milling around the track and went back to the car and put in a Signal 16, which is the riot call.

The next morning, the court attendant looked up and saw the judge was ready. With an unhurried municipal walk, the attendant went over to open the door to the detention pens and bring the morning's defendants into the courtroom. A wave of snarling people slapped into the attendant. Kid Sally Palumbo was leading them. He was in his T-shirt. His suit jacket was folded over his arm. Both knees of his pants were ripped. Behind him came a crush of bandaged, splattered, ripped people from the bike-race riot.

"And what's this?" the judge said.

"A company returning," the docket clerk said.

When everybody was released on bail, Kid Sally began to whisper and glance around to let his people know they were to show up at the street later in the day.

They came through the double doors of the courtroom and out into a shabby high-ceilinged lobby. Cigarette butts and candy wrappers littered the floor. Revolving doors opened onto the cold street. Through the door, Kid Sally could see photographers jamming together to get pictures of him coming out of court. Pictures ordinarily were all right, in fact Kid Sally once tried to pay a *Daily News* cameraman $25 to take a color picture for the Sunday roto section. But Kid Sally didn't want New York to see a picture of him in a T-shirt and with ripped pants. He stopped and looked around. The two old men working the shoeshine stand looked at him.

"Shine?" one of them said.

"No," Kid Sally said. "No, not a shine." He came over to the stand and took a tin of black polish. Using a courtroom-door window as a mirror, Kid Sally put his fingers into the polish and printed FUCK YOU across his forehead. Kid

Sally came through the revolving doors waving his arm at the pack of crouching, jostling, swearing cameramen, who laughed and then froze when they saw his forehead.

Chapter 11

Mario had gotten back to the hotel at three a.m. At nine a.m. the hotel cashier woke him up. The room bill had been paid, the cashier said, and Mario had until one p.m. to check out. After that, all bills run up by the bike-riders would be their own responsibility. If Mario intended to remain, the hotel suggested a deposit. Mario came down to the lobby, where the bike-riders were waving airline tickets and arguing over what had happened. The girl at the airlines counter in the lobby was busy booking the bike-riders on the afternoon and evening flights back to Europe. Mario handed the girl his ticket and said he wanted to cash it in. The girl gave him $311.35.

Mario took a cab down to 10th Street. He leaned forward on the seat and went through his inside pocket for the picture Father Marsalano had given him the morning he left for America. A small warmth ran through Mario when he felt the envelope. He looked at the words on the back of the picture: "Dear Friends Who Left

Catanzia to Go to America and Become Rich . . .” Mario patted the picture. No matter how tough it could get in America, he always had the envelope from home.

When the cab stopped on 10th Street, Mario saw the meter was $1.45. He became immobile. Slowly he handed the driver a dollar bill, two dimes, and a lire piece he hoped would pass for a quarter. The cabbie’s hand felt $1.45. The cabbie’s thumb ran over the palm trying to find a tip. The thumb found no tip. The cabbie wanted to shout, but his tongue already had gone into shock. Mario was halfway across the sidewalk when the cabbie finally broke the numbness.

“I could understand it if you was a Puerto Rican,” he yelled at Mario.

The veins on the sides of the cabbie’s head popped out in anger. Two blocks later, he was still muttering when he began to put the coins in his change-maker. When he saw the lire piece, he suffered a heart spasm.

Sidney had a more positive reaction when he opened the door and Mario pushed into the apartment.

“Kill yourself,” Sidney said.

Sidney was edgy because he did not like Mario, and also because he had been living without whisky. After Mario had shown up at the Plaza Hotel, Grant Monroe, in a rage, had come down to the apartment and frisked the place for whisky. Now Mario, who had caused all the trouble for Sidney, was sitting across from

160

him. And Mario, as payment for having discovered Grant Monroe's particular brand of larceny, was expecting help.

"Grant says we got no room for you," Sidney said. "We'll give you all the help we can, but we got no room."

"Just show me how you do this thing," Mario said. He thought that if he could just learn the game, the next step would take care of itself.

"Well, where are you staying?" Sidney said.

"The *chiti*," Mario said. Sometimes English words beginning with C came out "Ch."

"Cheatey is the right name," Sidney said. "I don't know what I can tell you. I think you're a natural thief myself."

He described his operation, which was very simple. Five years back, when Grant Monroe and Sidney met each other and started off, the usual route in art forging was to copy a Chagall or Modigliani. But apartments on Fifth and Park Avenues were becoming as crowded as subway trains with all the thieves selling phony Chagalls and Modiglianis to rich idiots. Grant came up with the idea of finding work done by artists who had lived in unrecognized ability and who died virtually unknown. Sidney would copy their works and sign Grant Monroe's name to them. Grant's great sales personality would carry it from there. He was great at selecting customers who lived far away from each other. They could be sold the same paintings. All Sidney had to do was sit in the apartment and work like a Xerox machine. It was a fine arrangement. Rather than pushing fake Chagalls for big, risky money, Grant Monroe sold phony Grant Monroes on a solid volume basis. The hundred-dollar bills added up. Of course, everything depended on Sidney's remaining hidden. This was all right with Sidney. He couldn't sell his own work. His personality was so bad the Chinese would not take free missiles from him. Besides, Sidney appreciated Grant. He felt Grant was removing the ultimate hazard of an art thief's life: a guard who won't allow you to mix paint in your cell.

"Just remember, only use dead artists," Sidney told Mario. "If they can breathe, they can sign warrants."

Sidney tugged open the doors of an old cabinet. Inside was a pile of reproductions and scarred originals of work done by people dead and unremembered. "Take your pick," he said to Mario. "Whichever you think is best for you. Don't worry what people like. They all got the taste of pigs. You can sell anything. The biggest art-collector in this city got a bum Picasso right in his living room."

Mario went through the pile. "Which one do you think I should use?" he asked.

Sidney said, "Hey, I don't even know if you can put a straight line on paper. Grant said help you out. That's what I'm doing. But you got to be able to do this yourself. If you're not a half an artist, then go find another way to steal."

Mario's chin came out in pride. "I can do it

162

myself," he said. He pulled out an original of a nude girl in her apartment. There was a rip through the girl's face. The rest of her was intact. Sidney said the picture was particularly safe to use. The artist, Peppis, was caught by the Depression and he wound up painting station signs in the subway for the WPA. He became drunk and tumbled off the platform and was killed by the Broadway local. "Even the motorman who killed him is dead," Sidney said.

Mario nodded and stepped around Sidney and Sidney tried to roll the wheelchair after Mario, but Mario was already whisking sheets from a stack of art paper. "The hell you will, they cost a dollar-fifty apiece," Sidney said. Mario was grabbing at charcoal nubs, paint tubes, brushes, anything that could be picked up.

"Thief bastard!" Sidney yelled as Mario walked out the door.

When Mario got back to the hotel there was a message from Angela. She would be at the hotel at 12:30. Mario was in front of the hotel at 12:15. He had his suitcase between his feet and the art paper tucked under his arm. The winter wind swirled out of a lifeless gray sky. The wind lifted newspaper pages and carried them along the sidewalk. Angela came around the corner from the subway. She had her chin buried into the collar of a navy-blue coat. She did not smile when she saw him. Her eyes teared in the wind and her face seemed drained. People who have been up all night always show it in cold weather.

She looked at the suitcase. "You're going home?" she said. Her voice had a hopeful rise.

"No, I'm staying here."

"Oh," she said. "Then what's the suitcase for?"

"The hotel costs too much. I have to find another place."

"You have to move *already?*" she said to him.

"They want money in deposit if I stay."

Angela's eyes narrowed. *"Che cazzo diavolo!"*

Mario thought he heard her say this, but he decided he had not. A woman hasn't talked like this since Mary Magdalene reformed.

"DeLauria," Angela said. "Chew!" She spat at the air.

The scowl on her face surprised Mario. He didn't think the girl was this tough. He immediately made his eyes wide and he let the rest of his face hang. He was pretty sure he looked like an orphan with sad eyes.

Angela looked at him and sighed. "Come on in and we'll have coffee and figure out something," she said.

She bought a copy of the *Village Voice* at the hotel newsstand, and they sat in the coffee shop while she read the ads. She went to the phone booth and made several calls. She came out smiling. "There's one down on Eleventh Street that's cheap."

The apartment was at 293 East 11th. The superintendent, a red-faced man in a dirty woolen shirt, led them up scarred staircases to the top floor. Pale afternoon light came through a skylight. The superintendent opened the door to number 20. It was three rooms in railroad-car alignment. There also was a small dusty kitchen and a crumbling bathroom. The wooden floor squeaked. White plaster showed through the dirt-streaked blue wall paint. The apartment was $36 a month. The superintendent wanted one month in advance and a month's security. Mario grimaced and took money out of his pocket.

"What can you do?" Angela said. "The least DeLauria could've done."

She spat at the air again. Mario paid the superintendent and was handed a key and a scrawled receipt. "It's yours as of now," the man said. "What do you want on the mailbox, Mr. and Mrs.?"

"What business is it of yours?" Angela said.

"I couldn't care less," the superintendent said.

"Well, then, don't ask," Angela said.

Downstairs, Angela looked at her watch. She had to get going.

"Good luck," she said. "I have a lot to do now."

She started down the stoop and turned to say good-by to Mario. He was standing on the top step with his face saying "War Orphan."

Angela stopped. "What are you going to sleep on?"

He shrugged and looked even sadder.

"Well, come on with me, you can't sleep on

165

the floor," she said. He bounded down the steps. They walked up to First Avenue and went past coffee shops and bars filled with young boys and girls wearing bell-bottom pants and Saint-John-the-Baptist hair styles. Two blocks up there was a store called Cheap John's. Angela left Mario on the sidewalk. She went inside and came out with a pillow.

"At least for your head," she said, holding the pillow out to Mario.

Two boys stopped on the sidewalk and watched. "We hope you'll be very happy together," one of them said.

Angela buried her face in the pillow. She was flushed with embarrassment. Mario was surprised to see her react this way. But when her face came out of the pillow it was straight and cold again. She handed Mario the pillow.

"All right," she said, "take care of yourself."

"When do you come again?" he asked her.

"In a couple of days," she said.

She was frowning as she went down the subway steps.

"No miss!" Big Mama said to Tony the Indian. He nodded.

"No miss!" Big Mama said to Big Jelly.

"Nobody miss!" she hissed at everybody.

They were crowded into the kitchen and the living room, thirty of them, standing around with plates in their hands, and when they came up to the stove Big Mama would plunge a

166

serving spoon into this big aluminum restaurant pot of lobster fra diavolo and heap it on the plates, all the time muttering, "No miss!"

They were going to shoot everything they could. The trouble had started predictably and easily. Kid Sally Palumbo, chewing a toothpick, leaned against the wall in Baccala's office. Kid Sally had been summoned because of the bike-race failure. The Water Buffalo and two black suits stood by the door. Baccala sat at his desk and looked at his hands in his lap.

"I like-a lunch," Baccala said.

Kid Sally said, "You wanna eat and talk? Good."

Baccala kept looking at his hands. "I said, *I* like-a lunch. I no say *you* like-a lunch. So *you* shut up-a you face!"

"Hey you!" Kid Sally said.

"Shut up-a you face," the Water Buffalo said. The two black suits stirred. Kid Sally bit his bottom lip.

Baccala looked up. His eyes were so narrow he could barely see through the slits. "What you do," he said to Kid Sally softly, "you drive-a me to lunch. You wait-a outside. When I finish-a lunch, I come out and you drive-a me back here." Baccala's voice rose. Every day you come here and you drive-a Baccala."

Coldly, almost offhandedly, Baccala was perpetrating the worst of all crimes against a gangster. He was trying to kill Kid Sally's ego. He was telling Kid Sally face to face — worse, in front of others — that from now on he was not the leader of a faction of a gang. He was to be a chauffeur for Baccala. Chauffeur, errand boy, footman, and lackey. And Kid Sally Palumbo, his face stinging, had to stand against the wall and take it without a sound. The Water Buffalo and the pair of black suits were only a few feet from him. The Water Buffalo had his eyes on the ceiling and he was praying to a saint whose name he knew, in hopes Kid Sally would say something fresh so Baccala would let the Water Buffalo kill Kid Sally right in the office.

The toothpick in Kid Sally Palumbo's mouth moved up and down. He said nothing. When he walked out of the place he took a deep breath because he was glad to be alive. Then he took a second deep breath. He would be back in that office someday with all of his people and they would make headlines because of the way they would kill Baccala and the Water Buffalo.

Kid Sally Palumbo stood alone, looking out the kitchen window. He trembled a little. Over the centuries, revolts in the Mafia have always been heavily sanctioned affairs. Just as no smart political legislator brings his bill to a vote unless he knows beforehand that he has the votes to win, so does an ambitious Mafioso operate. A revolt normally consists of the ambitious one becoming restless with an old boss, then subtly asking around the organization to determine if he has any support. If enough people in command tell him, "Old men, sometimes they better off they die," he knows he has assent. He then invites his boss out to dinner, and on the way home he drops the boss off in the nearest sewer.

But in this revolt Kid Sally Palumbo was starting, he had no official sanction at all. Instead, he was shaking the structure of the entire organization. This, he knew, normally was as sure a way to get killed as sky-diving from the Empire State Building. He had a group of, in all, 125 hoodlums from Marshall Street and the adjoining blocks. They were going against an organized Mafia family of perhaps 1000 members, full- and part-time. But Kid Sally Palumbo's group had youth and hunger for the money which Baccala had been denying them. And the Baccala Family, like any other institution in the country, was old and essentially sick with success. A small, determined group could topple it. The victory would require close teamwork and extensive brainwork. But the rewards could be incredible. If Kid Sally won control of the Baccala gang, all the other Mafia families in the country would automatically recognize him. He could get at millions. And there would be something so much more important than money. Revenge. As Kid Sally stared out the window, the wind gusted off the docks and the telephone lines began waving in the streetlights. Kid Sally could see Baccala hanging from the wires, his head flopping over on his broken neck, the wind blowing the body like wash.

"No miss!" Big Mama was saying. She was calling it out now.

Kid Sally knew she was right. It is not too good when you shoot at a guy and miss him. Sometimes the guy comes back and finds you asleep in your bed. Kid Sally also knew that it does not matter what you do in life, as long as you do it effectively. The people who shoot and miss are the ones who get in trouble. In a city like New York, failure is the real crime. But for those who shoot straight and get the job done, the rewards are immense. Society not only approves but gives adulation. They still write of Lucky Luciano as if he had been a fine Mayor of New York. Willie Moretti, who could have been as big as Luciano but happened to mess up a couple of key murders, was classified as a cheap hoodlum when he died.

"When you're broke, you're a joke," Kid Sally said. He took out a pack of cigarettes. He flicked the lighter deliberately. He took a drag on the cigarette. Everybody in the room watched him: young guys with dark hair and mean faces and cigarettes hanging from their lips. Kid Sally blew the smoke out in a stream. His lip curled. He began to giggle. Everybody in the room began to giggle with him.

"Old fuckin' greaseballs," Kid Sally said.

"I put out his mother's eyes," Big Jelly said.

"He don't give me nothin', I take it. I take it

over his fuckin' dead body," another one of them called out.

Big Mama stood in the kitchen doorway, drying her hands on her apron. Angela leaned in the doorway with her. Big Mama put out a hand to push her away. "Shoo. Go to your room."

Angela pushed Big Mama's hand back. "I spit on their graves," Angela said.

Big Mama clasped her hands and looked up at the ceiling. *"Madre di Cristo."*

"Nothin' means nothin' until we give them a present," Kid Sally said. "We give them a present of somebody's head in a box."

"Maybe they don't like it and they quit," Big Jelly said.

"We'll see what kind of chops they got," Kid Sally said.

Chapter 12

Joey Miranda, a good car thief, and his best friend, Julie DiBiasi, who does all sorts of evil things from his base as a gas-station attendant, were standing together and remembering certain things. This was a herculean thing for them to be doing. Joey Miranda had an IQ of 67 in grammar school and since has retrogressed to the point where he forgets his home phone number. And Julie DiBiasi always sneers at people and says, "At least I know I'm a dope."

With their heads together, the brain worms pulsed with great information. The much-hated Water Buffalo, Baccala's chief aide, always parks his car at night in the same spot on Bushwick Avenue. The spot is always open for Water Buffalo's car because there is a fire hydrant there. The cops put a $25 ticket on the car each night. The Water Buffalo uses the tickets to pick his teeth. When he parks the car at night, the Water Buffalo is well covered by another car, which pulls alongside him, the people in the back seat holding machine guns at the ready. The Water

Buffalo lives in a two-family house around the corner from the fire hydrant. When he gets to his house, the cover car leaves him, and his wife, Mrs. Water Buffalo, takes up the coverage. She peers out the door with a shotgun.

In the morning the Water Buffalo has no coverage. However, he walks on the street very close to people. He usually picks out a lady wheeling a baby carriage and he walks alongside her. If he sees any suspicious car, he bends down and kisses the baby. "Who could shoot if they thought they might hit a baby?" the Water Buffalo says. "The only person I know of who would do a thing like that is me."

"What happens," Julie DiBiasi wondered, "if he starts driving away in his car some morning and then the car stops on him and he has to get out and see what's wrong?"

Joey Miranda thought about this. "So many things could happen to you when the car stops and you have to get out and look at what made the car stop," he said.

"He could get his throat strangled," Julie DiBiasi said.

"No strangle!" Big Mama said. "It takes too long. Everybody walks by and see what you do. Just shoot-a him."

"The Water Buffalo gets hit right in the head," Kid Sally Palumbo announced.

Early the next morning Julie DiBiasi, working very carefully with a knife, started a slow leak around the valve of the Water Buffalo's left rear tire. At 11:30 the Water Buffalo came out from behind a lady who had twins in a stroller and got into his car and drove it off and turned a corner and went down three blocks and turned another corner. He felt the car pulling on the turn and he slowed down and stopped at the curb of a street that had garages and a factory on it. The car following him was driven by the best driver on Marshall Street, Ezmo the Driver. He was terrific at trailing people and not being noticed. Julie DiBiasi and Joey Miranda were in the back seat. They got out and strolled up to strike a blow for freedom.

The Water Buffalo was crouched over and feeling the flat tire. Joey Miranda and Julie DiBiasi swaggered up to him. The Water Buffalo saw them and he dove under the car and came up on the other side like a guy coming out of the pool. Joey Miranda and Julie DiBiasi bent over so they could shoot the Water Buffalo while he was under the car. But all they could see was the Water Buffalo's $110 Bostonians on the sidewalk on the other side of the car. They fired twice at the Bostonians, but the Bostonians were clomping up and down so fast that the bullets pinged off the cement sidewalk, and the Water Buffalo raced down an alley. Joey Miranda and Julie DiBiasi came rushing around the car and started into the alley. There was this big puddle in the way. The Water Buffalo, who had his adrenalin pumping because it was life and death, had taken the puddle in a big leap and hadn't gotten his $110 Bostonians wet. He was beating down the alleyway. But Joey Miranda pulled up short at the puddle in his $120 Footjoys, and Julie DiBiasi stopped dead in his $115 Johnson Murphys. They tiptoed around the puddle. Then they started down the alley in a fury. Running, running, running with guns in their hands and the fury of centuries racing through their blood. The alley was quite short, and the Water Buffalo had gone beating to the end of it. He skidded on his leather heels around the turn. Joey Miranda and Julie DiBiasi came around the turn flying, guns straight out. They ran into a ramshackle fence made of rotting wood. The fence closed off an area between two buildings. Joey bounced up and looked on the other side of the fence. Nobody was there.

"What do we do?" Julie said.

"We're in some trouble," Joey said.

"Yeah," Julie said.

"We could go back and say we got him and then we could go out tonight and get him for real," Joey said.

"What about Ezmo out in the car? He knows we didn't get him," Julie said.

"I know what to do," Joey said. He pointed his pistol at the fence and closed his eyes and pulled the trigger twice.

"Now run like we just done somethin'," Joey said.

The two of them came racing back out of the alley. Ezmo the Driver had the car rolling just slow enough for them to dive into the back seat. He hit the pedal, and the car was doing 60 by the time Julie pulled the door shut after him.

"Right in the head," Joey said loudly.

"Boy," Ezmo said.

"Right between the ears," Julie said.

"Boy," Ezmo said.

"What blood," Joey said.

"Boy," Ezmo said.

There was a large but quiet celebration at Big Mama's that night. There were fifteen guys sitting there like pirates but saying nothing about anything and Big Mama cooked zuppa di clams and spaghetti alla Carbonara and veal scaloppine alla Romana. There was Soave Bolla on the table, and after it was finished, everybody went to the Bardolino. They toasted Joey Miranda and Julie DiBiasi without saying what they were toasting them about because it was one of those things you don't talk about, and Joey and Julie looked at each other with nervous glances and then Julie decided the only way out was to go to the Bardolino heavy, and pretty soon his head was hanging in the spaghetti alla Carbonara and he was saying to himself, "I'm Al Capone."

The story of the Water Buffalo's murder was not in the *Daily News* when Beppo the Dwarf brought the early edition up at 9:30 p.m. And the story was not on the eleven-o'clock news on television. Big Mama stood in the doorway, drying a pot, and her eyes narrowed.

"Hey, Joey, what you do?"

Kid Sally Palumbo got up and walked over to Julie DiBiasi and slapped his face, and then he walked over to Joey Miranda and slapped his face.

"What is this?" he said.

"The body was in a alley, maybe nobody looked yet," Julie mumbled.

"Yeah," Joey said.

Kid Sally looked at them. "Maybe they're all keeping it quiet to see if we do anything stupid."

"That could-a be," Big Mama said. She glared at Joey and Julie. "It better."

"We seen the blood," Joey mumbled.

The party broke up and Joey Miranda was so drunk he got into the car and fell asleep at the wheel. Julie couldn't feel a thing and he stumbled along the street and tried to take in deep breaths to clear his head, but the wine was still coming up from his stomach and exploding in his head. He walked over to the gas station and passed out in a chair at the desk. You could have stuck pins in Julie, and he would not have felt anything. Which was a good thing because at 4:30 in the morning the Water Buffalo and three other guys walked into the gas station, and the Water Buffalo dragged Julie into the grease pit and it was a good thing Julie couldn't feel much of anything. The police-emergency-squad guy observed, "Dracula never did anything as bad as this."

At 9:30 p.m. the *Daily News* did carry news of the gang war. It read:

DIBIASI — Julie. Very suddenly. Beloved son of Carmela and Ralphie DiBiasi. Dear brother of Frankie, Anthony, and Salvatore DiBiasi. Dear brother of Mrs. Laura Ruocco. May he live forever in a thousand hearts. Reposing CAMPION'S Funeral Home, Inc., 56 Lockman Street, Brooklyn. Interment Thursday 9 a.m. private.

All over South Brooklyn, in every railroad flat, there could be heard the sound of hangers clicking while people took good black funeral clothes out of the closets. They began to get ready for as good a gangland funeral as Kid Sally Palumbo could put together under the circumstances of not having the big money to blow on the kind of funerals all gangsters dream of for themselves.

All major funerals in New York, including the funerals of some people who may have led legitimate lives, such as a Cardinal, basically are copies of Frankie Yale's funeral. Frankie Yale was a very good guy who lived in Brookyn until 1932, and then he became a very bad guy and somebody put a bomb in his car motor. The bomb worked.

They ran a funeral for Frankie Yale that was bigger than the Democratic National Convention. The great moment in the wake came when Dominic Monzalulu, the man who had coupled the bomb to Frankie Yale's car, stood in front of the casket and began crying and held out his hands and wailed to the flowers over the casket, "You got no idea of the respect I had for this here man." On the day of the funeral there were 21 flower cars and 103 limousines and 225 private cars following Frankie Yale's body. It was terrific, and all good undertakers have a mimeographed copy of the order of Frankie Yale's funeral just in case they get lucky with a bombing victim who was rich.

The funeral of Julie DiBiasi was different. Usually a gangland murder occurs as part of a drive by the established organization. A man drifting away from the fold is the target. The action is both approved and carried out by organization members. All attend the funeral. But for Julie DiBiasi's funeral, there was no way for the Baccala people to attend. Nobody likes to kneel in front of a casket if he knows somebody from the bereaved family is likely to open fire from his folding chair.

Campion, the undertaker, had an easy time with the funeral. Usually he has to spend a lot of time making up the deceased's face so everybody can say how good he looks. But after what the Water Buffalo did to Julie DiBiasi, Campion needed Rembrandt to straighten it out. It would be a closed coffin. Campion also had no argument about the clothes. Usually Campion pushed for the family to buy a new suit for the body and then Campion would pull the suit off the body just before the burial and go out and sell the suit or wear it himself. But with the closed coffin, Julie DiBiasi could be buried in his underwear. The problem of flowers was easily solved too. At an event like this, the prospect of a bomb in the middle of a cluster of roses is disturbing. But Campion had not had the body for an hour when a florist's delivery truck pulled up across the street and a deliveryman came in with a twenty-dollar piece. Campion didn't have to look up from the desk to know that it was a rat cop delivering the flowers. Only the Irish would send such a cheap piece of flowers to a funeral. The deliveryman went back to the truck. The truck did not move. This meant there was a camera in the back of the truck, taking movies through a peephole. This also meant that many strangers, more cops, would be attending the wake. Everybody in the Kid Sally Palumbo gang could now come to the wake. The Baccala mob would know the cops were on the scene, and Baccala's people would not do anything that might get a cop hurt.

The wake for Julie DiBiasi started officially at four o'clock in the afternoon, when Ezmo the Driver picked up old man Toregressa's wife in front of her house on Marshall Street and took her to Campion's. Toregressa's wife is called Mrs. Toregressa. She is the finest mourner in all of South Brooklyn. People from all over get in fights over Mrs. Toregressa so they can have her at their wakes.

Now Mrs. Toregressa sat quietly in the car while Ezmo the Driver drove the car to the funeral home. Mrs. Toregressa had a black shawl over her head and rosary beads twisted in her wrinkled hands. She had stayed up all night so she could have some good coffee circles under her eyes. She started warming up.

"*Gesù,*" she said softly.

"*Gesù.*"

"GESÙ!" She was quite loud this time. Her hands shook. She was ready.

She came into Campion's walking just behind Julie DiBiasi's brother-in-law and two of his sisters-in-law. There were eleven of Julie's cousins in the place already. The mourners walked in the pale sunlight coming through the windows of Campion's lobby and then into the dim hallway choking-sweet with the smell of roses. When Toregressa's wife came into the chapel with the flickering candles showing on the wallpaper, Toregressa's wife let out a wail which started low in her throat and then came higher and louder. It became a wonderful pitched scream.

"GESÙ! GESÙ!"

"A BONOM' JULIE!"

Julie DiBiasi's sister slumped against her cousin. The sister's legs buckled. Both women fell on the casket in screams. Mrs. Toregressa was directly behind them, screaming.

The immediate family, which includes to the fifth cousins, sat on the right-hand side of the front of the room. The father and mother sat on cushioned chairs facing the doorway so they

181

could wail at each person coming in. The rest of the family sat on wooden folding funeral-parlor chairs with the stenciled CAMPION FUNERAL HOME on the backs. Toregressa's wife sat on the left side of the casket, in the third row, so she could generate mourning that would run through the entire room. All people came in black. The only person who would wear a gray suit to a wake would be a rat cop. The conversation in the funeral chapel was standard. Between the wailing, a mourner observes that God took the deceased. He has six machine-gun bullets in him, or, in this case, was strangled by the Water Buffalo, but God took him. The only alluding to the manner of death is done with a gentle, "At least he didn't suffer." And in recounting the life he led, one sentence suffices: "He had a good life." Nothing else is said. If you begin to search for nice things to say about Julie DiBiasi you stumble onto the ten guys he helped to kill.

The big moment in the wake at Campion's came when Kid Sally Palumbo arrived. Entrances signify rank at gang funerals. A big shot does not walk in from the hallway and stand in front of the casket like any other mourner. A big shot forms up in the hallway with his bodyguards and he waits until the front of the room is clear and the seats are filled. Then he sweeps in. The level of murmur in the room attests to his rank. A buttonman gets a little gasp. A lieutenant gets a louder gasp. A captain gets tears. A *don beppe* or generalissimo creates screams. If you come in

182

front of a casket and create only silence, it usually means that you too could be on the road to the cemetery.

Kid Sally Palumbo came into the lobby of Campion's at 9:15 p.m. to make his entrance. In the absence of the Baccala organization, Kid Sally Palumbo now was the highest-ranking person at the funeral. When Kid Sally came through the door, he was with Big Jelly. He waited in the lobby while Big Jelly ambled down the hall to check the room. Campion asked Kid Sally if he wanted to sit down. Kid Sally shook his head no. He didn't want to crease the thighs of his black Italian-silk suit. Big Jelly stuck out his head and waved. Kid Sally came down the hallway, brushing against floral pieces. Big Jelly held him up for a moment in the hallway. Kid Sally stood clenching and unclenching his hands, waiting to go onstage. Big Jelly tapped him on the shoulder. Kid Sally Palumbo walked into the room like Maurice Evans.

His head was high and his chin was out and his shoulders weaved as he walked. He stood in front of the casket with his hands clasped in front of him. His feet were apart. He kept shifting from one foot to the other.

"*Che peccat'*," Toregressa's wife screamed.

"*O Dio.*"

Kid Sally Palumbo looked down fondly at the body.

"*È con Dio!*"

A woman in the back of the room picked it up. *"Gesù!"*

An old man in the center mumbled, *"A bonom' Julie."*

"Gesù!" Toregressa's wife screamed.

The father and mother came up and threw themselves, wailing, onto the casket, and Kid Sally Palumbo put his arms around them and rosaries were twisting in almost every hand and crying men kissed each other on the cheeks and bit their knuckles and women flung up their arms in despair. The wake of the beloved Julie DiBiasi, New York City Police Department identification number B-765379, FBI file number 129368742, United States Immigration and Naturalization Case 112-20-7143, was a great success.

Chapter 13

After the funeral mass, Angela did not go to the cemetery. She took the subway to school. She came up the subway stairs reluctantly and dawdled over a cup of coffee in a place on the corner. She started toward the school building and stopped. She felt like walking instead of sitting in a classroom. There was no use in going to school. Her nerves wouldn't let her concentrate. Nor was there much sense in going on any other day, as long as this business was going on. She began walking down truck-clogged streets toward the East Side. She knew vaguely where she was going, but she didn't think about it until she was on 11th Street and walking toward Mario's. It was all right to look in on him, she told herself. She didn't know anybody else she could stop to see at this time of day.

She was almost to Mario's building when he came out the door and stood on the top of the stoop. Mario had been up since seven o'clock, working on his painting. Since he had no easel or table in his apartment, he worked on his hands and knees, the art paper spread on the floor under him. Mario worked with his head hanging down like a collie's. After many hours of doing this, he became accustomed to having the inside of his head filled to the brim with downrushing blood. When Mario couldn't work any more, he stood up straight and the blood went rushing down from the inside of his head so quickly that his eyes rolled and he had to put his hands against the wall to keep from falling down. Now, outside on the stoop, he was still swaying. He held out his arms to make airplane wings for balance.

"What are you doing, exercising?" Angela called to him.

Mario felt himself falling. He rotated his arms violently to stay up.

"My knees hurt," he said.

"Oh," Angela said.

He came down the steps, keeping his legs stiff. He resembled Frankenstein.

They went up to a place on the corner and talked, over coffee. Mario was vague about the type of work he was doing, and Angela listened vacantly. She was still unnerved from Julie DiBiasi's funeral. He mentioned that he wanted to see some of the museums in New York. "Modern Art is only a few minutes from here," she said. "You ought to learn the way. Why don't we ride up there and I'll show it to you."

Mario pushed out of the booth and walked eagerly out of the coffee shop. Angela had to stop at the counter and pay the check. When they came out of the subway onto 53rd Street, Mario stooped down and pulled his shoelaces apart. He took his uncle's eyeglasses out of his jacket pocket. He immediately plowed into a woman. Angela had to take his arm and guide him across the street.

The museum had a weekday afternoon crowd of women in their sixties, their sagging chalk necks spilling onto the soft bristles of mink coat collars. There were a few college students, and also many men in the uniform of Wall Street retirement: black Chesterfield coat, rimless glasses, and the *Times* folded to the obituary page.

Two women were standing in front of a work by Andrew Wyeth. Angela and Mario stood alongside them.

"Simply fascinating," one of them said.

"God, such talent," the other said.

Sidney's voice was in Mario's ears. *Pigs.*

Mario stepped up and put his face inches away from the painting. He stared intently at it. *"Fromage,"* he said.

"Fromage," he said again.

The women stopped talking.

Mario stepped back His arm waved. *"Fromage!"* he shouted.

The women looked at the eyeglasses sitting on his nose, and open shoelaces.

"Maybe this really isn't one of his best works," one of the women whispered.

"Well, to tell you the truth, I really don't see much in it myself," the other one said.

Mario took Angela's arm and they walked away. Sidney was right; they all knew nothing. Now Mario was sure he would be able to sell somebody some of his work. He stuck his chin out like he was Mussolini. *"Fromage!"* he shouted at a group watching a Picasso.

In one hallway there was a spot from which a painting had been recently removed. Plain wooden brackets for holding the picture frame remained. The painting which had been removed had obviously been there for some time. The wall plaster inside the brackets was covered with a thick layer of dust. Mario stopped. He poked Angela.

A man in a Chesterfield coat and his mink-coated wife were walking along slowly.

Mario stared at the rectangle of dust. "Magnificent," he said.

The man and woman stopped and began inspecting the dust.

"Magificent!" Mario roared.

The woman sighed. "I wish the frame were nicer," she said.

"The frame doesn't bother me," the man said.

"There's just something," the woman said.

"Could it be hanging upside down?" the man said.

Angela was still laughing when the subway came into the Second Avenue stop, where Mario was to get off. She pointed to the door. He got up. He looked at her sadly. She started to get up with him. Then she sank back in her seat.

"G'by, I'll see you again," she said.

He went out the doors and the train started up again, and when it left the station the day's fun went out of Angela and Brooklyn came on her. She pulled the coat around her.

Between visits from Angela, Mario put together a narrow standard of living. It was unsatisfying, but he felt every day brought him closer to the afternoon when he could sell his first work to one of those ignorant women at the Plaza. He worked in three-hour shifts, resting for two hours, through an entire day, and brought the results to Sidney for help. Most evenings he sat in the coffee shop on the corner and went to the cheapest price on the sign, a 40-cent egg-salad sandwich. The place was frequented by wanderers who lived in the East Village. Mario got to know Simon Krass, a writer who specialized in articles on eroticism. Simon Krass usually came into the coffee shop carrying his cat, High Yellow, under his arm. He sat and commented on the world's latest sex habits. "Airedales are just magnificent," Simon Krass said. He thought Mario, with his eyeglasses and untied shoelaces, would be interested.

One morning the superintendent put Mario into shock by announcing the $36 rent was due. All day Mario was edgy. He kept walking downstairs to stand on the stoop and look for Angela.

She did not come. He went to bed heartsick over being stuck with the rent. In the morning he paid the superintendent the $36, went up to the coffee shop, and sat in the telephone booth. He looked at the names he had gotten from Father Marsalano. The third man on the list, Dominic Laviano, had two big checks after his name. The address was the Andrea Doria Club, 724 Knickerbocker Avenue, Brooklyn. Mario looked up the number and called the place. The old man who answered said Dominic Laviano was always there at seven p.m. Mario went through the classified directory and looked for religious listings. Nearly all the Catholic stores were on Barclay Street. He asked the waitress for directions.

After a month in the apartment, Mario had $159 left, and a little fear went through him when he began ordering things in McGowan's Religious Outfitters, 78 Barclay Street. Mario paid $85 for a priest's black suit. He told the salesman the suit was for his twin brother, who was a priest in Italy. The tailor at home would fix the cuffs, Mario said. He also bought a Roman collar and a black shirtfront to wear with it. The salesman wanted to mail the things to Italy. "We just don't like to give our clothes to anyone but a priest," the salesman said. "All these impostors." Mario sent the man to the back of the store for a cape and then ducked out of the door with the box. At 6:30 p.m., dressed as a priest, the pants cuffs dragging, Mario arrived on Knickerbocker Avenue.

The Andrea Doria Club was next to Dominic's Fruit and Vegetables, D. Laviano, prop. The store had crates of greens around the entrance. The greens had been washed and the outer leaves were glazed with ice. The club next door was an old storefront. The bottom halves of the windows were painted over with green and trimmed with red and black. The place had been an ice-cream parlor when Germans lived in the neighborhood. The Italians, who followed the Germans, sought out ice-cream parlors. They made fine social clubs, which are as important to an Italian neighborhood as dairy restaurants are to a Jewish neighborhood. The old marble fountain counter is perfect for holding a $1500 espresso machine imported from Milano. The wire-backed chairs and round tables are fine for card games. Even the big Coca-Cola syrup jugs have a purpose. They get filled with homemade wine.

There were a dozen old men playing cards at the tables when Mario walked in. Dominic Laviano sat at the counter by the wine jugs. He was a bald man with heavy-lidded eyes. Mario handed him the picture. Dominic Laviano's eyes glistened. Mario showed him the message on the back. Dominic Laviano's eyes narrowed. He had a basic conflict about matters religious.

Some years ago the pastor at his church in Brooklyn, Our Lady of Mount Carmel Church, had begun pointing out that the statue of the patron saint had no crown. The old women donated their rings to be melted down for a crown. Their diamonds studded the crown. It was worth $250,000 when finished. The crown was put on display in a glass case set in front of the church. Only the pastor and the sexton had keys. An electric eye would set off a burglar alarm louder than an air-raid siren if anybody tried breaking into the case. One night, with no breaking glass or siren, the crown disappeared. The pastor knelt in church and conducted a prayer vigil for its return. The old women knelt and prayed with him. The men of the church, led by Dominic Laviano, took the matter to another authority. They went to Baccala's office. That night Baccala appeared at the church. He walked up the center aisle and looked at the priest praying. He looked at the sexton, who was trying to hide behind a bank of candles.

"Hey!" Baccala called out. The sexton came out from behind the candles. Baccala whispered something in the sexton's ear. The sexton wet his pants. When the women came to the church to start praying the next morning, the crown was back in the case. It had slipped in and out without the alarm's sounding. The women began to thump their breasts. *Mirac'*.

Dominic knew otherwise. But there was a time when Dominic Laviano's sister from Poughkeepsie, Mrs. Regina Barbella, went home to Catanzia, and it still made Dominic wonder. During his sister's visit, Father Marsalano showed her the church doors, which were rotted.

She said she would pay for new doors. The doors took so long to arrive and be hung that she missed her return trip on the *Andrea Doria* from Genoa to New York. The *Andrea Doria* sank off Nantucket. Mrs. Regina Barbella still thumps her breast and tells everybody, *Mirac'*."

Dominic Laviano was not too sure it wasn't a miracle. He named his club after the ship. As he looked at the picture and the note on the back from Father Marsalano, Dominic was holding a little argument with himself. He really didn't trust priests. But he had also had a few whips of pain across the left side of his chest in recent months. Who knows?

"I had my own horse when I was a boy in Catanzia," Dominic Laviano said finally.

Mario could feel the money now. "The church doors of your sister are very beautiful," he said.

"They saved her life," Dominic said.

The two sat at the counter and talked about home for an hour. Across the street, Big Jelly twisted uncomfortably in the cold in his parked car. He and Tony the Indian had been there for two hours on the odd chance that Baccala might drop in to the club and see his friend Dominic. Every ten days or so, Baccala showed up at the Andrea Doria Club for coffee and messages.

"What's the priest doin' in there for so long?" Tony the Indian said.

"He's robbing that old man Dominic, what do you think he's doin'?" Big Jelly said. "Look at him. You could see he got more con in him than a legitimate thief."

At nine o'clock the fencing ended. Dominic took one more look at the picture of the ragamuffin in the lot. Eyes misting, Dominic told Don Mario, as he called him now, that he would have a contribution for him at four o'clock the next afternoon. Mario blessed him and left.

He walked across the street and he was almost up to the car when he remembered the subway was the other way and he turned around.

Big Jelly looked at Mario closely. "Young priest. I didn't think they hung out with old greaseballs like Dominic," he said.

"He could have them," Tony the Indian said.

"Let's go home," Big Jelly said.

Mario barely slept. He was back at 3:30 the next afternoon. Dominic came into the club with a stack of envelopes that were stamped and addressed to Father Marsalano. He showed the insides of the envelopes to Mario. In each, wrapped in paper, was a ten-dollar bill. "I mail them all," Dominic said. "If a letter gets lost, then we don't lose all the moneys." He asked Mario for the picture. During the night Dominic had woken up with a sharp chest pain. He was afraid it was the Lord, not marinara sauce. On the back of the picture Dominic wrote Baccala's name and the address of the trucking company. "I tell him you come to see him," Dominic said. Dominic felt better about the chest pain now. He was sure he had just saved his soul.

"*Grazie,*" Mario said. He held out his hand. Dominic handed him the picture. Mario held out his hand for the envelopes. Dominic sniffed. He led Mario out of the club and up to a mailbox on the next corner. "You watch, I mail," Dominic said. He stuffed the envelopes into the box. Mario smiled and shook hands good-by. Dominic went back to the fruit-and-vegetable store. Mario pretended to head for the subway. Dominic went into the store. Mario ducked into a doorway.

An hour and a half later the mail truck pulled up, and the driver was starting to shovel the letters into his bag when a hand came past his nose and started digging into the box.

"Scoose, please."

"Hey!" the mailman said. He grabbed the hand. He let go when he saw it was a priest. "Oh, I'm sorry, Father. Can I help you?"

"I mail all the letters and I forget to put something in them," Mario said. "I need back."

"Father, I'm not supposed to . . ."

Mario's hand kept digging. "Ah, here they are," he said. He grabbed a stack of Dominic Laviano's envelopes. "See, they addressed to my pastor, Don Giuseppe Marsalano," Mario said. "I send, but I forget to put inside."

"All right, Father," the mailman said. "Just don't say I let you do this. It's a big violation."

Mario counted the envelopes on the way home in the subway. There were fifty envelopes. He took forty of them, pulled out the ten-dollar

195

bills, and ripped up the envelopes. At the Second Avenue stop he dropped the remaining ten into the mailbox. He walked with his hand over the $400 in his pocket. In the coffee shop he looked over Father Marsalano's list. There were a number of women on it. Women are less suspicious than men, he knew. He wouldn't even need his priest's suit with the women. They would trust him to mail the envelopes himself. He ordered a meat-loaf dinner. The sign said it was $1.65, the most money Mario had spent for food. Soon he would spend much more, he told himself.

Kid Sally Palumbo was in the office. A cigarette was hanging from his mouth. The smoke ran up in front of his eyes.

Angela opened the door. "Well?" she said.

"Getoutahere, I thinkin'," Kid Sally said.

"Just think of one person," she said. She held up a finger. "One is all that it takes. Get Baccala, and the rest will fall in line." She shut the door.

"She's right," Kid Sally said. "This is one-hit proposition. We can't go after everybody. We just concentrate on the boss."

"Whatever you say," Big Jelly said. He picked up a paper bag of chopped meat from the butcher's. He opened the door to the cellar. There was a low roar from the lion, which was at the foot of the stairs. Big Jelly threw the bag of chopped meat. At the bottom of the stairs two lion paws snatched it. Big Jelly started to close the door. The lion's smell rolled up the stairs and hit him in the face. Big Jelly turned blue. Everybody in the office put a hand to his mouth and started to choke. Big Jelly just did get the door closed before the odor smothered them.

"Somebody got to train the lion," Big Jelly said.

"I never dreamt of the lion goin' to the bat'room," Kid Sally said.

"He could kill you quicker than anything they got in the drugstore," Big Jelly said.

"Look," Kid Sally said, "somebody figure out about the bat'room. I got to try and think like Baccala." He began hitting himself on the forehead to make his head think.

On the other side of Brooklyn, Baccala's manicured fingernails tapped his desk. He looked down at the desk as if it were a sand table. He saw all the great maneuvers of war spread in front of him.

"We just go slow," he said. "So far, it's nice. The other punks, they run around. They think they cowboys. We just go slow and we get every one of them." He leaned forward. "And I strangle Kid Sally personal!"

He got up to leave. Then he looked at the group of black suits standing around the office. "Somebody take a ride down-a their street. Be careful. Just look. You never know. They all craz'. Maybe one of them be standin' right there for you. Go see."

On Marshall Street the next afternoon, nobody was around. Who could get shot if he's not around to get shot at? Kid Sally's cousin Carmine Palumbo and Beppo the Dwarf were on guard in the office. Beppo had performed his duty. He had stolen two license plates in Staten Island. Carmine Palumbo was waiting around to kill somebody. They sat for an hour. Then Beppo the Dwarf's nose crinkled like a rabbit's. Carmine Palumbo's nose looked like a saxophone. He took a deep breath. When the air finally got up to the top of Carmine's nose, his eyes watered. The lion's smell had come all the way up the cellar stairs and was all over the office now. Five hundred cats on a rainy day could not match the lion in Kid Sally Palumbo's cellar.

"I can't take this," Carmine Palumbo said. He took a beach chair and set it up on the sidewalk in front of the office. Beppo the Dwarf came out and sat on the stoop.

"We better keep a eye open," Beppo the Dwarf said. "Who could tell?"

"I keep a eye open," Carmine Palumbo said. "I also want to keep my nose open. Jeez, that lion could put you on the critical list. Maybe the son-of-a-bitch don't bite good, but he sure as hell knows how to go to the bat'room."

Carmine Palumbo sat there with his eyes open, watching everything on the block, for about fifteen minutes. Because he could not concentrate on anything, even nothing, for any longer than this, Carmine Palumbo leaned back in the chair and closed his eyes.

Beppo the Dwarf was sitting on the stoop, looking at his fingernails, he was just looking at his fingernails, when the corner of his eye saw these two cars rushing down the street, rushing along close to the curb. The windshields showed both cars were filled with heads. Beppo let out a yell and threw himself back over a railing. Carmine Palumbo opened his eyes and he was pulling himself upright in the beach chair when the cars slowed and the lead car came up even with Carmine Palumbo in the beach chair. Carmine Palumbo saw machine guns coming out the front and back windows. The scene was just about to register in his mind when the machine guns blew Carmine through the back of the beach chair.

PALUMBO — Carmine. Unexpectedly. Greatly loved son of the late Joseph Palumbo and Teresa Palumbo. Dearly beloved brother of Alphonse, Anthony, Nicholas, Michael, and Pasquale Palumbo and Mrs. Loretta DeSalvio. Mourned uncle of Danny DeSalvio. May St. Michael the Archangel recognize his great strength. Reposing CAMPION'S Funeral Home, Inc., 56 Lockman Street, Brooklyn. Interment Tuesday 10 a.m. Private.

On the second night of the wake, late in the

going, when Toregressa's wife had shrieked herself into laryngitis, Beppo the Dwarf stood in
front of Carmine Palumbo in the casket.

"It's all on account of the rat bastard lion,"
Beppo the Dwarf wailed.

In the afternoon, after Carmine Palumbo's
funeral, Joe Mangoni was driving along Flatbush
Avenue, humming and slapping his right hand
against the steering wheel in time to the music
on the car radio. Joe felt very bad about losing
his good friend Carmine, but the music coming
into the car was making him feel better. A great
scream came out of the radio: James Brown
singing. Joe Mangoni began slamming his hand
hard against the steering wheel. He glanced at
the clock. He was right on time. At four o'clock
every day Joe Mangoni came into the College
Diner, right down the block from Saint Joseph's
College, and he had coffee and a Danish and he
collected money. Customers who owed shylock
payments shuffled in, handed him the money,
and walked out. Joe Mangoni always liked to collect money, even though it was just money he
turned over to somebody else. But today Joe
Mangoni had come up with a very terrific idea.
Normally he collected the money and gave it to
one of Baccala's messengers. But now, being
that he was with Kid Sally Palumbo and being
that there was all this trouble, Joe Mangoni
would not see any of Baccala's messengers. This
means, Joe Mangoni reasoned, that if there is no

messenger to give the money to, and if you still collect the money, then the money is yours.

"Smart guys do good when there's trouble," Joe Mangoni said out loud in the car. He looked at himself in the mirror. "You look real smart, baby," he said.

Joe parked his car on a side street and walked around to the diner, which was on the avenue. Only a couple of people were in the diner. "Hi, guys," Joe said to the countermen when he walked in. The countermen stared at him. When Joe ordered coffee, the counterman was so nervous he nearly scalded himself.

"What's the matter, you get nervous in the service?" Joe said. He laughed. This was one of Joe's best jokes.

Two priests came walking across the avenue from the block the college was on. The priests wore black fedoras and sunglasses and carried prayer books. The priests came into the diner and came up to take seats at the counter next to Joe Mangoni. Then the priests both stopped and came out from under the coats with guns. Each held the prayer book in one hand and the gun in the other. It was blasphemous, but highly effective.

MANGONI — Joseph. Very suddenly. Beloved, dear son of the late, beloved Luigi and Rose Mangoni. Mourned brother of Dominic Mangoni. "An eye for an eye. A tooth for a tooth." Reposing CAMPION'S Funeral

Home, 56 Lockman Street, Brooklyn. Interment Saturday 11 a.m., private.

"We gotta do somethin'," Kid Sally said when he got back from the funeral. "We got to get one back."

"I said just get Baccala," Angela said.

"We got no time for that today, we got to get one right away," Kid Sally said.

"She's-a right, just think of Baccala," Big Mama said.

"No, somebody right now. Today. They got three of our guys and we got nothin'." Trailing 3-0, Kid Sally was ready to bunt in order to get onto the scoreboard.

"You know who's a good friend of mine?" Big Jelly said.

"Who?" Kid Sally said.

"Albie."

"How good a friend?" Kid Sally said.

"He'd come and meet me," Big Jelly said.

The two of them got in a car with Tony the Indian and Ezmo the Driver and went to Patrissy's Lounge. The place was empty except for the porter. It was two in the afternoon, and Patrissy's doesn't open until nine p.m. The porter was told to get lost. The moment the porter left, Big Jelly reached inside his shirt and pulled out a coil of nylon rope. Sally began snapping the rope between his hands to make sure it wouldn't split while they were garroting Albie.

Albie was home. He never gets out of bed before the six-o'clock news at night. Albie is an air inspector. He stands all night on a streetcorner next to the newsstand on Coney Island Avenue and he breathes the air in and out. Once in a while Baccala sends somebody around to get Albie for something at which Albie is good. What Albie does best is to swing a baseball bat in a crowded bar. Albie has one personal weakness, which accounts for his friendship with Big Jelly. Albie is helpless in the matter of girls. "I like you," he told Big Jelly one night. "You are a real degenerate. Just like me."

All night while he stands on the streetcorner and breathes the air in and out, Albie reads the magazines from the newsstand. Albie reads *Sexology* and *Pervert* and *The American Orgasm*. His favorite is *Orgy Manual*, but this publication appears only when its publisher is between Supreme Court appearances.

So Big Jelly knew exactly how to activate Albie when he called Albie up at his house on the telephone.

"I'm at Patrissy's, where are you?" Big Jelly said.

"I'm home," Albie said.

"Oh, you're home," Big Jelly said.

"You're in some trouble," Albie said.

"What of?" Big Jelly said.

"You know," Albie said.

While Big Jelly talked, Kid Sally stood in front of the phone booth, pretending he was hanging

203

himself with the rope. Big Jelly giggled while he talked.

"What's goin' on?" Albie said.

"I got a girl in the phone booth with me and she is doing all these things to me," Big Jelly said. He giggled at the rope some more.

"She in the phone booth with you?" Albie said.

"Sure, the joint's closed and I'm in here with her. What do I care about what's goin' on? That's Sally's business. My business is bein' a degenerate with broads. You know that. Here, honey, stop it. You're drivin' me crazy here." Big Jelly giggled.

"Stay there," Albie said. "I'll be right down."

While they waited, Ezmo the Driver plugged in the jukebox and put the sound up very high so when it played it would drown out the noise of what they were going to do to Albie. Ezmo was proud of this move. "Sometimes I'm very shrewd," he said.

Albie came a half-hour later. He came into the place with a sex sweat on his forehead. He was so busy looking for a girl in the bar that he never knew what hit him. Kid Sally Palumbo jumped on his head and Tony the Indian got a thumb in Albie's eyes and Ezmo and Big Jelly fell on him and out came the rope and they looped it around Albie. They were going to garrote him, which is the best way in the world to murder somebody, particularly if the perpetrators are demented. Ezmo the Driver ran over to the jukebox with two quarters to play some loud music to drown out Albie's screams. Ezmo's eyes ran down the selections and he saw the Beatles. *Rock-'n'-roll. The Beatles. Good and loud kid stuff.* Ezmo dropped in the money and punched the Beatles' record, number B-6. He punched it for six plays. He ran back to help them garrote Albie.

Albie was in the middle of the floor and the rope was all around his throat and body and he opened his mouth for his first scream when the record on the jukebox came on. The record was "Penny Lane" by the Beatles. It is a soft, lovely tune, the new kind of thing the Beatles do, and even with the jukebox turned up full force, you have to cup your ear to hear the words. Albie's first scream drowned out the soft music.

"Change the music," Kid Sally Palumbo yelled.

Albie let out another shriek.

Here was Ezmo the Driver at the jukebox, kicking it with his foot to try and make the record reject so he could play something loud, and the Beatles kept singing "Penny Lane," and here was Albie on the floor, yelping with the rope around him, yelping way louder than the music, and old ladies began looking out the window across the street.

Kid Sally Palumbo, thinking under intense pressure, thought of an idea so terrific he didn't know why everybody hadn't tried it before. He had Big Jelly take one end of the rope in his hands and face the rear door of the saloon. He and Tony the Indian took the other end and faced the front door. This left Albie in the middle with the rope looped around his neck.

"When I say go, run as fast as you can to the door with the rope," Kid Sally said.

"Go!"

Big Jelly gripped the rope and started. Kid Sally Palumbo and Tony the Indian headed in the opposite direction. Each side in the tug of war had its back to the other. They did not see what was happening in the middle, where Albie, almost out of it, wobbled to his feet and hooked one leg over the rope, the end running to Kid Sally and Tony the Indian. Big Jelly barged ahead to the back door. Kid Sally and Tony started running to the front door. Albie's leg hooked down on the rope, and the rope snapped out of Kid Sally and Tony's hands. When the line slackened suddenly on Big Jelly's end, the fat man went into the door head first. Albie fell to the floor like a sack. Big Jelly stumbled out to the street knocked half dizzy. Kid Sally and Tony kept flying and they hit the car while Ezmo the Driver had it in motion. Big Jelly dove at the moving car, and they barely hauled him in.

"Boy, that was terrific," Big Jelly said to Kid Sally in the car. "His whole head must of come off."

"Wow! We got to do that again," Tony the Indian said.

Kid Sally Palumbo had his eyes half closed

while he blew out smoke. "I know what I'm doin'," he said.

When the police arrived at Patrissy's and took Albie to the hospital, there was no way of telling what had happened. Certainly Albie couldn't tell them. The rope had done so much damage to his neck that when the people in the hospital finally revived him with ammonia capsules he couldn't talk. His throat was closed. It would be days before he would be able to make a sound. When a detective gave him a pad and pen, Albie wrote down: "I got a bad stiff neck."

Chapter 14

After a week of working on copying the painting of the naked girl, Mario got off his knees and carried it over to Sidney's apartment. Right away, it was obvious to Sidney that the ripped face on the picture Mario was copying had caused him to shy away from that part of the body and invest great time and energy on other parts.

"Here and there it looks like a caveman worked on this thing," Sidney said. "But overall, I want to tell you something, you got a lot of long, hard work ahead of you, but you know how to express yourself all right. Oh, I don't think you can try with this thing yet. You still got a long way to go. For one thing, you're concentrating on this too much."

"What?" Mario said.

"The top of the thing."

"Top?" Mario said.

Sidney shouted. "The top of the tit!"

"Oh," Mario said.

"It gives you away that you're just beginning.

Too much detail, it's no good. It's what you suggest and leave out that gives a thing its strength. You paint every eyelash on somebody's eye? So why do you put down every bump on the top of her thing?"

When he got back, Angela was standing in front of the house. He started upstairs to put his work away. When she asked to see it, he covered it and ran. Then they walked up to the corner. In the early darkness the brightly lit coffee shop on the corner looked inviting to Mario. He hadn't eaten since morning.

"Let's go some place nicer," Angela said. "Have you ever had Chinese food?"

He shook his head no.

"There's a place right up there," she said, pointing up First Avenue.

They sat in a booth and she ordered. Mario did not inquire what he was eating. He put his head down and swallowed egg rolls, shrimp and lobster sauce, and sweet-and-sour pork without noticing what it was. Angela was comfortable in the place. It was empty and warm and dim and the booths and the white tablecloths and the curtained door closed around her and kept the cold wind of Brooklyn out of her mind. She held a cup of tea up and looked at Mario. She liked his thick hair. She liked his eyes too. He always looked directly at her, as if she were important. When she went to the ladies' room, she combed her hair carefully. She wondered what it would be like if Mario ever became even a slight success as an artist. She looked at herself in the mirror and shrugged. When she came back to the table, she was eager to take the check from the waiter. After all, Mario had nothing.

Outside the restaurant, Mario half waited for her to go to the subway, but instead she started walking with him. *Well,* she said to herself. *Well, who knows?*

The flights of stairs to Mario's apartment left the two of them panting when they reached his door. He opened it and stepped into the darkness with her. Mario shut the door with one hand and pulled her to him with the other. He kissed her with all the great romance of the Italian mountain country. She twisted her head. She couldn't breathe from the stairs, and now, with his pressing on her, she thought she'd faint.

Angela pushed him back. "Stop for a minute," she said. "Give me a second." She took a deep breath. "Where's the light?"

He flicked the switch. One bare bulb in the ceiling came on. Angela's mouth fell open. On the floor in the center of the room was the pillow. It was covered with a towel Mario had taken from the hotel. Over by the windows were the art supplies and a few smears of paint on the floor. Otherwise, there was nothing in the room.

"You didn't even buy a bed?" she said.

Mario, his eyes glistening, tugged on her arm. Angela went one step toward the pillow and then pulled back. Mario put both hands on her and tried to drag her as if she were a donkey.

"Are you crazy?" she said.

He tried to tug her again, but she wouldn't move. She kept looking at the bare floor. One word kept running through her mind.

Splinters!

She twisted away from him and got out into the hallway.

"What you want?" Big Mama said when she saw Angela in the kitchen the next morning.

"I'm just looking," Angela said. She was fishing in the papers on top of the refrigerator. When she felt her bankbook, she waited until her grandmother wasn't looking, and then she walked out of the kitchen with it. *The hell with it,* she said to herself. *Nobody can live like he is.*

An hour later, Angela banged on Mario's door. She stood in the hallway until he got his coat on. They spent the rest of the morning having a cheap kitchen set sent to his place, buying a second-hand easel and carting it back to the apartment, and going uptown to buy a studio couch at a furniture warehouse that was listed in the *Village Voice.* Mario spent the day staring out windows whenever the price was mentioned. In the furniture warehouse, the price tag on the studio couch read $219. Mario asked the manager if the men's room was available. When Mario came out, Angela said, "They can't deliver it for three days."

Mario put a hand under one end of the couch and lifted. It was light enough. Angela reached

211

down. Her end of it came up easily. They walked out of the warehouse and through the people on the sidewalk and down the subway stairs. Mario stopped at the bottom of the stairs. He timed his move with the subway change clerk. As the clerk's head went down to make change for someone, Mario rushed ahead, kicking open the gate with the NO ENTRANCE sign. When the downtown train came in, Mario backed into it, swinging the couch around until it was lengthwise in the middle of the aisle. He sat down on the couch, and Angela sat next to him. At 42nd Street, the first swirl of the rush hour came into the car. People fell into each other trying to go around the couch.

"Are you comfortable?" a man snarled down at Mario.

"Yes," Mario said.

An old lady with a shopping bag turned around and started sitting down. Mario tried to block her with his elbow. The old lady swung her shopping bag into Mario's face and wedged her way between Mario and Angela. The old lady spread her arms, the elbows coming out like gates. She was ready to hold her position.

The old lady made a sound like a whippoorwill and flew up from the couch. Angela put a hand over her face.

Mario was proud of himself.

Mario and Angela got the studio couch to his building. The superintendent looked out into the hallway to see what the noise was. Angela looked at him. The superintendent swore to himself. He took Angela's end of the couch. She reached over and grabbed the thick hair on the back of Mario's neck. She held it for a moment. It was just as well the superintendent had come out.

"I'll see you, get a night's sleep for once," she said.

Joe Quarequio is a cousin of Tony the Indian, and he is a very confident guy. His last name means "happy death" and Joe Quarequio always tells himself, "Nothing bad could happen to me because I'm going to have a happy death." So Joe Quarequio is not afraid of doing many things. To satisfy a curious parole officer, Joe works at construction. When he is not at work, he is open to any proposition. One day Joe was on a job in Long Island where they were excavating for an office building. The engineer planted dynamite and the workers spread huge steel mesh mats on the ground over the area to be blasted. An engineer blew his whistle and everybody scurried out onto the sidewalk. Joe saw the engineer take what seemed to be a television channel-selector out of his breast pocket. The engineer pressed a button. The dynamite went off. The sound was muffled by the woven mats. The exploding dirt and rock were held down by the mats. The whole thing worked beautifully. Joe strolled over to the engineer and asked him about the channel-selector. The engineer said it was an electronic detonator. Instead of the old-fashioned, time-consuming stringing of wires from the dynamite to a plunger-type detonator, the electronic detonator merely has to be pressed and a signal explodes the dynamite.

"It's *sim-u-lar* to changin' television programs, ain't it?" Joe Quarequio said to the engineer.

"With slightly heavier results," the engineer said.

"Oh, boy, I seen that," Joe Quarequio said.

Joe Quarequio also saw the toolshed where the engineer kept the dynamite sets. And when Joe Quarequio went home from work that night, he sat against the window in the train and whistled little tunes to himself. In Joe's shirt pocket was the electronic thing. In Joe's lap, inside a paper bag, was enough dynamite to end the rush hour. Joe Quarequio couldn't wait to show it to Kid Sally Palumbo.

"Infuckincredible," Kid Sally Palumbo said. He looked at the neat stapled pink and blue wires, batteries, brass conductors, and sticks of dynamite inside the paper bag. He fondled the electronic detonator.

"We change programs for Baccala," he said. "From livin' to dead."

Kid Sally giggled. Big Jelly slapped the desk. Joe Quarequio was very proud. He had done a very good thing. The bomb would give them a great chance at Baccala. There would be none of this work under the car hood, wiring dynamite to

214

the ignition system. It was slow and therefore quite dangerous. Anybody caught toying with Baccala's car would be immeasurably better off convicted of a major crime in the Orient. The new bomb merely required somebody to slip it onto the floor in the back of Baccala's car, where it would not be noticed, and then stand a block away with the electronic detonator and wait for Baccala to get into the car. A mere press of the thumb would handle the rest of it.

Big Jelly patted the dynamite sticks. "Beautiful," he said. He looked at a small dial. His fat fingers touched it. "What's this for?" he said. Big Jelly twisted the dial. "It goes around in a circle," he said.

"Geez, don't freak with nothin'," Kid Sally said.

"Yeah, I better not," Big Jelly said. He twisted the dial back to where he remembered it had been.

Kid Sally and Joe Quarequio left the office and got into a car with Ezmo the Driver at the wheel. For three days and nights they tried to find Baccala's car. They caught a glimpse of it one night, and Ezmo was about to step on the gas and catch up when he saw a second car slip in behind Baccala's. Ezmo knew the second car was a gun ship. He slowed down. On the fourth day, tired of looking, Kid Sally said he felt like something to eat at a place called the Lercarafriddi on Sackman Street. When Ezmo the Driver came onto Sackman Street he hit the brakes and put the car in reverse. Baccala's Cadillac, with the Water Buffalo riding shotgun, was pulling up in front of the Lercarafriddi. Baccala and the Water Buffalo got out. They went inside the restaurant. A black suit got out of the back seat and took up guard duty in front of the entrance.

Kid Sally peered around the corner. Any experienced thief, he figured, should be able to sneak up to the car on the street side, slip the paper bag with the bomb under the car, and then sneak away without being noticed. After that, all that remained to be done was to wait for Baccala to get into the car. A press on the electronic detonator would make the dynamite blow through the bottom of the car. The bottom of a car made in Detroit is not quite as sturdy as the woven mats used on construction jobs. The bottom of Baccala's car not only would not muffle the sound of the dynamite going off, but it also would not do much to prevent Baccala from riding in the lead funeral car.

"I tell you what," Kid Sally said. "There's been so freakin' much gone wrong, this one I wanna do personal."

"Hey," Joe Quarequio said, "what about me? Who brung you the bomb?"

Kid Sally fingered the detonator. "All right, Joe, you go put the bomb under the car."

Joe Quarequio held the paper bag in front of him as if it were being presented to the queen. Walking in a crouch, so he would be hidden by parked cars, Joe Quarequio slipped down the opposite side of the street from the restaurant. He took a deep breath and began to duck-waddle across the street to Baccala's car.

Inside the restaurant, Baccala had his head inside a big menu. The Water Buffalo watched the sidewalk to make sure the black suit was patrolling properly. The black suit looked up and down the street. He nodded to the Water Buffalo. Everything was all right. By now, Joe Quarequio was in the middle of the street, duck-waddling with his head so low it was impossible to see him as he came at Baccala's car.

Kid Sally leaned against the wall of the building up at the corner. He shook with excitement. It was unbelievable that he was getting this clear a shot at Baccala. He had imagined the death of Baccala would come after a pitched battle which would claim half of Brooklyn. He saw it with guns and ropes and curses and screams. But here in his hand was just a simple, innocuous plastic thing with a button on it. Just press it. "Inventions is unbelievable," he said to Ezmo. Kid Sally fondled the detonator. All the James Bond movies and the television spy shows, things Kid Sally had maintained were jerkoff shows, seemed like the Bible to him now.

A mile away, at the Bergen Street police station house, the desk lieutenant wanted to speak to Patrolman George Cusack, who was on traffic duty. In order to speak to Cusack, the desk lieutenant, under a system installed that day, was to push a button on a monitor board. This would activate a pocket beeper in Patrolman Cusack's pocket, and he would go to a telephone and call in. Patrolman Cusack's beeper was on wavelength 151.190.

When the desk lieutenant pressed the beeper, two things happened. A high-pitched but soft noise began in the beeper in Patrolman Cusack's breast pocket. And on Sackman Street, Joe Quarequio disappeared in the middle of a waddle.

QUAREQUIO — Joseph. Very, very suddenly. Son of Thomas and Donnette Quarequio. Beloved brother of George, Frank, Peter, Louise, and the honored Todo (Tommy Scratch) Quarequio. "Fire and brimstone shall descend on our enemies!" Family receiving mourners at CAMPION'S Funeral Home, Inc., 56 Lockman Street, Brooklyn. No interment.

Kid Sally Palumbo was rubbing his fist across his forehead so hard that the skin was peeling. Upstairs, his grandmother was sitting with her hands out while the water boiled in two big pots for the day's number-10 macaroni. There would be a little oil and garlic with it, and that would do it. The lobster fra diavolo and chicken cacciatore and veal rollatini were of the past. The organization not only was having trouble keeping its members alive, but also was having supply trouble.

There were two reasons for this. First were the supply routes. One morning Ezmo the Driver and Tony the Indian decided that at ten a.m. nothing could happen to them. They walked down to Columbia Avenue to buy some meat and a few cans of paint. They thought that fresh paint on the office walls would overcome the lion's smell coming up from the basement. They were two doors down from the paint store, hugging the building line so the people on the crowded sidewalk would be between them and the street. This gave them great natural protection, they felt. The trouble with this was that the Water Buffalo uses the same type of defense every morning and he understands its basic weakness. The basic weakness is that the people standing between you and the danger have a marked tendency to flee, leaving you alone with the danger. This is not good.

The Water Buffalo was driving slowly along Columbia Avenue just to see if he could get lucky. The Water Buffalo saw Ezmo and Tony and he rushed his car to the curb. He came bounding out with a gun in his hand. All the people on the sidewalk ran. This left Tony the Indian, Ezmo the Driver, and the Water Buffalo alone with each other. When the Water Buffalo got back in his car and began speeding away, he was swearing to himself. He had hit Tony the Indian only two out of three times. And all he had done to Ezmo the Driver was shoot him in the ankle. But after this everybody on Marshall Street was afraid to go off the block except in an armed caravan.

The other reason for the lack of food was the lack of money in the Palumbo organization. The subsistence payments — they amounted to little more than welfare — which Baccala paid to the Palumbo organization had been shut off. The few gambling and shylocking accounts which Kid Sally had kept for himself had displayed coolness to Kid Sally since the start of the revolt.

"What's doin', pal?" Kid Sally said to Norton the Gambler on the phone.

"Gee, I'm glad to hear from you," Norton the Gambler said.

"Don't you want to see me with somethin'?" Kid Sally said.

"Gee, I wouldn't like to get killed just now," Norton the Gambler said.

"Never mind that, what about what you're supposed to see me with?" Kid Sally said. Norton owed Kid Sally $500 interest on a shylock loan.

"Oh, that? Oh, I give that to Jamesy," Norton said. Jamesy was one of Baccala's finest black suits.

"You give it to who?"

"You see Jamesy," Norton the Gambler said. "And if he's not there, just ask for Baccala. I'm sure he'd be glad to talk to you and tell you."

Norton the Gambler hung up. Kid Sally began

banging his head against the side of the outdoor phone booth he was using.

He walked back down the block to the office and sat down. The fist started rubbing across the forehead. He took a deep breath. The ammonia smell from the lion caused his eyes to tear. "Geez." He took another deep breath. "Murder."

He put his hand over his mouth and opened the door. The lion slipped past Kid Sally's legs and came into the office. The guys in the office threw themselves at the front door. Big Jelly jumped up on the desk. After six weeks in Kid Sally's cellar, the lion had grown a full foot longer and gained about a hundred pounds, much of it in his head, which made him look frightening.

"He'll fuckin' eat me!" Big Jelly yelled.

Inspiration flooded through Kid Sally's head. He grabbed a rope and reached for the lion. "C'mere, you!" The lion ducked his head. He was still just a trifle young. But strangers to the lion would not know this. "He'll give out heart attacks," Kid Sally said, roughing the lion's mane. Kid Sally sniffed. "He needs a bath," he said.

There was, a little while later, a tangle of bumping cars and people threading their way through the cars and sprinting for their lives away from the Clean-Brite Car Wash on Carroll Street. An immense, prolonged roar came from inside the car wash. The lion was tied to a stanchion. The water came on and hit the lion from all sides. The lion came up on his hind legs, fighting against the rope and shaking his head in the water spray. After five minutes, Kid Sally pushed the lion into the rear of the panel truck. Ezmo the Driver was driving. Big Jelly sat in the middle with a shotgun, and Kid Sally was crushed against the outside door. The truck pulled away from the deserted car wash with the lion in the back growling and shaking himself dry.

Chapter 15

Nearly all the people in South Brooklyn play the policy numbers. And within close range of Kid Sally's headquarters there were a considerable number of places used as drops for the numbers gambling. The numbers play from these places belonged technically to the Baccala gang. But loyalty dips as chances of death rise. Kid Sally knew there was a chance, if proper strength was displayed, to grab the numbers play from these places. It amounted, each week, to a figure large enough to support a gang in a war. Once a week people handed a numbers runner anywhere from $1.50, to cover a quarter bet each day, to $12 and $18, to cover $2 and $3 play per day. Kid Sally knew his presence, or the threat of it, would not hold these places in line permanently. People figured, correctly, that Kid Sally was so busy defending himself against Baccala's mob that he couldn't concentrate on them. Kid Sally knew he needed something that would produce lasting fear.

The biggest numbers drop was Herman's

Luncheonette on Fourth Avenue. It was around the corner from two big taxicab garages. The place was always filled with drivers who left their numbers business with Herman, the owner. Herman stood ready to turn over his numbers each week to the collector who frightened him most. "Yell, shout, scream, but don't get physical," Herman kept saying. Herman was at one end of the counter, smoking a cigarette, when Kid Sally came into the place with the lion. Herman did not move. He stood with his cigarette held out and his eyes bulging. He then wet his pants. Ida, the waitress, had her back to the counter. She was looking in the refrigerator for sandwich meat. The lion's nose twitched. He jumped up on the counter. The customers at the counter, all male, wet their pants. The lion teetered on the counter, reached out with a paw and brushed it against Ida's shoulder, and pulled an eye round out of the refrigerator. Ida glanced at the lion and fainted. Herman was too frozen to look. He could hear the lion chewing on the eye round. He retched. He thought the lion was chewing on Ida the waitress.

"Are we friends?" Kid Sally said to him.

Herman, between trembles, was able to nod yes.

Kid Sally spent the next couple of days building a numbers route. At Jack Goldfarb's candy store, Mrs. Jack Goldfarb was bent down behind the counter looking for a box of El Productos. When Mrs. Jack Goldfarb looked up, she saw a lion eating her Hershey bars. Mrs. Jack Goldfarb went home later that day and was not to come out again for six weeks. In Ackerman's Bar, the lion gauged his distance and leaped onto the bar and began eating peanuts. Mickey, the bartender, broke a quart soda bottle off at the neck and stood with it in his hand, ready to fight for his life. His legs buckled and he passed out.

At the end of a week Kid Sally had things lined up. The numbers route was just large enough to support his outfit, and it was just small enough to be safe for a few weeks. By the time the Baccala people were ready to react to the loss by throwing in a large number of gunmen, Kid Sally expected to have Baccala dead and be in charge himself. Kid Sally was going to take over everything on Monday, the big day in the numbers business. On Monday people leave their bets for the week.

Early Monday morning, Kid Sally felt better. He stood in front of the mirror, flipping his tie and making faces.

"I'm starting to put things together now," he said.

"I hope so, I'm tired of goin' to funerals," Big Jelly said.

Kid Sally put the lion in the back of the truck and started out with Ezmo, Big Jelly, and Beppo the Dwarf. Beppo held a sawed-off shotgun and sat on Kid Sally's lap. They stopped at Herman's Luncheonette first. Kid Sally held the back door of the truck open so the lion could stick his head out. Which was all Herman had to see. He reached behind the counter and came up with a big shopping bag holding slips and money. The shopping bag is the carrying case of the numbers business. Numbers is the racetrack of the poor, and many women serve as runners. A shopping bag is their best disguise. Kid Sally took the bag and had a cup of coffee and left Herman's. At ZuZu's Bar and Grill, Kid Sally took the play, stuffed it into the shopping bag, and had a beer. At Ackerman's they all went inside and had a shot of whisky and a beer. Big Jelly went next door to the butcher and bought chopped meat. When he came back they had another drink and left. At Zanetti's Saloon they all had another round of shots and beer. By the time they hit the Cameo Lounge, three hours and five joints later, they all were shaky from drinking.

The Cameo is not much of an afternoon place. It has a barmaid whose name is Del.

"Hello, Del," Beppo the Dwarf said.

"Don't even talk to me, you're too small for me," Del said.

"I got a five-and-a-half-inch tongue," Beppo the Dwarf said.

Ezmo the Driver gripped the bar and began jumping up and down. Kid Sally sat Beppo the Dwarf on the bar. Del spilled water down the front of his pants. Beppo kissed her in the ear with his tongue. Big Jelly reached for a bottle of scotch. They all kept laughing and drinking and they were still laughing an hour later, when Ezmo was driving them back to Marshall Street. In the back of the truck, the lion was growling. Kid Sally remembered the lion hadn't been fed. "I put the meat on the floor," Big Jelly said. Kid Sally, still giggling, reached down and felt the paper bag. He threw it back over his shoulder. The lion fell on it.

Back on Marshall Street, everybody fell out of the truck, laughing, and Kid Sally reached down for the shopping bag. He felt the paper bag and fumbled for the handles. He didn't feel any. Instead, his fingers touched waxed paper from the butcher store. In the back of the truck, the lion was coughing to clear his throat of a ten-dollar bill.

Kid Sally did not remember coming out of the truck. He was unable to breathe, hear, or see. He went upstairs, like Stalin, locked himself in his room for two days.

Big Jelly sat downstairs with his eyes closed. *"Calamare,"* he said to himself. "Zuppa di mussels."

"You're makin' me hungry," Tony the Indian said.

"Shut up, I'm imaginin' I'm out eatin'," Big Jelly said.

That night Georgie, who was Tony the Indian's cousin, became uncomfortable staying on the block. He was uncomfortable because, as

227

he complained, "My thing don't know we got troubles, all my thing knows is that it's good and ready." At 10:30 Georgie wandered from Marshall Street and got in a cab to go to his girl friend's house in Bensonhurst. Bensonhurst was a bad place for Georgie. It was Baccala's home grounds. Georgie didn't care. "I follow my thing," he always says. "I trust it."

A guy got into the apartment elevator with him. Georgie stood facing the guy, just in case. In a one-on-one situation, Georgie was not afraid. Georgie's girl was on the fifth floor. The guy pushed the button for the second floor. Georgie relaxed. The guy was all right. When the elevator door slid open at the second floor, Georgie just did catch a glimpse of the four black suits before they came in on him.

At this point there were six dead and the situation was beginning to reach people beyond the Brooklyn South Homicide Squad. The matter by now had come to the attention of M. E. Landsman, a reporter on the *Times*. Mr. Landsman is in charge of the "Crime, Organized" department of the *Times* city desk. Mr. Landsman's first name is Morris, but the *Times*, German-Jewish oriented, apparently seems not to like the Eastern European "Morris" or "Abraham" to be used in its bylines. Landsman and all Abrahams on the paper either use initials or go on home relief. He has been writing stories about organized crime for three years. Landsman was born in White Plains and lives in Larchmont. The only real Italians he ever saw were atop a garbage truck.

As a reporter, however, he is considered an expert in what is known as Italian Geography. This is a practice of such as the FBI, various police intelligence units, and newspaper and magazine writers. Italian Geography is the keeping of huge amounts of information on gangsters: the prices they pay for clothes, the restaurants in which they eat, the names of all relatives out to the fifth cousins, their home addresses, and their visible daily movements. All this information is neatly filed and continually added to. It is never used for anything, and the gangster goes on until death. But Italian Geography keeps many people busy and collecting salaries, and thus is a commendable occupation. M. E. Landsman, just by digging into the cabinet behind his desk, could tell you the home address of Baccala (55 Royal Street), the number of guests at Anthony (Tony Boy) Boirado's wedding (732), the birthplace of Lucky Luciano (Lercara Friddi, Sicily), and the favorite dining spot and meal of dock boss Mike Rizzuto (Della Palma; veal marsala). All these little facts always add up to nothing in the geographer's mind. And every evening, sitting over a martini in the Oyster Bar at Grand Central Station, M. E. Landsman waits for his train to Larchmont and he says to himself, "I wonder what these people really *do*."

In the security of his office, however, he was without doubt. He submerged himself in his geography and wrote authoritative stories about the Mafia. Now, with the bare police details of the six recent murders in front of him, M. E. Landsman went to work. He went into his cabinet for the M's and brought out Joe Mangoni's file. It showed that Joe Mangoni had a cousin who married Carlo Gambino's niece in Saint Fortunata's Church in Bensonhurst. M. E. Landsman studied this information. He reached for the phone and called Sergeant Paul DiNardo at police headquarters.

Sergeant DiNardo was on the streets as a precinct patrolman for the first month of his first year on the New York City force. A desk lieutenant found DiNardo knew how to type, and for the next seventeen years DiNardo typed reports in offices in the Police Department. Because of the wave of talk about organized crime, the Chief Inspector, George Glennon, looked around headquarters one day and announced that DiNardo would be the department's expert on the Mafia.

"Why are you picking him?" The Commissioner, Michael McGrady, asked Glennon.

"Because he's a guinea," Glennon said. "He'll be able to spell the names right."

DiNardo grabbed the phone. "Organized Crime Special Attack Unit, Sergeant DiNardo speaking." Sometimes he said "Enforcement Unit," and other times he said "Investigation

Unit." It didn't matter. He was alone in his office and whatever he said was all right, as long as the names were spelled right on the records.

"This is Morris Landsman at the *Times*. All these murders in Brooklyn. Could you tell me anything about them?"

"Like what?" DiNardo said.

"Well, take the Mangoni killing," M. E. Landsman said.

DiNardo pushed a button. It caused a file drum to rotate. DiNardo stopped the drum at M. He grabbed the folder for Joe Mangoni. "Well, Mangoni cousin married Carlo Gambino's daughter."

"I know that too," Landsman said smugly.

"Well, what else can I tell you?" DiNardo said.

"What do you think about it?" Landsman said.

"You know I can't talk," DiNardo said. "There's an investigation."

DiNardo hung up and went through a newspaper to see if there was a movie he could see that afternoon. Morris Landsman pushed open the typewriter well on his desk and went to work. He turned his head, as he always did, while his fingers typed out: BY M. E. LANDSMAN.

His definitive story read in part:

High police officials today are investigating a series of murders in Brooklyn to determine if they have some connection to the operations of the criminal organization known as the Cosa Nostra, or Mafia. Police officials

231

pointed out that the murder victims, six within two months, all had police records.

The story was put on page one under a headline saying: POLICE PROBE 6 MURDERS IN BROOKLYN.

The next morning the pale sunlight came through the bare trees on the lawn outside Gracie Mansion, and the wind blew the branches, causing their shadows to flick across the newspaper the Mayor was reading at breakfast. The Mayor closed his eyes. They were red-rimmed and hot. He had been up until three a.m. unwinding after a two-hour session with 2500 angry people in a Jewish Center in Flatbush. He opened his eyes and ran them across the headlines on the *Times'* first page. There were three stories out of Washington, one out of Tel Aviv, others from Tokyo, Bombay, and Paris. The only New York story was M. E. Landsman's piece on gang murders.

"Shit!" the Mayor said. "Who the hell cares about gangsters? I mean, you'd think . . . Here I'm out all night arguing about housing, and what do they put on the first page? Gangsters. Shit!"

Harold Downing, his chief assistant, sat across from the Mayor. "He's got six murders to talk about, and he's the expert on gangsters. Maybe he'll try and stretch this out. Run one every day."

"Fuck that," the Mayor said. "There's problems in this city a little more important than

232

gangsters. The biggest one is me getting re-elected." He picked up a phone attached to the table. "Give me Commissioner McGrady," he said.

He waited a moment, cursing under his breath. "Michael, how are you? . . . That's right, that's exactly what I'm calling about . . . Yes, yes, yes. . . . Well, you see, I couldn't care if they killed each other forever. But I have this housing bill and, shit, I can't have gangsters on the first page. You know. . . . Oh, good. All right, thanks, Michael."

Commissioner McGrady put the phone down. He stood up and walked around the immense desk Teddy Roosevelt had used when he was the city's Police Commissioner. He looked down at the thick rug for a moment. Then he pushed a buzzer. His secretary, a detective, walked in.

"Tell Gallagher to meet me at Emil's," he said.

Emil's is an old, dark-walled German restaurant a block and a half from City Hall and Police Headquarters. A corner table in the rear is always reserved for the Police Commissioner.

The place was empty. It was only 9:30. McGrady was on his second scotch by the time Gallagher walked in.

"I know what this is about," Gallagher said. "One fuckin' story in a newspaper."

"I just wanted to congratulate you on your dead guineas," McGrady said.

"Thanks," Gallagher said. "And I'd have

more of them if I had my way."

"You can do two things for me," McGrady said. "First, you can have a drink. Second, you can get them to go some place else with their troubles. I had the Mayor on the phone the minute I got in this morning."

The waiter brought two shot glasses of scotch, with water on the side. "Here's how," Gallagher said. He threw a shot down, Irish style, his tongue showing as it went into the shot glass. He put the glass down. "It's this fuckin' punk Sally Palumbo," Gallagher said. "He's pushin'."

"What does Baccala have to say about that?" McGrady said.

"Well, what do you think the shootin' is about?" Gallagher said.

"Well, get on him," McGrady said.

"I'll get on that fuckin' Palumbo, that's what I'll do," Gallagher said.

"I don't care what you do, just do it," Mc-Grady said. "Just keep the Mayor off my back."

At three a.m. the squad rooms and all the offices of the 79th Precinct were filled with detectives talking to Kid Sally Palumbo's people. Gallagher, his eyes bloodshot, walked from office to office, conferring with detectives out in the hallway. Gallagher liked the way it was going. His men had grabbed the Palumbo outfit after midnight. By the time lawyers could drive in from Long Island and scream about civil liberties, he would have the Palumbos exhausted and

234

bothered. Gallagher had told his detectives to abuse them. "It takes them a week to get over it when you treat them like shoeshine boys," he said. "Their guinea egos suffer."

A week would give him time. He could take it up with Baccala and see if there was a way to end it. But that was for later. Right now, all that counted was abusing everybody.

From each office, Gallagher could hear a voice saying the same thing.

"What could I tell you?" Kid Sally Palumbo was saying to two homicide detectives.

"What could I tell you?" Big Jelly was saying.

"What-a could I tell-a you?" Big Mama was saying. When she saw Gallagher, her thumb and forefinger shot out in horns.

Gallagher smiled. "Dead guineas and niggers, that's what I like," he called out. "The more I see of dead guineas and dead niggers, the better I like it."

He looked into one small office. A thin smile came onto his face and he stepped inside. "Good evening," he said.

Angela sat in a chair with a cigarette in her mouth and no make-up on her face. She inhaled and put the cigarette carefully in the ashtray. She let the smoke come out of her nose slowly.

"Get cancer," she said quietly.

"What's that?" Gallagher said.

"What could I tell you?" Angela said.

"You weren't this way the last time I saw you," Gallagher said.

The young detective talking to her was sitting on the other side of the desk. Gallagher motioned with his head for the detective to come around the desk and sit alongside her. The young detective frowned. He didn't know what Gallagher meant.

Gallagher smiled again. "Be nice to her, she's a nice college student," he said.

Angela sat and stared at the ashtray and said nothing. She was reminding herself that once you say anything except the one rote line, "What could I tell you?" you open yourself up for a slip.

The cameramen were at the bottom of the stairs, and the doors behind them were open to the morning rain. Angela held her head high and started down the stairs. She looked over their heads, at the rain in the doorway, but her eyes caught the cameras being held up. An arm in a blue rain jacket held a television floodlight high over the heads of the other cameramen. Angela was halfway down the stairs when the floodlight came on — glaring, bare light that brings up the rust on the railings and the cigarette butts and gum wrappers on the steps and the soot coating on the walls and the stale faces and the munic- ipal smell of a police station when you are in trouble. Angela's head was high and she felt her- self coming down each step and there were no more steps and the cameras were all around her and her ears became filled with the *shhhhhhh shhhhhhhhh shhhhhhh* of the cameramen shuffling backward while they kept filming her, and then there was nobody around her and she was in the morning rain on the steps of the police station. It was a winter rain. The wind blew it in gray sheets. The cold touch of the rain came through her hair and to the scalp.

"Miss Palumbo, Miss Palumbo," a woman's voice said.

Angela kept her head high and came down the steps to the sidewalk and she heard the footsteps coming alongside her.

"Miss Palumbo, are you going to your classes at college now?"

Whoever she was, she was on the left. Angela's left shoulder came up in self-protection.

"Miss Palumbo, I went to NYU myself, and I was just wondering . . ."

Angela kept walking, controlled, erect, the rain coming into her face and soaking through the shoulders of her cloth coat. She could feel the presence on her left going away. Angela's left shoulder came down.

"Artie, she won't say anything," the female voice behind her was calling out.

They had let Angela go first. It was 7:30, and she walked up to the corner and into the rush hour on an avenue in Brooklyn. The street was a wall of trailer trucks and buses with steamy windows. The sign hanging from the corner drugstore squealed while it swung in the wind and rain. A light changed, and the traffic in the street began to move. The Diesel trucks and buses shifted gears with a roar, and the squeal from the drugstore sign mixed in with the roar, and Angela walked in the heavy rain with the noise hurting her ears and her back in a little bunch against the hand she felt would touch her, a cop's hand, a cameraman's hand, somebody's hand, and nausea started in the back of her head and ran to her stomach. She swallowed against it and kept walking, controlled and erect, and people began brushing against her as they ran in the rain to the subway. She slipped into the middle of a crowd going down the steps. The train was packed and hot, and the smell of wet clothes was thick. People dressed in rainhats and raincoats stared at Angela. There had been no rain when the detectives came the night before, so she was not dressed for it. Her blue coat was dark with water, her wet stockings stuck to her legs, and her hair dripped. Angela stared out the window and was motionless all the way to Manhattan. She did not notice the stations, or the people getting on and off the trains. She thought about nothing. She was frozen. Vacantly, automatically, she got off at Second Avenue and began walking in the rain. At Mario's corner the sewer was stopped up and a puddle was spreading into the middle of the street. A cab ran through the puddle and threw a spray of water. A sheet of dirty water splashed into Angela's face. She walked through it.

Mario was in a T-shirt and his shorts when he answered the door. He said something to her, but she didn't hear it. "I'm wet," she said. She walked past him. "I just want to get dry," she said. She picked the hotel towel off the doorknob. She started into the bathroom, then went over to a chair and picked up his raincoat. In the bathroom she took off her coat and hung it on the door hook. Her plaid shift was soaked. She took it off and hung it on the shower-curtain rail. The bra felt damp. She took it off. She reached down and began to unhook her stockings, but her fingers fumbled. She peeled the girdle and stockings off at once and threw them over the rail. She put on the raincoat and started rubbing her hair with the towel. She gave a little shudder and fell on her knees and began vomiting into the toilet. Her body shook all over. When she began screaming, Mario opened the door.

He helped her to the couch and she buried her face and Mario could see her body shaking through the raincoat. He ran his hand on her back in a slow circle. She lay on her face on the couch for a half-hour and sobbed. She twisted around to look up at him. Her mouth was trembling with shock. Mario's face came down to her. He kissed her, and she was whimpering and moaning in shock and fear, and then all the trouble inside her came out in a wave of need and she had her mouth on his and her legs stretching and moving and her fingernails digging into his back while she drew in a sharp breath through clenched teeth.

She listened to the rain against the windows

for a few moments. She held up her arm and squinted at the watch. It was 2:30. Mario was sitting at the easel, which he had set up in front of the windows. She put her head down and pulled the blanket up over her shoulders.

"Don't tell me you went out and bought a blanket," she said.

"People help me," Mario said. He smiled. He wished Sidney could hear that. He got the blanket one day by waiting until Sidney was stuck in the bathroom and then whisking it off Sidney's bed. Sidney heard the movement and knew he was being robbed, but he couldn't do anything about it except to scream from the bathroom, "Thief fuck!"

Angela put her head back and stretched. The police station started in her stomach. She closed her eyes against it.

"What are you doing there?" she said.

He grunted something. He had been working for five hours, using Angela's face to make up for the torn face on the painting he was copying.

"You've been working too long," she said. She shook her head against the light. He stood up and stretched. *Now all I have to do is finish this painting and find some old lady and make her buy it,* he said to himself. He had everything else he needed. He walked across to the couch.

They woke up in darkness. Angela stiffened. "My God, what time is it?" He got up and pushed the light switch. She squinted in the light from the bulb in the ceiling directly over her head. "Oh, five o'clock." She fell back. "I thought it was late, I didn't know what time it was. I have to call home. They'll be crazy if I don't call them soon." She yawned. "The light. Don't have one bulb in a room like this. Get a lamp. You'd be surprised what one lamp would do for you. We'll have to get one. But right now I'm starved." She sat up quickly. "Oh, I don't know what I have in my purse."

She pulled the blanket around her and slid off the couch and went over to the kitchen table and began going through her purse. The blanket slipped from one shoulder. Mario's eyes followed her back slanting in from the shoulder and then rolling, white, into the top of a long leg.

"I hope you have some money, because I have exactly two dollars and some change," she said.

"Nothing, I have none," he said. He swung onto the floor and went for his pants. He put them on carefully, so the change wouldn't jingle in the pocket where he had the money.

She ran a hand through her hair. "Well, what are you going to live on? I mean, you've got to eat."

"I have no money," he said. He put his hand in the pocket that had the money.

She went into the bathroom and dressed. She was running a comb through her hair when she called out, "Get dressed."

"I'll stay here," he said.

"Just get dressed," she said. "I can't leave you here like this."

"To go where?" he said.

She came out to him and kissed him. "Come home with me and get something to eat. And if anybody asks you, I met you after school."

Chapter 16

In the City of New York, in the ninety minutes between six and seven-thirty p.m. each weekday night, there occurs the greatest flood of information directed at man in the history of the world. On the major television channels, a group of men who appear to be either studying or teaching undertaking appear on the screen with the news of the day in words and film. The film, running from talking heads in a hallway at the Board of Health to F-4 planes dropping napalm canisters into trees, comes into nearly every house, apartment, furnished room, saloon, and office in the city. And on almost every evening this television news, merely by displaying a subject, can raise the level of annoyance over a minor matter to the point where it becomes a major crisis.

Which is what was occurring around the city when, after the billboarding and commercials, the first set of straightfaced television newsmen came on camera to give all New York the lead story of the day's news.

"Good evening. Police early this morning conducted a lightning raid on a gang of Brooklyn hoodlums who were alleged to be at the bottom of the series of Cosa Nostra murders which have occurred in that borough in recent weeks. Sixty-three of the men, and two women, were brought to the 91st Precinct and questioned for several hours by homicide detectives under command of . . ."

The Mayor kicked his wastepaper basket, spilling it across the red carpeting of his office at City Hall.

"Shit!" the Mayor said.

". . . gang, which operates in Brooklyn, is said to be under the control of Salvatore (Kid Sally) Palumbo . . ."

Harold Downing stood up. He smiled. "I wish I could be the mayor, so everybody would do exactly as I tell them."

"I ask them to get rid of it for me, and what do I get?" the Mayor said. "The police running a publicity stunt for a couple of lousy gangsters."

In Baccala's office they were standing around the boss, who sat in a chair and looked at a new color set which he had set up next to the statue of Saint Anthony. On the news show there was a film clip of Angela coming down the stairs, her face set against the light glaring into her eyes.

"That's the sister," one of Baccala's black suits said.

"Who sister?" Baccala said.

"Kid Sally's sister," the Water Buffalo said.

244

"I make him watch while I shoot her," Baccala said.

The film now showed Kid Sally starting down the stairs. On camera, Kid Sally brought his right arm up in an elaborate movement. He was just starting to slap his left hand on the inside of his right elbow when the film clip dissolved.

"Punk!" Baccala said. His head went far back, then came forward as he spat at the television set. "Die!" He said it from deep in his throat. The Water Buffalo jumped up and spat at the television. All the black suits ran up to the set, clearing their throats to spit.

In Kid Sally Palumbo's front room, twenty of them were crowded in and watched the show the way big football teams look at game films. "Here I go," Kid Sally said, looking at himself. Everybody groaned when the film was cut before his gesture. Big Jelly now appeared. "Watch me shine," Big Jelly said. On television he came strutting down the stairs with his tongue sticking out of the right side of his mouth. One hand was on his hip. The other hand made a fist. The fist was just starting an up-and-down motion when the film clip was dissolved.

There was a great noise in Kid Sally's front room. There was a small noise in Baccala's office. "Punk!" Baccala said again. In the office of the Mayor there was the most dangerous sound of all. Silence.

The Mayor sat immobile for several moments. He reached for an old black phone which con-

245

nected him directly to the Police Commissioner's office.

"Hi. You know, I was just sitting here thinking. We're having an Urban Task Force meeting tonight, and I thought at the end of it a couple of us ought to sit down. We're a little out of sync. When? Oh, I'd say, let me see, somewhere around eleven o'clock tonight at the mansion."

At Police Headquarters, McGrady had one hand reaching for the intercom while he put down the Mayor's call. "This Protestant bastard will have me sitting up all night on account of these guineas — yeop, get me Chief Gallagher in Brooklyn South, will you please?"

The switchboard operators had left the Brooklyn District Attorney's office. The patrolman at the reception desk answered the night line. "Mr. Rogin?" The patrolman checked the list in front of him. "No, I'm sorry, he left for the day. Would you care to leave a message? Oh, excuse me. The Mayor's office. If you'll hold a minute, I'll get Mr. Goodman."

Benjamin Goodman, the chief assistant district attorney, sat hunched over his municipal green metal desk. A small round mirror, the kind women take along when traveling, was set up on top of a pile of trial minutes. Benjamin Goodman looked into the mirror while he combed his red hair.

"Mayor's office," the patrolman said.

Benjamin Goodman was on his feet in one

246

motion. He jogged out of the office. In the hallway he began to sprint. He slid up to the phone.

"Rogin?" Goodman said to Harold Downing, "Well, yes, he's been working on this gang business. But . . ." Goodman took a deep breath. He did not need to pause. He knew what he was going to say without having to think about it. "But he's merely been assigned to it. Actually, in view of the worsening situation, I think I'd better step into the case personally. When? Gracie Mansion at eleven tonight? Of course."

In the City Room of the *Times*, a voice came over the loudspeaker. "Mr. Landsman, please report to the metropolitan desk. Mr. Landsman . . ."

M. E. Landsman walked through the long rows of desks to the front of the room, where three men in shirtsleeves, all wearing glasses, were standing in front of a television set.

"Mersh, what do you plan to do with this Palumbo business?" one of the men in shirtsleeves said. "They were just on television. God, what despicable characters."

"Oh, I'm putting up something on them," M. E. Landsman said.

"Well, we'd like to use it fairly strong, perhaps out front," the man said. "When can we see the lead?"

"Oh, I'll have it coming up right away," M. E. Landsman said.

He walked back to his desk with a sinking feeling. He had planned to write the story the next morning. Now he was going to miss his regular train home to Larchmont. He sat at his desk and took the Associated Press copy on the arrests and began to write it in different words. There was no use in trying anything else. He had nothing on Kid Sally Palumbo in his files. And he had spoken to Sergeant DiNardo earlier in the day, and DiNardo had assured him Kid Sally Palumbo was a soldier in the Mafia family in Youngstown, Ohio.

Landsman's story ran on the bottom of page one. At 10:45 p.m. the Mayor had his secretary circle it on each copy of the newspaper that was on the long conference table in the basement at Gracie Mansion. At eleven o'clock the Mayor sat down at the head of the table. He nodded to everybody and then picked up a paper. The Mayor was wearing a short-sleeved blue knit yachting shirt. This made everybody at the table think of one word: *Protestant.*

"Well, gentlemen, I want to thank you for coming," the Mayor said. "The purpose of this meeting is to further the coordination of our efforts in regard to this damnable mess in Brooklyn."

Benjamin Goodman picked up a pencil and began to scrawl on the pad in front of him. *What is this guy worrying so much about a few guinea homicides?* he thought. Idly, Goodman wrote "2%" on the pad. The Mayor, running on a

248

Fusion ticket, had defeated the regular Democratic candidate because of a shift of 2 per cent of the Democratic voters. Goodman, like any other fifty-one-year-old clubhouse Democrat, could recite the names of party defectors.

"Look," the Mayor said, "I don't have to tell you people that if there's one thing people react to these days, it's something about crime. Hell, anything about crime. I'm up half the nights worrying about street crimes and burglaries. I couldn't care less about gangsters killing each other. But you put just one dead body in a gutter and the public reacts. It's an issue."

Goodman's pencil tapped on the pad. Goodman began drawing rows of "2%." He ripped the page off and stuffed it into his pocket. Carefully he printed a newspaper headline.

BROOKLYN DA GOODMAN MOUNTS
INTENSIVE DRIVE ON MAFIA

Goodman looked at Gallagher. The inspector's pouchy eyes returned the look. *Maybe,* Benjamin Goodman thought, *this drunken slob could help a nice alert Jewish Democrat to get 2 per cent of the vote back. Who knows? Who knows anything?*

"Am I given to understand," Goodman called out, "that Chief Gallagher will be running the Police Department's end of this?"

"Yes," McGrady said.

"With a little less noise than in the past, I

249

would hope," the Mayor said sharply.

"Fine with me," Goodman said. "That's fine."

Later the Mayor's wife served coffee in the living quarters. Benjamin Goodman stood at the living-room windows, looking at the dark lawns that run down to the East River. The Mayor's wife was bringing Benjamin Goodman cream and sugar and she heard him muse to himself, without knowing he was saying it aloud, "This would be a helluva place for me to live."

Just before they fell asleep that night, the Mayor's wife said, "This Goodman is a slimy worm, you know."

"Why?" he asked.

"Because he's a slimy worm, that's why," she said.

Mario and Angela had come into the Palumbo apartment just as the news program started. They stood in the doorway between the kitchen and front room and watched, she in silence, Mario with little noises coming out of him when he found he was so afraid that he could not inhale. When the television announcer changed subjects, Kid Sally turned off the set. Everybody in the room looked at Mario.

"This is Mario Trantino, he is one of the boys who came here for the bike race," Angela said.

"How do you do, pleased," Kid Sally said.

"How do you do, pleased," Big Mama said.

They all reached out and shook hands with

Mario, and Big Mama took him into the kitchen. "I want to change," Angela said. She went down the hall to her room. Right away, Big Jelly closed his eyes and put his head against the wall. Tony the Indian sat with both hands on top of his head. He began scratching his scalp. He knew a lot of people do this when they think, and he wanted to try it out. Big Jelly opened his eyes. When he saw Tony the Indian trying to think too, it came to him.

"That guy is a rat priest hittin' on your sister!" he snarled.

Kid Sally Palumbo picked up his head. "Who rat priest?" he said.

"Me and Tony seen him," Big Jelly said.

"Seen him where?" Kid Sally said.

"Seen him in his priest's suit," Tony the Indian said.

"By Dominic's when we was watchin' that night," Big Jelly said.

"I could of touched him . . ." Tony the Indian said.

". . . same guy . . ."

". . . rat priest . . ."

". . . I don't hafta swear, I got eyes, I could see . . ."

". . . yeah . . ."

Mario, sitting at the kitchen table, picked up a few stray words of the jumbled conversation in the front room. Therefore he knew enough to drop his chin onto his chest when Kid Sally exploded into the kitchen. With the chin down,

Kid Sally could not get his hands on Mario's throat. Big Jelly grabbed Mario by an ear in order to yank the head up so Kid Sally could do some strangling. Big Mama had a bread knife in one hand. With the other hand she tried to flatten out the fingers of Mario's right hand onto the kitchen table. Big Mama intended to saw off the thumb and forefinger of the hand. These are the fingers which are anointed when a priest is ordained. Mario made a fist so the fingers wouldn't stick out. Big Mama jabbed the tip of the knife into the fist. Mario yelped. The fingers of his hand jumped out in pain. Big Mama tried to hold them flat so she could begin sawing. Mario pulled the fingers back into a fist. Big Mama jabbed him again with the tip of the knife.

"The hell with it," Big Jelly said. He bent over and sank his teeth into Mario's ear. Mario made a loud noise.

When Angela heard Mario shriek, she tumbled out of her room. At the kitchen doorway she started to scream, but put her hands to her mouth instead and stood motionless. Centuries of Sicilian blood cause a woman to stay out of a thing like this, even if her greatest love is about to be murdered. Weep for his soul, yes. But never interfere with the necessary rite of his murder.

Beppo the Dwarf got a hand inside Mario's jacket and pulled out the picture. He turned it over and saw the writing on the back. He held the picture in front of Kid Sally's face. He turned

252

it around so Kid Sally could see the writing.

"What's it say?" Beppo the Dwarf said.

Kid Sally's hands dropped from Mario's chin. He pushed Big Mama's knife hand away and slapped Big Jelly on the head to make him stop biting Mario's ear.

"Let's talk a bit," he said to Mario.

"I never touch!" Mario said, gesturing to Angela. "On my mother's grave, I never touch!"

"That means he touch!" Big Mama shrieked. She waved the knife. "Open his fly, I cut off!"

Kid Sally held his arm out to keep her away. He sat down across the table from Mario. "You're on the film with the priest suit?" he said. He held his hand out as if it were a boat rocking. This is the international semaphore for larceny. Mario said yes with his head. With a few more words and several hand signals, Kid Sally got the general flow of Mario's life in America.

He held up the picture. "This name on the bottom, are you *congeal* with him?"

Mario didn't understand.

"*Congeal,* he means do you know him good?" Big Jelly said.

"I don't see him yet," Mario said.

"Do you know who he is?" Kid Sally said.

Mario shook his head no.

"Dangerous old man, he finds you out, he cuts your whole head off," Kid Sally said.

Mario clutched his chest. "Then I cross out his name."

"He has money," Kid Sally said.

Mario let go of his chest. "How much money?"

"A whole roomful of money."

"Then I keep his name on the list."

"You meet him," Kid Sally said, "and we'll snatch him and get his money. I'll let you count the money while I cut his heart out." Kid Sally began to giggle. "Unless you're afraid of kidnaping an old man."

Mario closed his eyes to show fear.

Big Mama had everybody sit down for plates of spaghetti and olive oil. Nobody grumbled. They had prospects now. Angela ate in silence. She said she needed air. She and Mario went down the block to Nunzio's. An old car with dented fenders was parked a few doors up from Nunzio's. The car was parked in the wrong direction, facing the docks. Four of Kid Sally's guys, leather jackets pulled up to their cheekbones, sat in the car. Their job was to shoot at anybody or anything coming onto the street from the dock end. Another car was doing similar guard duty at the other end of the block.

Nunzio stood behind the counter, picking his silver teeth with a hunting knife. The jukebox was playing his favorite record, "Mala Femmina." The title means "Bad Woman." Nunzio always plays the record and thinks of the girl who once robbed him. While the coffee dripped from the espresso machine, Nunzio hummed and muttered his own special words to the song.

". . . whore-a basset . . ." Nunzio sang softly. As the music rose, the image of the girl who had done him wrong grew clearer in his mind. Nunzio's hand slapped down on the counter. "Rat-a whore!"

They looked out the window and did not talk. The pier was across the street from the store. The water in the slip alongside the pier was black and motionless. At the end of the pier, out in the channel, the strong night tide created ripples. Light from a slim moon splashed over the black water, and the ripples turned the light into a corrugated tray of diamonds. A tug, the running lights rigged like a necklace, moved against the tide, its snub bow throwing white water into the moonlight.

"My greenhorn," Angela said. "God knows what you *really* know." He was surprised at the tone of her voice.

"Did you bring the priest's clothes with you from Italy?" she said.

He shook his head no.

"At least," she said.

"I came here for a race and there is no race," he said. "What do I do? You know all I want to do. The painting."

"Well, that's one thing," she said.

She started to pick up the cup and stopped. The car must have been three blocks away, but it was coming so quickly its noise was clear. The car was coming from the left, racing along the deserted street in front of the piers. Nunzio stepped behind the pizza oven. Angela pulled Mario by the arm. They crouched. The car, twin exhausts booming, swept down the street along the docks and crossed Marshall Street without stopping. The four hoodlums ran from the parked car to the bundle of clothes that had been thrown from the speeding car. The bundle comprised Ezmo the Driver's new sports jacket and his slacks. Ezmo's tie was knotted around the bundle. One of the four hoodlums pulled the bundle loose. The neon from Nunzio's sign fell on the white belly of a fluke.

"They put Ezmo under the top of the water," one of the hoodlums from the car yelled.

Angela turned her head and started walking quickly. Mario caught up with her and they went along in silence. She paused for a moment in front of the house, looked up, and put her arm through his and made him keep going.

Detective Donald Jenkins, dressed in a milk-delivery uniform, sauntered out of a doorway on Columbia Avenue and followed them to the subway. As the train swayed to Manhattan, Jenkins noticed Angela taking Mario's hand and holding it tightly. He hoped they were going to a hotel. It would make surveillance easy. Twenty minutes later, when Angela and Mario went into the building on 11th Street, Jenkins watched from the corner. "I don't even know the name of the bum with her," he muttered.

In bed, Angela buried her face in Mario's chest. She shivered and tried to get the picture of the fish out of her mind. Her bare legs rubbed against Mario's. In the emptiness of the hours of the days since she had stopped going to school and begun living with slurred curses and funerals and fish in the street, Mario, simply being there, had become the only real thing in Angela's life.

Mario did not notice the softness against him. He was thinking of what it would be like to drown: thrashing in the black water, his eyes rolling wildly, his body trying to move in the chains wrapped around it, going down, down, down, realizing that he would not come up, opening his mouth to scream and immediately choking on water.

"Wa." The noise came from the bottom of Mario's throat.

"What's the matter?" Angela said. She was looking into his face.

Mario closed his eyes. Slowly, gracefully, another thought slipped into his mind. *A roomful of money.* The fear went away and he opened his eyes and smiled at her. His hands pressed on her shoulderblades and he began to come onto his side against her.

"Just remember to say that we went to an all-night movie," she whispered.

Chapter 17

She slept late in the morning. He was up early and went right to the painting, which he kept carefully covered when Angela was around. He moved the covers from her face so he could follow the cheekbone. At 10:30 the sounds he made getting dressed woke her up. He pointed to the work under his arm. "I'll be back in one hour, two hours," he said.

She sat up. "Oh, let me look at it," she said.

He stepped away from her. "When it's finished," he said. He certainly didn't want her to see he had copied somebody else's work and tossed in only her face, or at least her cheekbones. He checked to make sure the torn original he'd been copying was under his arm too. He didn't want to leave anything around for her to see.

"I'm going to go out and get some coffee," she said.

"Uhuh."

"But I'll come right back. I don't want to be out some place and have you back here looking for me."

He walked down the staircase wondering if he wanted all this strange dependence and compliance she was showing.

He woke up Sidney again. Sidney rubbed his hands over his face to get rid of the sleep. He looked at Mario's work and let out a deep breath.

"I guess so," Sidney said.

"Yes?" Mario said. His hands were waving over Sidney's shoulder.

"I told you I guess so," Sidney said. "I don't know how the hell you did it. You got it looking like a face, not a sketch of a face."

"What should I do now?" Mario said.

"Stop breathing in my ear," Sidney said. "See Grant for anything else. The next one you do should be fast. Do ten of this thing, unload them on ten people, you'll have some sort of a living. Anyway, get the hell out of my life."

Mario was fumbling with excitement when he got to the luncheonette on his corner and dialed Dominic Laviano's number.

"Don Mario?" Laviano said. "It's good you call me. I spoke to my friend. Do you have a paper to write something down?"

Mario ripped a page out of the front of the phone book and scribbled in the white space while Dominic talked.

"Tomorrow is Wednesday. Then come Thursday. On Thursday afternoon, we see my friend. Now I have to be at the market in the Bronx. So I give you the address and you ask and get to the place yourself. I be there at three o'clock. My friend, he be there at three o'clock. So maybe you be there at three o'clock too, Don Mario?"

Dominic read off the address of a restaurant called the Della Palma on Queens Boulevard in Queens. "God bless till Thursday," Dominic said and he hung up. Mario knew he was close to money. And his art would work. Someday he would be a painter of his own. All that was in his way was a little danger.

Mario was thinking of Catanzia in the morning while he walked back to the apartment. The smell of cow and goat urine, which hangs in every house, came into his nostrils. He thought of the white belly of the fluke in the clothes on Marshall Street. He thought of the urine smell again. It hung in his nose. He was more afraid of going back to the urine smell than he was of the fluke in the clothes.

At seven p.m. Mario took a pear from the tray on the kitchen table at Marshall Street. Casually, he took the piece of phone-book paper out of his pocket. He read out the restaurant address.

"And what time on Thursday do you meet this-a certain party?" Big Mama said.

"Three o'clock," Mario said.

Angela got up and walked out of the kitchen. She didn't want to hear. Mario put the slip of paper back into his pocket. He picked up the pear and took a deep bite.

All the years on all the streets kept running through Kid Sally's mind. He sat in the vending-machine office, rubbing his fist across his forehead, thinking slowly, step by step, of how the kidnaping and torture-death of Baccala should be done. The mistakes and missed shots and the funerals, they would all be made meaningless by one pull of a trigger. People now taking oaths on their mothers' graves to kill Kid Sally on sight would get down on one knee and kiss Kid Sally's hand if he ever got Baccala. The police would not knock on the door and bring everybody to a precinct house for questioning. Instead, they would make appointments through Kid Sally's lawyer. There would be pressure from nobody and money from everywhere.

"The truck," Kid Sally said.
"What of the truck?" Beppo the Dwarf said.
"Put a sign on it that says FISH."
A fish truck near a restaurant would seem normal.
"We need a strange car, too," Kid Sally said.
Beppo nodded. "I'll get one."
Big Mama held up her hand. "Make-a sure you throw the license plate away."
Beppo the Dwarf nodded. The art of stealing cars for purposes of murder requires, besides a stolen car, that a set of license plates must be stolen from still another car. The stolen license plates are put on the stolen car. The stolen car's

261

plates are scaled into the river. This is because the police looking for stolen cars check license-plate numbers. And people whose license plates have been stolen never report this. They blame it on kids and go stand on line at the Motor Vehicle Bureau to get new plates. So the police are unlikely to look for any car which travels with stolen license plates. It takes at least six months for the Motor Vehicle Bureau to circulate stolen-license-plate numbers. In six months a good murderer using a stolen car in reasonable condition can cause overcrowding at a cemetery.

"We better get a couple of pieces of iron, too," Kid Sally said.

A kid named Junior and his friend, Jerry the Booster, got up and stretched. Stealing guns was their department. All shooting requires a gun that can't be traced. If you happen to shoot somebody with a gun that can be traced to your hand, jurors might happen to vote for conviction. Therefore, stolen guns are necessary.

The meeting broke up. Kid Sally, Big Jelly, Tony the Indian, and Big Lollipop went out to the car. "I got to relax a little bit so I could think clear," Kid Sally said.

The car drove off. Beppo the Dwarf went out to steal a car and license plates. And Junior and Jerry the Booster went down to the docks to steal guns and ammunition. This was one of the hardest jobs of all. Not that Junior and Jerry the Booster couldn't get onto the docks. This was easy for two tested thieves. The problem was finding the right guns and ammunition for the gang to use. The largest area of the South Brooklyn waterfront is the Brooklyn Army Terminal, a complex of gloomy gray government warehouse buildings with many piers jutting into the oily water. Large freighters load at the piers and slump through the water on the outgoing tide. They carry the basic American export. Which is why Junior and Jerry the Booster had trouble. The first pier they tried was stacked with cases of 122-mm. rockets for shipment to Haifa, Israel. On the second pier there were tarpaulin-wrapped 105-mm. howitzers addressed for shipment to Beirut, Lebanon. Junior and Jerry the Booster couldn't see how they could catch Baccala by surprise with any of this equipment. They spent the night working through crates of napalm for India and mortars for Pakistan. Finally, in an area marked for use by a United Fruit Company ship, Jerry the Booster found crates of .32 Smith and Wesson revolvers marked for Guatemala. Junior found crates of ammunition, the stencil saying it was for .32 Savage automatics.

Junior looked at the number. *Aah, .32 is .32.* "You got .32s?" he asked Jerry.

"Yop."

"I got .32s too," Junior said. He broke into the crate and began stuffing boxes of bullets into the canvas bag he was carrying.

Kid Sally and his group were taking a risk by going out. If Baccala knew about it, he would send all four hundred of his people after them. But Kid Sally was going to a place where nobody would expect him, a loud, dark discothèque named the Dream Lounge, on Bedford Avenue. To reduce the risk further, three shotguns were in the car. Kid Sally began to rock back and forth in the seat when the car pulled in front of the Dream Lounge. "This is just what I need, I need a place to think," he was saying.

Tony the Indian and Big Lollipop got out of the car first, with shotguns under their coats, and they walked into the place. Tony the Indian looked out the door and waved. Kid Sally got out of the car and smoothed his jacket. He craned his neck and fixed his tie. He put a cigarette in his mouth and lit it slowly. He hadn't felt this good in weeks. He knew that anybody looking through the door at him was looking at a real gangster. A big-league gangster. Kid Sally's shoulders swung while he walked into the place.

Big Jelly did not go directly into the Dream Lounge. He went to a drugstore on the corner. A little dark-haired man with thick glasses was behind the counter. He knew who Big Jelly was.

"Hello, baby," Big Jelly said. "How about a little something to step me up?"

"Like what," the druggist said.

"Like a fistful of red birds," Big Jelly said.

The druggist filled a small envelope with triangular-shaped red pills. He handed them to Big Jelly and then turned away to other business. He knew there was no sense in waiting to be paid even for an illegal prescription. Big Jelly ambled out and went down to the Dream Lounge. Inside, he blinked in the darkness and smoke. Tony the Indian and Big Lollipop were standing alongside the checkroom door, the shotguns bulging against their coats. They could see the street clearly. Kid Sally was on the other side of the bar. Big Jelly put two barstools together and heaved himself up on them. "One for each cheek, baby," he said to the bartender. "Now give us two glasses of water, sweetheart." Big Jelly spilled the red pills on the bar. He took three of them and swallowed them with water. Kid Sally blew smoke at the pills on the bar. He giggled and picked up three of the pills and shook them through his hand and into his mouth like peanuts.

"All right," Big Jelly said. He clapped his hands together. "Let's have a taste, sweetheart."

"What'll it be?" the bartender said.

"Double scotch and a large sauterne on the side."

Kid Sally giggled. "The same."

"Yeah!" Big Jelly said.

There was a whine from the loudspeaker system, and a four-piece band, back from a break, got set on the bandstand. The name of the band was Looey and the Birds. With a crash of electric guitars and drums, they started playing a tune whose key line was, "Your fat ass!"

The music pepped up Kid Sally. "Yeah!" he yelled out and swallowed the scotch. He banged his shot glass on the bar for more. The bartender poured scotch into the glass, then turned around and took a pencil from his ear and marked the drink down on a sheet of paper. A big sign on the register said: WE GIVE CREDIT ONLY TO A REAL CORPSE. The bartender knew enough not to bring it up. Kid Sally brought the shot glass to his mouth. He tilted his head back a little, then more, and finally, his head all the way back, his eyes looking up into the blinking psychedelic lights, he threw the scotch down and came rocking forward and slapped the shot glass on the bar with one hand and raised the sauterne with the other and threw the wine down and then he let out another shout.

"Could you see us when they hear what we done to that old greaseball?" he said to Big Jelly.

"There'd be a line-up of guys wantin' to kiss my ass that'd be longer than the two-dollar window at the track," Big Jelly said.

"Yeah!" Kid Sally said.

"And you," Big Jelly said. "They'd be lightin' candles and prayin' *to* you. You hear me? Prayin' *to* you."

"Yeah!" Kid Sally said.

"Let's have a taste, sweetheart," Big Jelly yelled to the bartender.

On the bandstand, Looey and the Birds screamed, ". . . Your fat ass! . . ." and Kid Sally and Big Jelly swallowed more scotch, and the red pills were putting glass into their eyes. A girl in a Curley McDimple wig came past the bar from

266

the ladies' room, and Kid Sally grabbed her by the arm and pulled her to him.

"Hey," she said.

"Hey, what?" Kid Sally said.

"Buy baby a drink," she said. She chewed gum methodically and her head bounced in time to the music.

Big Jelly shook more pills onto the bar and he grabbed a couple and Kid Sally grabbed a couple and the girl looked at the remaining pills, made a face, and said, "Oh, medicine? All right, baby takes her medicine." She pushed the pills into her mouth and reached for a scotch to wash them down. Kid Sally began clapping his hands to the music. Big Jelly grabbed the bottom of her skirt and lifted it up.

"You show me yours and I'll show you mine," he said.

"Fresh," she said, hitting his hand.

"What about me, can't I show my thing to somebody?" Kid Sally said.

The three began slapping the bar and yelling for something to drink and the girl kept chewing gum and rocking to the music. Big Jelly was having trouble keeping his eyes straight, and when Kid Sally tilted his head back to throw down the double scotch, some of it ran out of the corners of his mouth and he was licking with his tongue and he kept his head tilted back, looking straight up into the maze of blinking lights, and he saw himself, very clearly, riding to Baccala's funeral in an open car, with the sidewalks of

South Brooklyn lined with people clapping for the new boss of the outfit.

Mrs. Maxine Finestone was telling Mrs. Lucille Goldman, over tea and watercress sandwiches in the Plaza, that "We would never go to Lauderdale, but the boat *was* there, so you see we really had no choice. Now, to get on the boat, you had to go across this skinny little plank, just a splinter really, and in the darkness, my Lord, you could see nothing but all this water underneath you, and who knew how deep it was? So here's this little splinter of wood and do you know what Jack said? 'Maxine, you go first.' I said, 'Me? Why should *I* have to?' Jack said to me, 'I want to make sure the board won't break.' Well, dopey me, I start going out on this piece of wood. And here is my husband, standing there holding out his hand. 'Maxine, first give me the diamonds.' "

"Oh, that's your husband," Lucille Goldman said.

"You're telling me," Maxine Finestone said. "Oh, hello, isn't this nice? Grant, how *are* you?"

Grant Monroe was trying to say hello when Mario, lockstepping behind him, tripped on one of his open shoelaces and shoved Grant into Maxine Finestone's lap.

"Maxine," Grant Monroe said, "this young man is from Italy, and — Oh, Maxine! Isn't that a striking pin! Yes, this young man is from Italy. His name is Mario Trantino. This is his very first work and I was thinking to myself, *Now who could look at this?* Of course I could only think of one person."

"Why, *thank* you."

Mario bent down to kiss Maxine Finestone's hand, but because of his uncle's glasses he couldn't see and missed the hand completely. He stuck his tongue out and caught the hand with a dog lick just as his mouth went by. He swung into a chair. Grant Monroe began walking backward. Grant shook his head at Mario's paint-splattered hair. He could see Mario had twirled a paintbrush through it just before coming to the Plaza. Grant was not happy to duck away from Mario. Grant was in ecstasy.

"This painting is a very low price because it is the first I ever have done," Mario said to Maxine Finestone. "But someday, when I am very famous, this painting will be a very rich thing to have in your own house." Mario had rehearsed the line with Grant out in the lobby. It is the major line all artists have used on buyers since Michelangelo tried it on the Pope. Maxine Finestone smiled as she heard it. Her qualifications as one of the city's best-known supporters of young artists consist of a taste acquired in commercial courses at George Washington High School, a year behind the counter of her family's dairy delicatessen, and a husband named Jack, who runs a big junk business. Jack loves any painting that is explained to him in terms of an investment. For pure art, Jack Finestone will

269

place Delco Battery posters on his walls.

"Well," Maxine Finestone said, "the face is *quite* interesting."

"Think of what this will be worth when I am famous," Mario said. Maxine Finestone nodded.

Mario tripped out of the hotel with his chest pounding. Maxine Finestone had taken the work home to her Fifth Avenue apartment. She told Mario she would have her mind made up the following afternoon. Mario almost expected to hear her say she would pay about $300 for the work. If he could put ten of the same painting on the market in a hurry, he would have the beginning of a career that one day might even become completely honest.

"So if she buys it," Angela was saying later, "that means I'll never see the first thing you ever did."

"The next one you'll see," Mario said.

"But it won't be the same thing," she said.

"It's all the same thing," he said.

He dropped the subject before it got him into trouble. They were walking into the doorway on Marshall Street, and Beppo the Dwarf stuck his head out of the vending-machine office and called Mario. Angela kept going upstairs. She did not want to hear any of it.

In the office, Kid Sally was tilted back on a chair so the rear of his head would press against the wall. This relieved some of the throbbing from the hangover the whisky and pills had left. The last thing he remembered about the night before was being in somebody's apartment and watching Big Jelly try something involving a kitchen chair and a naked girl. Big Jelly was still in the apartment.

"Now is tomorrow all right still?" Kid Sally said. Mario shook his head yes. "Then why do we got to be in suspansion all day here? Why didn't you come here early?"

"Forget. Say something important," Big Mama said. She was standing by the door. She motioned Mario to sit down.

"Let's see how we do this," Kid Sally said. His eyes, pulfy, closed.

Big Mama snorted. She pointed to Mario. "You just sit in-a restaurant. When two men come in deliver the fish, you get-a you ass up and you get-a you ass out of the restaurant."

Kid Sally's eyes opened. He pointed two fingers at Mario. "Two guys with white coats on, they'll be carrying baskets of ice and fish. They'll come in like they're delivering to the kitchen. You get up like you got to go to the bat'room. Only you keep goin'."

"Where to?" Mario said.

"Right out to the subway. Go right home and stay there until you hear from one of us," Kid Sally said.

"No stop!" Big Mama said.

"If you said it, don't stop," Kid Sally said. "You just make sure you're not inside that restaurant when the two fishmen get to the table."

"Sally Kid," Beppo the Dwarf said, "when we bring this old man here, how are we goin' to get all his moneys out of him? He won't have all his moneys on him."

Kid Sally's lip came up in his sneer and he began to giggle. "We bring Baccala here, and we all say to him, 'Baccala, you nice old guinea, where you keep all your moneys hid?' "

"But he no say," Big Mama said. "But we no get mad at him. We take-a off his shoe. Rub the foot. Nice rub. Then we cut off the little toe!"

Kid Sally gazed fondly on his grandmother. "He still don't tell us. What do we do? We're stuck. The man won't talk. We tell him, 'Old man, you go home now. You look tired, old man.' But we can't let him go home like he is. He walks all crooked with the one toe off one foot. So we even up his balance. We take off his shoe and cut off the other little toe!"

"He no like that," Big Mama said.

"He tells us where he got his money," Kid Sally said. "He tells us because he got ten whole toes and he got ten whole fingers, too. We either get it in ransom or we go right to where it's hid. Whichever. But we're going to keep slicing until we get moneys."

"And then we come right back here and we cut out Baccala's heart and throw it to the lion!" Big Mama said.

Big Mama cackled. Beppo clapped his hands.

Kid Sally giggled uncontrollably. The giggle became a roar.

Mario was not quite sure whether or not he actually passed out during the conversation. He did know that both his little toes had severe pains shooting through them. Dimly he heard Big Mama lecturing him about getting a night's sleep so he would be alert. He left the office and wandered up the street like a piece of frozen wash. He heard Angela running up after him and Big Mama calling to her, "Where you go?" and Angela, putting her hand on his arm, calling back, "I'm going, that's all." All the way to the subway, Mario struggled for breath. "A roomful of money," he kept repeating. He imagined Mrs. Finestone's voice on the telephone, telling him how beautiful his work was and to come up for the money any time. The two thoughts kept him on his feet until he got home. He fell onto the bed and was asleep immediately. Angela pulled the blanket over him. Exhaustion from fear made his face break into a heavy sweat while he slept.

Chapter 18

The Della Palma Restaurant is on Queens Boulevard, in the Queens section of New York. To get there you take the Queensboro Bridge, a maze of gray spiderwork which rises out of the East Side of Manhattan and climbs across the East River. You begin the trip watching a maid cleaning the picture window of a $2000-a-month Sutton Place apartment. When you come out on the other side, there is a workman staring out of a factory window and eating a hero sandwich for lunch. Queens Boulevard starts there, amidst the el pillars and industrial slop of a place they call Long Island City. Queens Boulevard becomes a broad, crowded avenue which runs past the Irish bars of Sunnyside, grows side walls of apartments in Rego Park and Forest Hills, and comes to an end with one last apartment house, a gas station, a supermarket, and, sitting by itself, in a one-story building erected for a store, the Della Palma. Queens Boulevard then ducks down onto an expressway that goes into Kennedy Airport, two miles away. The Della

Palma has always been a quiet, almost sleepy restaurant with most of its trade coming from nearby apartment houses. It became an odd-hours favorite of Baccala's because of its closeness to the airport. Big guys from out of town flew in, had shrimp and clams oreganato with Baccala, then flew out without being seen.

At ten on Thursday morning a black-haired, dark-eyed guy of about twenty-five sat in a booth against the window of the Empress Diner, three blocks from the Della Palma. He looked out at housewives talking in the bright, cold, windy morning on Queens Boulevard. Jackie Dunne is from the Horseshoe Bend section of Jersey City, which is perhaps the world's leading supplier of Irish gunmen. He is so dark that he uses Italian names, particularly the one he had chosen for the day, Vincent Scuderi. The only thing that gave Jackie Dunne away as being Irish, and you had to be Irish yourself to notice it, was the way he sat in the booth and drank his coffee. The coffee was too hot, so he spilled some of it into the saucer and picked up the saucer and began blowing on the coffee to cool it. He slurped coffee from the saucer. He did it carefully, holding the saucer far out over the table and craning his neck to it. When he set the saucer down, he ran the thumb and forefinger of each hand down the lapels of his gray suit. He began to fuss with an already immaculately knotted tie.

A probation report once devoted three full pages to Jackie Dunne's fastidiousness. The report urged he be sent to a place where young psychiatrists could study him. "He is the perfect psychopathic gunman," the report concluded. The judge, a sixty-seven-year-old product of political clubhouses, detested psychiatrists. He threw out the medical testimony and sentenced Jackie Dunne seven and a half to ten years at Attica. Jackie Dunne for three years was the star halfback of the same D Block football team on which Kid Sally Palumbo played quarterback. Jackie had seen Kid Sally off and on for the last year. Two days ago Kid Sally had sent a messenger, Joe the Sheik, over to a poolroom in Jersey City to make Jackie Dunne an offer. Kid Sally would pay $1500 for Jackie's services on Thursday. Payment would be within three days. He was to tend bar in the Della Palma Restaurant and put things in the drinks of any bodyguards Baccala came into the place with. Jackie Dunne had a face none of the Baccala people knew. When the bodyguards were out of the way, Jackie Dunne could split.

"What if the geepos with Baccala don't drink nothin'?" Jackie Dunne said.

"Hey, don't *axt* me, go axt Eisenhower," Joe the Sheik said.

Jackie Dunne thought the arrangements were sloppy, but he still took the job. For $1500, Jackie Dunne would fight tigers.

Now, right on schedule, Jackie Dunne sat in the diner booth with envelopes of chloral-hydrate crystals in his pocket and a .38 stuffed

276

into the front of his belt, right behind the buckle.

Ten blocks down Queens Boulevard, Tony Lombardo came out of the elevator and pushed the door to the basement garage of his apartment building. Tony didn't have to be to work at the Della Palma until eleven. But he liked to get in early and dawdle over coffee and arrange the small bar so he could handle the lunchtime rush without having to keep reaching for bottles left in the wrong places. Tony liked the job at the Della Palma. The lunch hour was busy, but it tailed off sharply at two, and the restaurant was usually totally empty until five.

Tony Lombardo had the door open and he was walking into the garage when somebody put a gun to his left ear.

"You're dead," Big Jelly said to him. "Take a deep breath and you're dead."

A few minutes later a blue fish truck came slowly past the Empress Diner on Queens Boulevard. Beppo the Dwarf began waving out the window of the truck. Jackie Dunne, sitting at the diner window, nodded.

Big Jelly was wiping his forehead while he drove the truck. "I should of gone to the Turkish bath," he told Beppo the Dwarf. "I'm still shot from the other night." In the back of the truck Tony Lombardo was tied up like a chicken. He was so frightened that he fell asleep.

One of the waiters in the Della Palma was fixing up the tables in the front, so he answered the phone when it rang. "This is Sailor, the agent for Local Fifteen," a voice, Kid Sally Palumbo's, said. "Your regular bartender, Tony, he won't make it today. Guy's sick. He called in a half-hour ago. So we're sending a very good man down to you. Name of Scuderi. He should be there ten, fifteen minutes from now."

The waiter said he guessed it was all right and hung up. He walked back to the kitchen and told Nick, the owner. Nick said he hoped Tony was all right. Ten minutes later, exactly, Jackie Dunne walked into the restaurant. "You got coffee made yet?" he asked a waiter. Jackie hung his jacket in the checkroom and put on the red bartender's jacket that was on the hook. He checked to make sure the jacket came down far enough to cover the pistol in his belt. He went behind the bar and moved his shoulders around inside the red jacket. This was, he told himself, going to be the easiest $1500 he ever earned.

On one side, the Della Palma is separated from the supermarket by a large parking lot. On the other side of the restaurant there is an empty lot. The restaurant is in a long, narrow building. You enter a small vestibule which has a cigarette machine and two pay telephones on the wall. You step to the left and come into the bar area. Used mainly for service, it is a small bar, which faces you as you come out of the vestibule. At one end the bar stops at the storefront plate-glass window half covered with drapes. Opposite the bar is the checkroom and a staircase going down to the men's and ladies' rooms. The bar area ends at a breakfront. Behind it is the long, narrow restaurant, running back to the kitchen. Deliveries to the restaurant are made through the front door, to save the deliverymen the trouble of slogging to the back of the store. There is no room behind the Della Palma for anything to park. The Della Palma keeps its back door locked and barred. Which is another reason why Baccala always liked the restaurant.

At 10:30 Mario and Angela sat next to each other in a booth in the coffee shop on the corner near his flat. The windows of the shop were frosted in the cold and the wind. Brightness from the unseen sun flooded through the frosted windows and spilled onto the aluminum and formica of the coffee shop. Angela tucked her legs under her on the seat and leaned against Mario. She spooned grape jelly onto a half-piece of toast and held the toast up to Mario. He took a bite of it. They smiled at each other. Mario sat and drank coffee with the steady, gentle weight of her body against him.

It was nearly 2:15 p.m. when the waiters in the Della Palma moved through the dining room, changing tablecloths and putting out water glasses and silverware shining from the dishwasher. Three salesmen, sitting over espresso, were the last customers in the restaurant. One of the men picked up the espresso pot and tilted it over his cup. A small black trickle ran out of the thin spout. He put the pot down and asked the men with him if he should order another pot. They shook their heads no. The man waved for a check. When the three salesmen took their coats out of the checkroom and walked past the bar to go out, Jackie Dunne slipped a hand under his jacket and patted the gun stuck into his belt. *I'm on next,* he said to himself.

Dominic Laviano walked in at a quarter to three. He nodded to Jackie Dunne and stood at the breakfront until a waiter came and helped him out of his coat. "There be three or four of us," Dominic said. The waiter led him to a table in the middle of the room.

Ten minutes later a black Cadillac pulled in front of the restaurant. Two black suits got out of it and came into the restaurant. They waved to Dominic Laviano and went back out to the car. Baccala, flanked by black suits, paraded into the Della Palma. He walked past the bar without looking at Jackie Dunne. He took no notice of the waiter helping him out of his coat. If royalty were to acknowledge each chambermaid, royalty would become painfully common.

Baccala went to the table. The two black suits took up posts at the bar.

"Help you fellas?" Jackie Dunne said.

"Gimme dimes for the meter," one of them said. He put a dollar on the bar.

"Somethin' to drink too?" Jackie said.

"I said gimme dimes for the meter, that's all I said," the black suit said.

Jackie gave him ten dimes. The black suits walked out to the car. The Water Buffalo had already eaten lunch. He did not care to sit through a conversation with some priest. If Baccala wanted to talk and buy his way into heaven, that was fine. But the Water Buffalo was not interested. "I'm going to take a ride aroun' for a half-hour or so," the Water Buffalo said. The black suits asked him for the dimes back. The Water Buffalo spat at them and started the car up.

"What am I, a dope? He beats me for a whole dollar," one of them said. The black suits came back and sat at the bar and kept looking out the window to check the street. Jackie Dunne could see the outlines of the pistols in shoulder holsters under their suits.

Mario's knees buckled when he came through the door. The two black suits jumped up, hands inside their jackets. Mario threw open the raincoat to show the priest's collar. Dominic Laviano, who had been watching for Mario, waved to him. Mario walked to the table, torn by a tremendous fear of what was behind him and a tremendous greed for the man in front of him. Baccala had been breaking off pieces of bread to chew on with his wine. He had the tablecloth and the floor around his feet covered with brown breadcrust. Dominic Laviano presented Don Mario Trantino to Baccala. Baccala grunted. For a cardinal, perhaps, Baccala would extend a hand and rise.

"Now I bless this table and all who eat at it," Mario said.

"*Grazie,*" Baccala mumbled.

Mario's right hand rose. He murmured in Latin.

"You say one more prayer?" Baccala said.

"Certainly," Mario said.

"Say a prayer that all people who don't like Baccala will get cancer."

Mario pretended not to hear this.

Dominic Laviano waved for a waiter. The waiters were all in the kitchen, reading newspapers and listening to a radio. None of them got up. Dominic sat with his hand waving over his head like he was a helicopter.

Baccala took a breath. "Hey!" he shouted.

Waiters spilled out of the kitchen, the napkins over their arms flapping as they ran to the table.

Mario looked at the menu. He was about to talk to the waiter when Dominic Laviano nudged him into silence.

"You like-a shrimp and clams oreganato?" Baccala said to Dominic.

"Yes."

"You like-a?" he said to Mario. Dominic nudged again.

"Yes."

Baccala smiled. "Then we have spaghetti alla Carbonara, right?"

"Right," Dominic said.

"And veal alla marsala."

"Good," Dominic said. He nudged Mario

again. Mario smiled that it was fine.

Mario waited until Baccala finished mopping a piece of bread through the last gravy from the shrimps and clams before bringing out the picture. He handed it to Baccala.

"When did you leave Catanzia?" he asked Baccala.

"I come from Sicilia," Baccala said.

Mario's throat stuck together. Baccala studied the picture. He turned it over and read the note. He went back to the picture again.

"*Che peccat'*," Dominic Laviano said. "And the people from Catanzia who are here, they don't have so much money."

Baccala looked at the picture. He seemed indifferent. He put it down and leaned forward.

"You hear my-a confess'?"

"Yes," Mario said.

"And when you hear this-a confess', you give the absolution?"

"Oh, of course," Mario said.

"You guarantee I go to heaven?"

Mario nodded vigorously.

Baccala leaned back in his chair. He pursed his lips. "Now, what if I no tell you everything in this confess'? You still put me heaven?"

"How could a man of such bearing as yourself not tell the truth?" Mario said.

"I no lie," Baccala said. "I just no tell."

"If you don't tell me a thing in confession, why, it means you just forget to tell it," Mario said. "This does not mean you lie, or you hide

283

something. You just forget."

Baccala poked Dominic Laviano. "Young priests, they the best of the best. These old geepos, they sit there and they say, 'Baccala, go 'way.' "

Baccala leaned forward with his chin almost touching the table. He whispered.

"Besides, I only peek up the little girl's dress. I no touch."

"Oh, you are a man of honor," Mario said.

Baccala raised his wineglass. *Salut!*"

At the bar, Jackie Dunne was getting a little nervous. The two black suits had ordered nothing. Jackie fingered the chloral hydrate in his pocket.

"Time for a drink, fellas," he said.

"Screwdrivers," one of the black suits said. Jackie's eye caught the fish truck puffing up outside.

Big Jelly pulled the truck into the same space the Water Buffalo had pulled out of. Kid Sally sat alongside him. Both were wearing long white deliverymen's coats, gray truck-driver's caps, and big round sunglasses.

"Don't look, but the two bums is right there in the window," Big Jelly said.

"What the hell is Jackie doin' in there?" Kid Sally said.

"We'll just have to wait, what can I tell you," Big Jelly said.

Beppo the Dwarf crouched in the back of the truck. Two baskets of chopped ice and codfish were on the floor by the doors. Tony Lombardo was asleep with his head against one of the baskets. The ice water seeped out of the basket and went into his hair. Tony shivered in his sleep. He was dreaming that he was in Antarctica. Beppo sat with coils of nylon rope, four sets of handcuffs, and Johnson & Johnson five-inch adhesive tape. He had to be ready for fast moving. The plan was to load Baccala onto the truck, kick Tony Lombardo off it, then truss up Baccala while the truck sped away.

He had one other thing to do. He reached into a paper bag and brought out three of the stolen blue-black Savage automatics. He opened a box of the stolen bullets. He had a little trouble loading the automatics.

"Here you go," Beppo said. He held out two loaded automatics. Kid Sally took them. Beppo stuffed the third into his belt.

Just up from the Della Palma, in front of the supermarket, Mrs. Rosalind Seneca Wiggins, who is known to her friends as Roz, sauntered along in her brand new size-46 blue-gray Meter Maid uniform. Roz was big enough to be listed in *Jane's Fighting Ships*. Roz had been on the job for three days. She was hired at a salary of $75 a week by the City of New York. Her job was to patrol a six-block stretch of Queens Boulevard and put tickets on all vehicles that were illegally parked. Illegal parking includes all those cars parked in front of meters which have a red flag showing to indicate the half-hour has expired.

Roz loved her new job. Instead of scrubbing floors for white people, she could walk along and give them $15 tickets. She stopped in front of the supermarket for a moment. She had a few more meters to check; then she could start on the opposite side of the boulevard. She glanced at the clock in the supermarket. It was almost 3:30. Roz quit at four.

From the window by the bar, the two black suits were unable to make out who was sitting in the front seat of the fish truck. They began muttering about the truck being parked and nobody coming out of it. Jackie Dunne heard this and picked up two glasses and began grabbing ice cubes, swirling orange juice and vodka bottles around. He made two drinks and put them on the sink under the bar. He went to his pocket for the chloral hydrate. The crystals dissolved into the orange juice. They dissolved into a heavy smell of chlorine, a stronger smell than a swimming pool gives off. Jackie let the drinks stand for a moment. He hoped the smell would go away. He was becoming very nervous now. He had never used knockout drops before. All he had ever done was hear about them. Just put them in a drink, everybody said, and the other guy never knows the difference and the next thing you know, he's on the floor. Like most of these things, it was nonsense. Jackie Dunne bent over and sniffed the drinks again. His stomach turned. The odor was even heavier now. Nobody sane would touch a drink like this.

Jackie draped a towel over his hand and went to his belt for the pistol. He kept the gun hand down. He put the drinks on the bar with the other.

"Fellas," he said.

The two black suits turned around. They picked up the glasses. The smell hit their noses at once.

Jackie's hand brought up the pistol under the towel. "Right there," Jackie said. The hands were tense and shook a little. They stayed motionless holding the drinks, but Jackie knew he had only a few seconds to keep them under control.

Jackie made sure the gun did not move a fraction of an inch. One show of motion, even tiny motion, would send both these guys flopping to the floor and pulling out their guns. Jackie could feel his weight automatically come back on the heels so he could pull away if one of them threw a glass.

"Very slow, bring your mouth down to the glass. Down, not up." They bent over, their eyes glaring up at him the way a dog does when he has a bone in his mouth. *Look out, look out, or here they go,* Jackie said to himself.

"Now drink the whole thing," he said quickly.

In the tension and fear, the two black suits knew the smell was there, but they didn't really notice it. The word "poison" ran through their minds.

Jackie Dunne pushed the gun at them and their bodies jumped. "Drink!" he said.

Each of them took a small gulp.

"I said drink!" Jackie said. His nerves were beginning to take over his voice and his body. His voice was tight, and the gun waved quickly.

The black suits, still looking at him, began swallowing. When they got near the bottom, Jackie waved the gun at them again.

"All right. Slow. Glasses down. Both hands on the bar. Slow."

The two stood hunched over the bar and Jackie held the gun on them. Three pairs of hands were twitching, and three sets of lips were trembling. Jackie knew it was going to start any fraction of a second. His finger was wet on the trigger.

One of the black suits felt his insides falling into his pants. He put a hand over his mouth and threw up into it. The other black suit exploded from every opening in his body except his ears.

They were coughing and retching and Jackie went inside their jackets and pulled out the guns. He dropped them into the sink. He stuffed his own pistol back into his belt. With a deep, free breath he came out from behind the bar and took each of them by the arm and tugged them to the stairs leading to the men's room. Jackie glanced into the dining room. Through the breakfront, he could see the three at the table busy talking. He pushed the two black suits onto the stairs. Throwing up, gagging, coming out of both ends, the black suits staggered down the steps.

Jackie stepped into the checkroom. He took

off the red jacket, grabbed his suit jacket, and swung out of the checkroom. He was out on the street in two steps, heading for the subway.

Kid Sally jumped. "That's it," he said. He fumbled with the door and tumbled out of the truck onto the street side. Big Jelly, wiping the hangover sweat from his face, came onto the sidewalk. He felt himself bumping into something while he was heading for the back of the truck.

"Please watch where you goin'," Roz said. She was standing with her Meter Maid book open, standing right in front of the meter the fish truck was parked at, the meter with the red flag showing.

In the back of the truck, Kid Sally and Big Jelly were grabbing the baskets of fish from Beppo the Dwarf. They each put a basket on a shoulder and started for the restaurant.

"What's this?" Kid Sally said. Roz was copying down the license-plate number from the front of the truck.

"Get rid of her," Kid Sally said. He kept walking to the door.

"Come on, lady," Big Jelly said to Roz.

"Just as soon as I finish my job," Roz said.

Kid Sally was in the Della Palma vestibule now, leaning against the cigarette machine. The ice water was running out of the fish basket and down his arm and onto his hand. He was afraid the hand would be slippery when he held the gun. *Come on, Jelly,* he said to himself.

Big Jelly was standing chest to chest with Roz. "Hey, lady, we're workin', go bother somebody else," he said.

"When I finish," Roz said. She said it slowly and without looking up from the pad on which she was writing.

"Come on," Big Jelly said.

Roz did not answer.

"Oh come on, you fuckin' nigger," Big Jelly said.

Roz put the top back on her pen.

"Black cunt," Big Jelly said.

Roz put the pen back into the breast pocket of her uniform.

"Old nigger cunt."

Roz tore off the parking ticket from her pad. She was careful to tear it on the perforated line.

"I'll piss on your leg, you fuckin' nigger."

Roz walked over to the truck and began to stick the ticket to the windshield-wiper.

"Fuckin' nigger cunt."

"You know," Roz said very softly and very off-handedly, "you know, you should of been a cop. Yes, you should of been a cop. Because your father was a police dog, you fat mother-fucker."

Big Jelly held the basket of fish over his head like he was King Kong. He brought it down onto Roz's head. He threw a kick at Roz's legs. Roz twisted away, and the kick missed. She pulled the basket off her head with one hand. The other was out in front of her, reaching and pawing and finding Big Jelly's fat cheek. Big Jelly threw a wild left hand onto the side of Roz's head. Mrs. Rosalind Seneca Wiggins, who has a head that has broken a thousand bottles, took the punch, blinked, and reached for Big Jelly's private parts. She had to dig hard through the apron, but she got them. A scream went up from Big Jelly's mouth. His left knee came up to his chest.

Kid Sally banged his head against the cigarette machine. He dropped the basket onto the floor and pulled out the automatic. Now there was no plan and no time. Now he could only do one thing: go inside and kill Baccala cowboy-style and come running for his life. Kid Sally's lip came up in a sneer. He began to giggle. The gun out, giggling, the giggle becoming very loud, he came into the Della Palma Restaurant for a shooting that would go down in gangland history, go down with the killing of Albert Anastasia in the barber chair and Vincent Coll in the phone booth and Willie Moretti in a clam bar.

The waiter and Mario saw Kid Sally at the same time. The waiter was coming out of the kitchen with a pan of spaghetti alla Carbonara to serve the table. The spaghetti alla Carbonara went into the air and the waiter belly-whopped under a table. Mario saw Kid Sally because for the last fifteen minutes Mario had been watching the door out of one corner of his eye so he could run the moment the fish deliverymen came in. Now, when Mario saw Kid Sally coming in with the gun out, a roar filled his ears. He came out of his chair with his hands out and a scream.

"Gesù!"

Dominic Laviano dove to the left. Baccala, mouth open, eyes wide, tried to get off the chair. He could not move.

Kid Sally brushed through two tables, giggling, the gun coming out farther. Mario fell over him.

"Gesù!"

Kid Sally's left hand pushed against Mario. The giggle now turned into a shriek. Kid Sally jammed the gun against Baccala's temple. Baccala's eyes closed. His face twisted. Kid Sally could hear Big Mama in his mind, Big Mama shouting at him, "No miss!" Kid Sally pulled the trigger, and the explosion filled the room and Baccala tumbled from his chair. Kid Sally had wanted to empty the automatic into Baccala's head, but he could not do this because the wrong-sized ammunition blew up the gun right away. In one flash Kid Sally's hand was shredded and his dreams and chances were gone and he was in shock, with blood from his hand running all over him. He turned and did not remember running out of the place and into the brightness and the wind and the cold and Big Jelly screaming on the sidewalk.

The side of Baccala's head burned. He could feel the huge hole in his head. He closed his eyes tighter. He was afraid to open them and have to look at the Sacred Heart. His heart pounded so hard that he heard nothing else. Then his leg began to ache from being doubled under him.

Baccala's heart slowed. Why should his leg hurt him when he was dead? Baccala opened his eyes. He saw the floor of the Della Palma and Dominic Laviano's ass. Slowly Baccala's hand reached for the hole in the side of his head. There was no hole. His fingers touched the hair over his ear, which had been singed by the powder burn. His fingers ran over the entire side of his face. There wasn't even blood.

Baccala got up from the floor. He looked into Mario's eyes. Baccala bowed his head. He clasped his hands.

"*Mirac*'," Baccala said softly.

He looked up into Mario's eyes. "*Mirac*'," he said to Mario.

Baccala looked up at the ceiling and shouted it. "*Mirac*'." Baccala came around the table and jumped into Mario's arms and began licking Mario's face with his tongue. "*Mirac*'," he kept slobbering.

Chapter 19

The Water Buffalo turned the corner slowly and came back onto Queens Boulevard. As he was thinking quite hard about women's underwear, the full impact of what was happening did not reach him all at once. First his eyes focused, and, three-quarters of a second later, his mind registered on Beppo the Dwarf tumbling out of the back of the panel truck in front of the restaurant. "Germ!" the Water Buffalo's mind shouted. His foot came down on the gas. The car shot toward the dwarf. Beppo darted for the sidewalk. The Water Buffalo had to swerve the car and hit the brakes. The Water Buffalo's head nearly went through the windshield. When the Water Buffalo righted himself, he saw Kid Sally Palumbo, hands pressed to his midsection, hopping around in front of the restaurant like a chicken. The Water Buffalo did not see Big Jelly, who was pounding both his hands on top of Roz's head. This was being done in order to force her teeth to slip loose from their tight grip on Big Jelly's left ear. Big Jelly was also bleeding from the nose. Roz had bitten him there first.

So the Water Buffalo jackknifed over the car seat and began fishing for the shotgun on the floor in the back and he was figuring only on Kid Sally Palumbo and he never saw Big Jelly reel up to the car. Big Jelly reached through the driver's window and put his pistol into the back of the Water Buffalo's neck. Beppo the Dwarf opened the back door, grabbed the shotgun away from the Water Buffalo, and pressed an automatic into the Water Buffalo's cheek. Kid Sally Palumbo, trying to wring the pain from his bleeding hand, pushed into the back seat. He was closing the door with his good hand while Big Jelly got the car going. Big Jelly had Baccala's limousine up to 65 by the time it hit the corner. The Water Buffalo sat in a daze in the back seat. Kid Sally Palumbo, giggling through the pain, held the shotgun muzzle right under the Water Buffalo's chin.

There was so much traffic on the parkway going to Brooklyn that Kid Sally and Big Jelly agreed it would be foolish to kill the Water Buffalo and throw him out of the car. "Besides, I want to have some fun with this punk," Kid Sally said. He slapped the Water Buffalo in the mouth with the shotgun muzzle. At Marshall Street, they pushed the Water Buffalo into the vending-machine office. Beppo went into the desk and came out with a pair of handcuffs and a roll of his Johnson and Johnson five-inch tape. They handcuffed the Water Buffalo's hands behind his back, slapped tape over his mouth, and used most of the roll to bind his ankles. Beppo opened the cellar door, and Big Jelly half lifted and half kicked the Water Buffalo down the stairs.

"Get me some rope," Kid Sally said to Beppo.

Beppo clapped his hands. "Geez, a garrote!"

"I'm gonna get somethin' out of this freakin' day," Kid Sally said.

The Water Buffalo tumbled down the cellar stairs in the darkness. Right away, his nostrils flared in the urine smell. The Water Buffalo rolled onto his stomach on the floor at the foot of the cellar stairs. He heard a rustle off to one side. His eyes darted around. Five or six steps away, framed in the half-light from a cellar window, was an apparition, a tousle-haired lion. The Water Buffalo slipped into mild shock. He exploded out of the shock when the apparition began moving. The Water Buffalo started rolling to get away from the lion. This had the same effect on the lion that a rolling spool of thread does on a cat. The lion leaped. The lion then pounced on the Water Buffalo. The Water Buffalo was in the face-down section of his roll when the lion landed. As the Water Buffalo came face up, he was looking straight up into the lion's face. It was the last thing the Water Buffalo ever saw. He did not go into mild shock this time. He went into straight heart failure and was dead in a moment.

"Come on, come on," Kid Sally Palumbo was saying a few minutes later. He pinched the

Water Buffalo's cheek. There was no response. He began twisting the cheek. Nothing happened. Kid Sally bent over and looked closely.

"The freakin' rat lion killed him!" he shouted. He jumped up and went for the lion. The lion scuttled into a hole in the piles of junk in the cellar.

"Just when we were going to say somethin'," Big Jelly said.

"This rat bastard," Beppo said. He kicked the Water Buffalo. "This guy never was no fun in his whole life. He just proved it."

"We got to split out of here right away," Kid Sally said. "When the cops get here they'll stay for breakfast they'll be here so long."

Big Jelly slapped the cinderblock wall. He went to the toolbox under the stairs and pulled out a sledgehammer and chisel.

At 5:45 the three of them came out into the early winter darkness with the Water Buffalo's body, which had a cinderblock tied to the ankles and another tied to the neck. The vending-machine office was crowded.

"What you hang here for?" Kid Sally said as he struggled out the door. "You know how many cops is going to make it here?"

"Will the cops shoot us?" one of the crowd said.

"No, but —"

"Then we stay here," the guy cut in.

They threw the body into the back of Baccala's car. Big Jelly drove. They had hours to kill before the street emptied and they could get rid of a body without having an audience. Big Jelly drove to Dr. Lambert's office. Lambert was trembling. He had received rumors, and now, looking at Kid Sally's hand, he knew he was seeing direct evidence. He cleaned the hand and put in seven stitches. With each stitch, he shook a bit more. By the time he got to Big Jelly, Lambert was an epileptic. Roz the Meter Maid's worst bite had been on Big Jelly's nose. Lambert slipped, bit his tongue, tried again, and, accompanied by a long wolf howl from Big Jelly, succeeded in stitching Big Jelly's nostrils together. Big Jelly came out of the office with his nose covered with tape and his mouth hanging open so he could breathe. Kid Sally's hand was wrapped in bandages, but the trigger finger was usable. Beppo the Dwarf opened the car door for them and they drove off.

A mile away, in the Brooklyn Municipal Building, Benjamin Goodman was sitting in his office with Inspector Gallagher and a detective from the 103rd Squad in Queens, which had caught the trouble at the Della Palma.

"All right now, let me see if I have this," Goodman said. "Inside there was Baccala, a man named Laviano, and a priest."

"That's as far as we know. Plus the help."

"All right. And outside there was who, now?"

"Catalano . . ."

"Is he the fat slob?" Goodman asked.

"Yes. And the dwarf, and we're pretty sure there was one or two others in a getaway car some place but they never showed. They must of panicked."

"And Kid Sally, of course," Goodman said.

"What else?" Gallagher said.

"And you have Baccala, Laviano, and the priest here now?"

"Well, they just come with me," Gallagher said. "I mean, we got no reason to, you know . . ."

Goodman smiled. "I know all about it. You can tell Mr. Baccala he can take his priest with him and go home and pray that he's still alive. We're not interested in him. Then come back here and let's sit down and we'll give this Mr. Palumbo something to think about for a couple of years."

Gallagher had one of his people take Baccala out the back way so he wouldn't have to pass the news people in the outer lobby. Baccala held tightly onto Mario's arm. Dominic Laviano walked behind them.

"Is this your first *mirac'*?" Baccala whispered.

"It is the first time I have been this blessed," Mario said.

Detective Donald Jenkins was sitting on a wooden bench by the door leading to the staircase. The floor around his feet was littered with cigarette butts. For three hours now, Jenkins had been waiting for Inspector Gallagher to come out and tell him what to do.

Jenkins decided to throw the stare at Baccala. *It's the most they'll ever do to this freakin' old guinea,* Jenkins told himself. Jenkins clenched his teeth on his cigarette. His eyes flashed steadily at Baccala. When Baccala wouldn't look at him, and kept talking to this fellow walking down the hall alongside him, Jenkins became irritated. He glanced at the one Baccala was with. Jenkins' hand went right away to the cigarette gripped in his teeth. He pulled the cigarette out and held it away from his face so there would be no smoke in his eyes while he looked at this priest. The same priest he had seen in civilian clothes taking Angela Palumbo in the subway over to 11th Street in Manhattan.

Jenkins came off the bench and walked very quickly down to Benjamin Goodman's office and knocked on the door.

Big Jelly and Kid Sally drove through the streets of Brooklyn, listening to the radio. Big Jelly drove with his right hand on the wheel and his head hanging out the window like a police dog's, so the wind would rush up any tiny passageway in his nose left by the stitches. At midnight, there still was no news of the Della Palma incident. The police were keeping the lid on it. There was no news of Red D'Orio yet, either. This was not because of any official reluctance. The delay was merely the result of slow typing in Brooklyn South Homicide.

Early in the evening Red D'Orio had become

bored hanging around the vending-machine office. He decided to go out for a drink. "I'll be a moving target," he said. Which he was. He had four scotches in Esposito's on Carroll Street. He promptly swung over to Busceglia's in Williamsburg. He had four scotches in Busceglia's and whisked across town to the Caprice on Fourth Avenue. An hour later he was in the Showboat Bar on Atlantic Avenue. "Beautiful," Red D'Orio complimented himself. "How could they get me when they never see me? Just keep walkin' and talkin'." He held his glass out for another drink. Nothing happened. Blearily, Red D'Orio looked down the bar. There was no bartender. This was because the bartender had just received a phone call telling him to get into the men's room or stand a chance of getting shot too. The rest of the place was empty. "Where did all the guys go?" Red said. The door to the Showboat opened. Red D'Orio brightened. He needed company. He turned to the door. "Hi, guys," he said. "Hi," one of them said. The other two did not talk. They were too busy shooting.

Rain began to fall at midnight. It rapidly turned into heavy rain, with the cold wind blowing it in sheets. The rain emptied the streets. Kid Sally, sitting in the front seat of the car, began hitting himself on the forehead. It was time to think of a good place to dump the body. He decided on the weed-fringed industrial slop of the bay on the far side of Staten Island. No human being would be in the vicinity on a night like this. Big Jelly drove onto the parkway that goes to the Verrazano Bridge. The bridge runs across the Narrows of New York Harbor to Staten Island. As they came up the approach ramp, the rain was so heavy that Big Jelly had to drive slowly. The windshield was covered with running water. The reflection of the bridge lights on the running water made Big Jelly blink. The car crept onto the wide, brilliantly lit bridge runway. Kid Sally was staring moodily out the window on his side. He rolled the window down and put his head out into the rain. He looked ahead. He turned his head and squinted to see behind the car.

"Nobody's on the whole bridge," he said.

"Everybody must of got smart and pulled off the road," Big Jelly said.

Kid Sally giggled. "Stop the car in the middle," he said.

"The middle?" Big Jelly said.

"Just stop the car in the middle," Kid Sally said. His lip curled into a sneer. He began giggling.

Big Jelly pulled the car to the side of the bridge and rolled to a stop.

"The greatest." Kid Sally giggled.

"What greatest?" Big Jelly said.

"Just let's go," Kid Sally said. He opened the car door.

"Go what?" Beppo said.

"Go to watch the first man ever to come off of the bridge," Kid Sally said.

"Wow!" Beppo said.

"That's different," Big Jelly said. "Whyn't you tell me?" He pushed his door open.

Kid Sally stood in the rain, tugging the Water Buffalo by the shoulders out of the back seat. Beppo stood in the back and kicked the body. Big Jelly reached for the legs. Grunting against the weight of the body and the cinderblocks, the rain washing their hair into their faces and soaking through their clothes, the three of them staggered with the body to the low battleship-gray wall on the side of the roadway. High above them, on the towers and cables, the bridge lights were strung out in a burning necklace that can be seen for thirty miles. Straight out, and below them, there was only blackness with rain whipping out of it. They heaved the Water Buffalo's body on top of the wall. The three of them went back a couple of steps. "Now!" Kid Sally said. They rushed forward, arms straight out in what football people refer to as a forearm shiver. They hit the Water Buffalo's body and sent it out into the blackness. Under the roadway, a great steel beam protrudes. The cinderblocks hit the lip of the beam and bounced off into the black air. The Water Buffalo's body followed. The bridge is 228 feet in the air. The rushing water below it is 180 feet deep. The initial airdrafts caused the cinderblocks and the body to wiggle a bit, as bombs do when they begin falling. The wiggling stopped, and the Water Buffalo and cinderblocks fell straight and true through the black air.

The three of them dove back into the car. They were laughing and hitting themselves while Big Jelly got the car going.

In the harbor water under the bridge at this time was the tugboat *Grace Moran*, pushing against the tide on its way to a scow-hauling job at Erie Basin. Also, the Greek freighter *Olympic Zenith*, which was sliding on the tide to the ocean. The *Olympic Zenith*, Theodore Kritzalis commanding, was carrying a cargo of steam turbines for Athens and also letter mail and printed matter for Lisbon, Naples, Piraeus, and Cyprus. The entire ship seemed to shake when the Water Buffalo hit the front hatch.

One crewman on duty at the bow, Peter Chingos, fainted. Captain Kritzalis, brought up under German dive bombing, instinctively fell to the bridge deck. When there was no immediate explosion, Captain Kritzalis crawled to the intercom and ordered the crew to run to the stern of the ship. Captain Kritzalis had seen these delayed fuses before. The American harbor pilot, George Edmundson, tried to speak, but his voice failed to come out. He scribbled on a sheet of paper, "Raise Coast Guard!" A mate rushed the paper to the radio shack.

Within minutes the Coast Guard cutter *Lawson* was streaming down the harbor toward the *Olympic Zenith*. Also converging on the freighter were the New York City Fire Department boat *John F. Kennedy* and New York City Police Department Harbor Launch No. 7. The

Olympic Zenith lay dead in the water and search-lights poked through rain and fell on the bow. The searchlights intensified the light cast by the worklights on the winches over the front hatch. And now, through the heavy rain and blackness, the damage could be seen. Sticking up from the hatch cover, which had been smashed almost completely through, were the Water Buffalo's still magnificent $110 alligator Bostonians. The rest of the Water Buffalo was dangling in the air in the front hold.

Preliminary reports reached all responsible parties.

Louis Samuels, night man in the Mayor's office at City Hall, scribbled quickly on a yellow legal pad while the communications man from Police Headquarters read off the report.

"Uhuh," Samuels said. He flicked the call off and then pressed down another key on the small monitor board and began to flick it up and down rapidly.

"What?" The Mayor's voice was husky with sleep.

"Mr. Mayor, the police say that a gangster was thrown off the Verrazano Bridge and the body landed on a Greek freighter."

Samuels' ear was filled with the hollow sound of the Mayor's phone falling from the night table and dangling in the air. He could hear a rustle and the phone being picked up again.

"Hello," the Mayor's wife said. "I don't know

what it is, but he'll have to call you back. He just had to go to the bathroom."

In Brooklyn, Benjamin Goodman leaned over a sink in one corner of his crowded office. Goodman ran cold water and slapped it over his red-rimmed eyes. He took a paper towel and dried himself. His face felt a little better now.

"All right," he called out to the crowd of detectives. "Now let's go over this again. I want the timing checked out step by step. I want to have this thing come off smooth, and I don't want to miss one of these animals."

It was eight a.m. in London. Georges Pappajohn, a silk robe wrapped around his 5-foot-4, 265-pound body, stood at the living-room window of his suite in the Dorchester. He looked down at the morning traffic in Hyde Park and muttered impatiently while the overseas operator put his call through to Washington. Pappajohn, seventy-one, is known as the Floating Greek because of all the ships he owns.

"Come on, come on," Georges Pappajohn snarled at the operator. "I buy your company and fire you."

"What's the matter, Georgie?" His wife, Rona, almost eighteen, stood in the doorway in a Baby Doll nightgown.

"I'm busy, can't you see?" Pappajohn said.

"Oh, Georgie, always business." Rona Pappajohn pouted. "And you promised."

"Hello, operator!"

"Georgie, you promised to buy little Rony a bracelet today so she won't be mad at you for running out of ink in your pen."

"Allo, allo," Pappajohn said. "Ah, Meester Assistant Secretary of State. How are you, Meester Assistant Secretary? I don't like to wake you up at this hour, but I have a question to ask of you. Meester Assistant Secretary of State, what is this *bullshit* with my ship?"

In Washington, in his house in Georgetown, MacGregor Wallingford of State listened glumly while the world's biggest shipping magnate screamed about an accident in Brooklyn involving gangsters. Wallingford didn't know what it was about. When Pappajohn hung up, Wallingford clicked the phone and told the State Department operator to get the Attorney General at his home.

Chapter 20

In the morning after the rain, the breezes coming down the street did not cause the usual swirl of soot to rise from the sidewalk on 11th Street. The streets seemed washed, and the air was clean and cold and sparkling in the sun. At the subway station, the lightshafts coming down the subway stairs made even the dingy change booth seem pleasant.

Angela and Mario were holding hands while they came down the stairs. They stopped in the pool of light in front of the change booth.

"I'll be back soon," he said.

"Well, I don't know, I have to be home," she said.

"Why go there?"

"Because I have to."

He let go of her hand and thought for a moment. He pulled out the key to his apartment.

"Go back and wait, it won't be long," he said.

"I have to see. I'm afraid there's so much trouble."

"Don't go home any more. I don't want you

near the trouble."

"I just don't know." She bit her lip.

She took the key from his hand and lifted her face and kissed him. He took her hand.

"I just have to see the woman about my painting and come back," he said. He took out twenty dollars. He felt strange when he held it out to her. He had never given away anything in his life. "Buy something if you need something," he said.

She gave him another quick kiss. He went up to the change booth. She spun and went up the stairs with her legs kicking freely. She had her head down and was humming something to herself and she didn't see the two men at the top of the stairs until one of them reached out and took her by the arm. The other pulled a warrant out of his jacket pocket.

Mario got to the fountain in front of the Plaza Hotel at 11:15. His date with Maxine Finestone was at noon. Over the phone the night before she had told him her husband was excited about the painting. That meant money, Mario knew. He sat down on one of the benches around the fountain. He was shaky, as are all veterans immediately after a battle. But the proximity of success soothed him. The woman would pay for the painting, and Baccala, between kisses, had given him a private phone number. He would be able to raise so many thousands out of Baccala that a subsidy for an art career, and also a good start toward building an orphanage in Catanzia, seemed assured. Mario thought it was so good that he would have to steal only one-third of the money for Father Marsalano, instead of half. He bent down and pulled his shoelaces apart. He reached into his pocket and took out his uncle's eyeglasses. He got up and began stumbling over to the steps of the Plaza.

Detective Donald Jenkins came off the bench on the other side of the fountain.

"Now where is he going?" Jenkins said.

"Look at the walk," a detective with him said.

"He's a pisser," Jenkins said.

"What the hell is he doing?" the detective said.

"I don't know," Jenkins said. "One day he's a priest, and now he's blind, I guess. The hell with it, let's start finding out right now what this son-of-a-bitch does."

They came onto Mario from each side. They guided him to a black Plymouth which had pulled up in front of the hotel a few minutes before.

The raid on Marshall Street took place at 10:15. It would have been much earlier, but Benjamin Goodman, in making calls to news desks, found that two of the local television channels did not have camera crews scheduled to work before nine a.m., and there was no way to get them in earlier. Goodman postponed the raid until the crews reported for work, picked up announcers, and drove to Brooklyn. The raid itself went off smoothly. Cops hit the block in battalion strength. No resistance was offered. They arrested Kid Sally Palumbo and fifty-nine others without incident. The day's only accident came when Benjamin Goodman, charging the vending-machine office for the television cameras, pulled open the cellar door and the lion flew out at him. This caused Benjamin Goodman to faint, but his reputation for fearlessness was saved by television cameramen who fled when they saw the lion.

The bridge man in Part I, Brooklyn Criminal Court, needed cough drops near the end of the afternoon to finish calling out the various charges against the sixty defendants. The charges began with homicide and attempted homicide and ran through conspiracy to commit homicide, felonious assault, possession of automatic weapons, unlawful possession of a lion, and, as the last line on Big Jelly's warrant, illegal possession of narcotics.

"It was only marijuana, I'm allowed to have that," Big Jelly said.

"What do you mean by that?" the judge snapped.

"I'm a high-school student," Big Jelly said.

There were sixty people in the courtroom. Bail was set at $100,000 each. The total came to $6,000,000, highest bail figure ever heard in a courtroom anywhere. Benjamin Goodman rushed into the men's room and began combing his hair. He came out into the television lights and gave interviews for an hour. It was after six when he got back into his office. Gallagher was tapping Mario's passport against the desk.

"What are we supposed to do with the girl?" Goodman said.

"Do what we're supposed to do," Gallagher said.

"What am I going to hold her on?" Goodman said.

"What you got now is good enough. Material witness."

"Where does that take us?"

"Right to here," Gallagher said. He slapped the passport against the desk. "He gets us everything we need."

"All right. Put the girl up in a hotel, like any other material witness," Goodman said. "Then let's bring this wop of yours in here and have a talk with him."

"How do you want to work it with him?" Gallagher said.

"Put him into the grand jury with immunity, and when he's through, your lovely Italian girl is no longer a material witness. She's a defendant. And I've got myself a good witness as a little insurance policy in case the rest of these bums try to go to trial with this."

Jenkins had been sitting with Mario in a dingy room at the end of the hall. Now he brought Mario into Goodman's office.

"Did you advise him of his rights?" Goodman said.

Jenkins shook his head yes.

"All right, you can go," Goodman said.

He leaned back in his chair. "Want a lawyer?" he said to Mario.

"I don't know one," Mario said.

"You better get one, you're in a lot of trouble," Goodman said.

"You're going to jail," Gallagher said.

"Have you ever been locked up with fags?" Goodman said.

Mario didn't understand the slang.

Goodman smiled. "A man of the world like you doesn't know what fags do to you in jail?"

"I don't know what they do in Italy, but in this country they make a big line in jail and they all rape you," Gallagher said.

Mario clutched his chest. But he said nothing.

Goodman leafed through the passport. "Pretty serious matter," he said. "Impersonating a priest, conspiracy to commit murder." He shook his head. "Why did you come to this country?"

"I think the big question is, how does he like it here?" Gallagher said. "Would he like to stay here, or would he like to get sent home right away?"

Mario picked him up on it. Now they were telling him what they had on their minds.

"What do I have to do?" he said.

Goodman and Gallagher smiled at each other. "You know, you're pretty cute," Goodman said to him.

313

"You're going into a room where nobody can see you," Gallagher said, "and you're going to tell a jury, a private jury we call a grand jury, you're going to tell them what you've seen and heard."

"Nobody can see me?" Mario said.

"Nobody."

"Who will know what I say?"

"Nobody," Goodman said. "I'll be there, you'll be there, and the jury will be there. Nobody else. You understand? Nobody else. Grand-jury testimony is secret."

"What do I have to say?"

"Just what you've seen and heard."

Mario nodded.

"If you don't, you get sent home. Bingo. Home to sunny Italy. Right to the town you came here from."

"All right," Mario said.

"Did the girl use to sit down with them and talk about what they were going to do?" Gallagher said softly.

Mario took a sharp breath.

"Didn't she?" Gallagher said.

Mario looked carefully at their faces. "Does she get in trouble?"

"You get sent straight home to Italy," Gallagher said.

"I never said that," Goodman said. "I never said we'd forgo criminal charges before deportation."

It was a very easy thing for Mario to do. He simply nodded yes, and he stood up, and this detective, Jenkins, came and took him out of the building and they drove to a new motel overlooking fishing piers in Sheepshead Bay. They ate in the room and sat and watched television, and Mario felt nothing.

All the next morning Mario sat in Benjamin Goodman's office and went over what he was to say in front of the grand jury.

"And who came into the restaurant?" Goodman said.

"Kid Sally Palumbo," Mario said.

"And what did Mr. Palumbo have in his hand?"

"A gun."

"All right," Goodman said. "Now, let's go back. When you sat in the kitchen at fifty-one Marshall Street, with whom did you sit?"

"The grandmother, the brother, the little man you call dwarf, and the fat one, Jelly, and the sister."

"The sister's name is?"

"Angela."

"And during the conversation did Angela Palumbo contribute anything?"

"Contribute?"

"Yes, say anything. Did she say anything?"

"Yes."

"What did she say?"

"She said, 'Don't forget to steal license plates for the truck.' "

Goodman sat back. Gallagher smiled. "Accessory before an attempted homicide," Goodman said.

"All right, tomorrow is your big day," he said to Mario.

Mario felt good the next morning. One of the detectives had bought him a new shirt. Mario whistled while he buttoned the shirt. All he had to do was walk into this room where nobody could see him, say what he had been told to say, then walk out of the room and go back to the apartment on 11th Street. When he thought of the apartment, Mario could feel Angela next to him. He reached for his tie and began kotting it. Maybe, he thought, it was better that he hadn't met Mrs. Finestone at the Plaza yesterday. It would make him seem more independent, like a real artist.

The hallways at the District Attorney's office were crowded in the morning with assistants coming in and out of their offices and going down to the courtrooms. Jenkins took Mario to Goodman's office and Goodman, leafing through a briefcase, told Jenkins to take Mario down to the grand-jury room. He would follow. Jenkins led Mario down the hallway toward the rear elevators. A policewoman was standing in a doorway near the end of the hall.

"Hi," she said to Jenkins.

"Who's that?" Jenkins said.

"You know," the policewoman said. She glanced into the office.

"Hey!" Jenkins said. He put his arm out to stop Mario. The policewoman tried to step inside the office and close the door. But Mario was even with the doorway and he could see Angela sitting inside. She was in a chair by the window. She had her coat on, and her hands were in her coat pockets. Her face was very white, and she looked very small and very young. He was looking at her, with no expression on his face, and Jenkins' hand pressed against his back and moved him on down the hall. While he waited for the elevator, Mario wondered if Mrs. Finestone would pay more than $300 for the painting.

The twenty-three people on the grand jury shifted around in red leather chairs when Mario came in. He sat facing them. Goodman walked in, carrying a bundle of yellow legal pads and crinkly onionskin paper covered with smeared typing. He put the bundle on the desk and began going through it. Mario sat in the chair and looked around. Fluorescent lights played on the brown walnut paneling of the room. There were no windows. The people on the grand jury were men, old men mostly, with chicken skin hanging over their collarbuttons. Most of them wore these dark ties with tiny dots.

"Good morning, gentlemen," Goodman said. The light played on his red hair.

He turned to Mario. "All right, now would you please tell these gentlemen if you know an Angela Palumbo."

"Parlo solo Italiano," Mario said.

Goodman smiled. "No, no, just relax. Answer

the question in English."

"*Parlo solo Italiano.*"

"What are you saying to me?" Goodman said.

"*Io no sache.*"

"Can't he speak English?" the foreman of the grand jury, a retired bank official named Everett Cashman, said.

"*Tu pari ca ti chiavi a mammata,*"[*] Mario said to the foreman.

"What's that?" the foreman said.

"One of the words was your mother, I know that," a man sitting next to Cashman said.

Mario smiled and nodded in agreement. "*Sorita sa appaura di te la notta,*"[**] he said.

Benjamin Goodman's eyes widened. His lips pursed. His finger shot out at Mario. "Now you listen to me . . ."

Mario stood up, made a courtly little bow, and came out of the bow with the middle finger of his right hand held up.

"*A foongool a bep!*"

Mario never did stop to think about what he had done. He just sat in one office while everybody screamed and cursed at him, and then went with the detectives over to another building, the Federal Court Building, and two other men who looked like detectives put him in an office and somebody brought him a sandwich and

---

[*] "You look like you have sex with your mother."
[**] "Your sister must be afraid of you at night."

cup of coffee. Late in the day he was brought into a huge paneled courtroom. A man from the Italian consulate was there. Mario heard discussions about whether he wanted a hearing and when the judge glanced at him, Mario said, *"Tu si nu porco grasso."**

The man from the consulate spoke to Mario in Italian. He said Mario could have an immigration hearing at a future date, but he would have to stay in jail while awaiting it. And there would be a chance he would have to face criminal charges. Or Mario could just sign a waiver and be sent back to Italy immediately. Mario shrugged. Anything but jail. At dusk two men who looked like detectives drove Mario through the heavy traffic to Kennedy Airport. At the Alitalia terminal they were ushered into a small cinderblock office.

"You've got about two hours before the plane leaves," one of the men with Mario said.

Mario folded his arms and closed his eyes. He wondered if Mrs. Finestone would have paid $350 for his painting.

At the Brooklyn District Attorney's office there had been so much shouting and commotion in the hallway that the policewoman was afraid to put her head out and ask for anything. Finally, when the office was getting dark and she had to put on the light, she decided to

---

* "You fat pig."

319

look outside and ask.

"Hey," she said to a detective, "what do I do with her?"

"With who?"

"I've got Palumbo's sister in here. Been here all day. Nobody told me what to do with her."

"Stay there and I'll find out," the detective said.

He walked down to Goodman's office. Goodman ran a hand over his eyes.

"I don't have time to start on her," he said.

"Well, the policewoman wants to know what to do with her."

"Throw her out of here," Goodman said. "I got no use for her now."

"Just send her home?" the detective said.

"I don't care where she flops, just throw her out of here without me seeing her," Goodman said. "And this old broad the grandmother, too. She's in detention. Release her. I can't hold her now. Just make sure I don't see them walking out of here."

"You can go home," the policewoman said to Angela.

Angela was still sitting motionless, hands in her pockets, by the window. She looked up.

"Home?"

"That's right, dear, you can go home."

Angela got up slowly. The policewoman held the door open.

"If I were you, just between us girls, I'd go

right home and write your boy friend a thank-you note."

"A note?" Angela said.

"Yes, dearie, I think you'll find your wonderful boy friend has just had his ass thrown out of the country."

"Out?"

"Today. Bang! Out on his ass."

"When did he go?"

"Don't ask me. Just get yourself together and leave so I can go home too. I didn't even get lunch here today."

In the hallway, Angela asked a detective if he knew about Mario Trantino.

"Who?" the guy said.

She looked around at the faces walking past her in the hall, and she left the office. She came running out of the lobby into the start of the night and her arm was up to call for a cab but two lawyers edged in front of her and took it. She stood on the crowded downtown Brooklyn street, waving her arm. All the cabs were filled. After fifteen minutes, she turned and ran into the subway.

The train went to New Lots Avenue station in the East New York section, which is close to Kennedy Airport. Angela wedged into the car and rode with a musty-smelling workman's jacket pushing into her face. The train made every stop and people wedged their shoulders to get out each time. Some of them got stuck in the doors while the doors were closing, and the conductor had to reopen the doors and try to close them again. At Kingston Throop Station a man stood with his shoulder blocking the doors. He wouldn't move. The train did not move while the door was still partially open. After what seemed like five minutes, the conductor walked down and pushed the man's shoulder into the car so the doors would close. The conductor walked back to his position between cars and pressed a buzzer. The train started slowly.

Angela came up onto the street at New Lots Avenue at 6:40 p.m. There were three cabs sitting at the corner. The drive to Kennedy took twenty minutes.

"What airline?" the driver said as he came into the maze of purple and blue and winking yellow lights of the terminal section.

The first terminal building handling overseas flights was the Pan American. Angela got out into the glare of lights and uniformed baggage-handlers and trim blond passenger aides. She ran into the crowded terminal and started one way and she saw the information sign and doubled back. A man in line in front of her wanted information on a flight to Karachi. The girl behind the counter patiently went through folders. Another girl was free and she nodded to Angela.

"Rome?" the girl said. "Flight 101 departing at 8:30 p.m."

Angela gave her the name. She picked up a

white telephone and dialed a number.

"Hello, on flight 101. Passenger Trantino, Mario. Is he on the list? Hmmmmm. All right."

She put down the phone. "No, he isn't. Are you sure he was on this flight?"

"No, I'm not," Angela said.

"Alitalia has a 7:40."

Angela ran out of the terminal and down the circular driveway. She ran over a plot of dead grass and onto the driveway of the next terminal and then onto the long, crowded, brightly lit sidewalk running in front of the international terminal. The Alitalia terminal was halfway down the long building.

"Trantino?" the clerk said. He looked at a typewritten sheet. He looked up at Angela.

"Just a moment," he said. The clerk stepped away from the counter and went through a door.

One of the United States Naturalization and Immigration agents sitting with Mario got up and answered the knocking on the door to the cinderblock office.

"Yeah?" he said to the clerk.

The clerk whispered to the agent.

The agent shook his head. "Fuck that," he said. "No."

The door shut and the clerk came back into the space behind the counters. He was walking over to Angela when a man at a desk reached for his arm and handed him the phone. The clerk took the phone and began talking over it. He talked for minutes. People were pushing into the lobby, and a family escorting a priest wedged past Angela to the counter. When the clerk got off the phone and came back to the counter he had his head down and he was looking for something and a man in the family was pushing the priest's airline ticket at the clerk and the pink pages were flapping in the light and the loudspeaker called for boarding and people were pushing and Angela was trying to step through and now she spat out a word and slashed at the crowd with her hands. People looked at her in surprise and stepped away.

The clerk bent over the counter. "I'm sorry, I'm sorry, I got so busy all of a sudden." He paused. "Why don't you go up to the observation deck? It is straight up the stairs here." He glanced up at the clock. "Don't say I said anything."

The observation deck at Kennedy Airport is one flight over the planes. There is a railing on it and you can lean over the railing and look down at the people walking onto the plane and call to them and wave to them. It is crowded in the summer, but few people stand on it in the winter. They say good-by inside the terminals.

Angela was the only person on the observation deck over the green-striped Alitalia plane. She stood with her hands gripping the railing and her eyes burning on the foot of the staircase leading to the plane. A mechanic in white coveralls and a blue baseball cap walked down the staircase. An airlines official in a navy-blue uniform and white hat stood at the foot of the ramp. A slow whine came from one of the engines. A blue tractor drove away from the nose of the plane, pulling empty baggage carts with it. Another whine started in another engine. The sound was very loud now.

Very quickly, with two men flanking him, Mario walked out into the whine. The two men held him by the elbows. Mario trotted up the steps and he was at the top and through the doorway and into the lighted cabin. The two men with him stood in the doorway for a moment. They stepped back and the airlines man in the uniform came up the steps and tugged on the plane door and slammed it shut.

The plane was parked at an angle to the observation deck so that when your eye tried to sweep along the egg-shaped lighted windows, the windows seemed to run together. Angela was trying to see into each window, and her eyes were smarting and she could not see Mario, and the whine of all four engines became loud and stabbed into her ears. Her hair began to blow in the kerosene fumes of the jet exhaust. The engines made more noise and her hair was whipping and the bottom of her coat was blowing and the plane was moving and Angela Palumbo put her hands over her ears and screamed into the noise of the plane and the fumes whipping into her and the lights and the night beyond them.

Two months later, after considerable legal

maneuvering, the Kid Sally Palumbo mob, in toto, agreed to plead guilty to charges of conspiring to kill approximately every citizen in the borough of Brooklyn. For this chance to get sixty hoodlums off the street without the expense of a trial, the state agreed to one-year sentences for all. A year does not sound like a lot in print, but it is a very long time in jail. All authorities agreed it would be long enough to end the great gang war and take much of the ambition for any future trouble out of nearly all the Palumbo gang members.

There was only one small hitch to the deal. Just before sentencing, with all sixty crowded in front of the bench, Kid Sally Palumbo looked around and saw his sister and grandmother. He whispered to the lawyer. The lawyer asked for a very short recess before sentencing. Kid Sally waved to his sister and she came up to the railing and he called out something to her. She looked up at the ceiling. Her lips moved in a short prayer. She ducked out of the courtroom. She returned in five minutes, holding a paper bag from the chain drugstore down the block from the court building.

"What's that you got there?" a court attendant said.

"He forgot a toothbrush," she said.

At 11:30 a.m., out in Beachhaven, Long Island, Mrs. Baccala started the car. When the car did not blow up from a bomb, Baccala got up from the kitchen floor and walked out into the driveway, patted Mrs. Baccala on the head as she came out of the car, got in, and backed down the driveway to start another day as a major American organized-crime overlord.